Unholy Death
in
Princeton

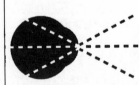

This Large Print Book carries the
Seal of Approval of N.A.V.H.

Unholy Death
in
Princeton

Ann Waldron

WHEELER PUBLISHING

Published in 2005 by arrangement with The Berkley
Publishing Group, a division of Penguin Group (USA) Inc.

Wheeler Large Print Cozy Mystery.

The text of this Large Print edition is unabridged.
Other aspects of the book may vary from the original edition.

Set in 16 pt. Plantin by Elena Picard.

Printed in the United States on permanent paper.

Library of Congress Cataloging-in-Publication Data

Waldron, Ann.
    Unholy death in Princeton / by Ann Waldron.
      p. cm. — (Wheeler Publishing large print cozy mystery)
    ISBN 1-59722-023-X (lg. print : sc : alk. paper)
    1. Princeton Theological Seminary. — Fiction. 2. New
Jersey — Fiction. 3. Large type books. I. Title. II. Wheeler
large print cozy mystery.
PS3573.A4226U54 2005
813′.54—dc22   2005008746

Unholy Death
in
Princeton

As the Founder/CEO of NAVH, the only national health agency solely devoted to those who, although not totally blind, have an eye disease which could lead to serious visual impairment, I am pleased to recognize Thorndike Press* as one of the leading publishers in the large print field.

Founded in 1954 in San Francisco to prepare large print textbooks for partially seeing children, NAVH became the pioneer and standard setting agency in the preparation of large type.

Today, those publishers who meet our standards carry the prestigious "Seal of Approval" indicating high quality large print. We are delighted that Thorndike Press is one of the publishers whose titles meet these standards. We are also pleased to recognize the significant contribution Thorndike Press is making in this important and growing field.

Lorraine H. Marchi, L.H.D.
Founder/CEO
NAVH

* Thorndike Press encompasses the following imprints: Thorndike, Wheeler, Walker and Large Print Press.

Author's Note

Princeton Theological Seminary is, of course, a real place. I have used it for the setting of this book, but peopled it with characters who are totally imaginary. I have taken a few liberties with geography and placed the seminary campus closer to the Delaware and Raritan Canal than it really is.

I am delighted to acknowledge the enormous help of the Rev. Pat Miller. He suggested this book, and with his wife Mary Ann Miller, answered with admirable Christian patience my thousands of questions about the work and life of the seminary. My friend of fifty years, Virginia Thomas, was also generous with facts about God, the Bible, life at a seminary, and many other subjects.

Other people who provided helpful information about seminary life include John Gilmore, the Rev. Carolyn Nichols, the Rev. Max Stackhouse, the Rev. Cathy

Cook-Davis, the Rev. Daniel Migliore, Kate Skrebutenas, Heather White, the Rev. Katharine Doob Sakenfeld, the Rev. Mark Orten, the Rev. Sue Anne Morrow, Mary Grace Royal, Michael Davis, and Carol Wehrheim.

My questions about everything from law to accounting to ancient manuscripts to rattlesnakes were answered by Kim Otis, Lt. John Reading, Chris Harrell, Lois and Jack Young, W. A. P. Childs, James Gould, Lynn Sanders, Sam Hynes, Larry Parsons, and Ann Zultner.

Thomas William Waldron went beyond the call of filial duty, reading the manuscript and providing invaluable advice and suggestions. Amanda Matetsky was a great cheerleader throughout.

As usual, I depended on my wise and infinitely patient editor, Susan Allison, and my trusted agent, Elizabeth Frost-Knappman.

— Ann Waldron

One

McLeod Dulaney was walking on the tow path beside the Delaware and Raritan Canal in Princeton, thinking about Elijah P. Lovejoy, when she kicked the corpse.

It was a beautiful autumn morning, and McLeod kept looking up to marvel at the cacophony of crimson and scarlet and ochre of the leaves on the trees on both sides of the canal. On her left, the canal gleamed in the sunshine and rippled in the breeze. On her right, the woods. Keeping an eye out for late wildflowers, she saw what looked like an autumn crocus blooming in the fallen leaves under trees several feet away. She left the path to get a better look. Glancing up again at the bright blue sky through the leaves of an intensely red maple tree, she hurried toward the pale lavender crocus — and stubbed her toe.

What had she kicked? Looking down,

she saw it was a garment bag — a green and blue Stuart tartan garment bag that lay in a patch of poison ivy next to a bright red sumac bush under the maple tree. It was mostly hidden in the ivy and sumac, but one corner protruded. She bent to look at it.

Curiosity was McLeod's salient characteristic, and she moved closer to the sumac and the bag. What was it doing in the woods beside the tow path? She hoped her jeans and socks protected her ankles from the poison ivy, which grew in ominous profusion. She hesitated about putting her hand through the tendrils of poison ivy to unzip the garment bag, but she could not resist. She reached down and unzipped the garment bag partway. A horrid smell — "the sweet smell of corruption," she remembered someone had once called it — assaulted her.

She screamed when she saw the bag contained a human foot and the top of a human head. She jerked her hand away, stood up, and got back to the tow path — away from the body in the bag — as quickly as she could. She never got a closer look at the crocus.

Back on the path, she took her cell phone out of her pocket — thank God for

10

cell phones! — and called 911.

The police dispatcher wanted her exact location and she had trouble thinking. "I'm on the tow path, west of Alexander Street," she said. "Headed toward the golf course. About a half mile from Alexander Road, I'd say." The dispatcher kept her on the phone. "A patrolman will be there soon. Just hang on. Tell me your name and address . . ."

He continued to ask her questions until two uniformed policemen came hurrying, not quite running, down the tow path. They must have parked at Turning Basin Park on Alexander and come the rest of the way on foot. When McLeod pointed toward the garment bag, one officer put on a plastic glove and paused. "Did you touch anything?" he asked McLeod.

"I unzipped the bag a little bit and saw the body," she said. "I didn't even zip it back up. I just got back to the tow path and called the police."

The officer went over to the garment bag and began to unzip it further. "Well, it's not a suicide, is it?" he said with what McLeod thought was inappropriate levity. "I mean he couldn't have put himself in this garment bag and zipped it up." McLeod turned away.

"Hold it," said the other, older officer, popping his walkie-talkie from its shoulder mount. "We've got a murder here," he said into it. "At least foul play of some kind. Send an ambulance, a forensics team. We'll secure the site." He then said that he would meet the detectives, the forensic team, and the ambulance at Alexander Road.

When he was through he turned to McLeod. "Are you all right?" he asked kindly. "Come with me, and we'll go back to Alexander. We can sit down at the park at the Turning Basin. The detectives will want to talk to you as soon as they get here. Sammy will take care of things here, won't you, Sammy?" The older cop tucked a hand under her elbow and guided her down the tow path. "Did you recognize him, Mrs. . . . ?"

"No, of course not," McLeod said. "I didn't see his face. My name is McLeod Dulaney. And I hate it when people take my elbow. It's hard to walk when somebody is holding your arm like that."

"I don't want you to fall," said the policeman mildly.

"I won't fall," McLeod said. "I walk on the tow path a lot." She shouldn't be cross with the policeman, she realized. Her white hair often made people behave in an excessively helpful fashion. Her hair had been bone-white since she was in her thirties and twenty years later she still didn't think she was old enough to have white hair.

"I want to get you to where you can sit down, ma'am. I know you've had a shock."

"We're almost there and I won't run away, if that's what you're afraid of."

"All right, all right." He withdrew his hand from her arm.

"What's your name?" McLeod said. "I told you mine."

"Kevin Makowsky."

When they reached the steps that led from the tow path to Turning Basin Park, Makowsky stopped and said she could sit there on the steps.

"What *is* the Turning Basin?" she asked him.

"I don't know," he said and looked baffled.

The ambulance arrived. "You can sit down here, ma'am," Makowsky said, pointing to the steps. He turned then, going over to talk to the paramedics who had gotten out of the ambulance. When two more police cars drove up, Makowsky left the paramedics to speak to the new arrivals, who were not in uniform. He pointed down the tow path, and the police car, followed by the ambulance, made a U-turn and went into the parking lot for Turning Basin Park. The men in the car, who were not in uniform, got out and walked toward the place where McLeod had found the garment bag. The medics stood about aimlessly — apparently they had to wait before they could get to the scene and pick up the body. In a few minutes, the forensics team and two photographers arrived and hurried down the tow path. Another police car drove up, and two uniformed men got out and began stringing yellow crime scene tape to keep joggers and hikers away from the tow path.

"Did they put somebody up at the other end to keep people off?" Makowsky asked.

"Yeah," said one of the uniformed men.

"The other two men are detectives," "her" uniformed officer told McLeod when he came back to sit beside her on the steps. "They're going down to the scene, but one of them will be back. He wants to talk to you."

"All right," said McLeod, sighing. Then she thought of something. "I have a friend who's a policeman in Princeton. Nick Perry — he's chief of detectives. Do you think he'll be along?"

"Don't know him," said Makowsky.

"That's funny," said McLeod.

"Wait a minute. He must be with the Borough Police. Princeton Borough. We're Princeton Township. We're in the Township now. The Borough is just the hole in the doughnut of the Township. The Borough boundary is up by the Wa-Wa." The Wa-Wa was a convenience store near the railroad station.

"Oh, I see," said McLeod, who was very sorry she wouldn't soon be seeing Nick Perry again.

In a few minutes, one of the plainclothes officers came back up the path and said he'd like to talk to McLeod. "Let's go sit at a table in the park," he said. When they were settled, he took out a notebook. "I'm Detective Sergeant Lester Brasher," he said. "And you are . . . ?"

McLeod told him and spelled it for him.

"Your home address?" he said.

"313 Virginia Avenue, Tallahassee, Florida," she said.

"Do you have a local address?"

"I'm staying in Erdman Hall at the seminary — Princeton Theological Seminary."

"Are you on the staff there?"

"No, I'm only here for a few weeks. I'm working on a book and using the library at the seminary. They sometimes let researchers stay at Erdman Hall if they aren't filled up with guests for a workshop or seminar. I'm doing research for a book on Elijah P. Lovejoy."

Lester Brasher looked up. "Who's he when he's at home?"

McLeod had disliked the policeman named Sammy when he said that the body couldn't be a suicide; she had detested Kevin Makowsky when he had tried to hold her elbow on the tow path, and now she hated this detective for his scornful attitude toward Lovejoy.

"Elijah P. Lovejoy was the first martyr to freedom of the press," she said frostily. "He was a newspaperman in St. Louis and then he came back here to the seminary — he did the three year course in thirteen months — and became a Presbyterian minister. When he went back to Illinois, he started publishing an abolitionist newspaper and was lynched by a pro-slavery mob in Alton, Illinois in 1837. I'm writing his biography."

"I see," said Brasher. "How did you find the body, Ms. Dulaney?"

"I was walking on the tow path. I love it this time of year, and I went over into the woods because I thought I saw an autumn crocus —"

Brasher interrupted. "What's that? A crocus? How do you spell that?"

McLeod spelled it for him.

"Go on," he said.

"I left the path to go look at it, and then I kicked this thing and looked down and it was a garment bag, lying there in the poison ivy, right by a sumac bush."

"Sumac?" said Brasher.

McLeod spelled it for him, and then went on. "I wish I'd never done what I did next," she said. "I unzipped that damned garment bag." She paused. "As soon as I saw it was a person, I left it and went back to the tow path and called 911."

"What time was it when you found the body?"

"I don't know," said McLeod. "I called 911 immediately and waited there until the police came. I waited here until you came to talk to me."

"We appreciate your cooperation, Ms. Dulaney," Brasher said. "Did you know who this person was?"

"No idea at all. I didn't see the face. The body was doubled up."

Brasher took her back over it all, checking every move she had made. When had she left Erdman Hall?

"I left from the library. It was about

eleven. I thought I would get out of doors for a while before lunch," she said.

And had she walked down to the tow path or driven?

"I walked," said McLeod. "That was the point, to take a walk."

"Lots of people drive down and park in the parking lot for Turning Basin Park and then go for a walk," Brasher said.

"I walked. It's just a few blocks down Alexander Street to the canal. I stopped at the Wa-Wa and got a sandwich to bring with me. I haven't eaten it yet. I don't feel like eating."

"You're quite a walker," said Brasher. "Now, you've been very helpful. Just a few more questions. Why were you walking along the tow path?"

"I like to walk beside the canal. It's a beautiful walk any time, and this time of year, it's stupendous."

"Stupendous?"

"It's the colors," she said, and felt like adding, "Stupid," but didn't. "We don't get fall colors where I'm from."

"So you had no special reason to walk here today?"

"No." He took her through the crocus and the garment bag and the sumac and the call to 911 again.

"Did you walk here yesterday?" he asked.

"No, I didn't. Why?"

"We think the body has been there some time, and we wondered if you had noticed the garment bag there yesterday."

"No, I wasn't here yesterday. But lots of people walk and run on the tow path. Somebody else might have noticed it but not unzipped it."

"All right, Ms. Dulaney. Thank you very much."

"Can I go now?"

"I'm sorry. I have to ask you to wait until they bring the body out. I want you to look at the face and see if it's anybody you know."

"I'm sure it isn't," said McLeod. "But the medics haven't even gone down there. How long will it be?"

"The photographers have to finish before they can take the body out," said Brasher.

"I see," said McLeod. "I guess I'll have to wait." Then she decided to try again: "Can you tell me what the Turning Basin is?"

Brasher looked at her as though she had gone mad. (Maybe I have, thought McLeod.) "I don't know for sure," he said.

★ ★ ★

While they had talked, other policemen had arrived, and other people not so easily identified. McLeod longed to see for herself exactly what law enforcement people did at the scene of a crime, but decided not to ask if she could go back. The medics left, carrying a stretcher, and went down the tow path. Brasher summoned another uniform to sit with her. McLeod was so cowed by the events of the past hour that she didn't even ask him his name.

She sat there and wondered what a Turning Basin was. She wondered why she was here, trapped in a murder investigation. It seemed to happen every time she came to Princeton. Maybe she should just stay in Tallahassee, where she had lived for more than thirty years, ever since she was married. She had gone there when she married Holland Dulaney, who had just finished graduate school and won his first teaching job at Florida State University. When he died, she had gone back to work as a reporter on the *Star of Florida* and raised two children alone. Tallahassee was a wonderful place to live, so why did she love coming to Princeton once a year? Because it was a change, she answered herself, because it was stimulating. Stimulating? This was stimulating? Sitting beside the Delaware and Raritan Canal waiting to get a good look at a dead body? Was she crazy?

At last the medics came up the tow path bearing a stretcher, with the body, covered in a blanket, on it.

Lester Brasher, following the stretcher-bearers, signaled to the uniform to bring McLeod down to the tow path. The medics stood quite still at the rear of the ambulance while McLeod walked down to meet them. Brasher pulled back the blanket and McLeod stared at the face. Brasher looked at her inquiringly.

"No, I don't know him," she said. The face was young and his hair was blond. "He looks vaguely familiar," she told Brasher. "But I don't know who he is. I really don't."

"All right. Thank you. You can go now. I'll have Makowsky drive you back to the seminary." They walked away from the ambulance.

"Thanks, I'd appreciate a lift," said McLeod, to her own surprise. She was tired, and it was uphill to the seminary, and she would be glad of a lift. She even allowed Makowsky to hold her elbow and help her into the patrol car.

Two

McLeod was in what her great-aunt Nannie used to call "a weak and rundown condition" when the policeman dropped her off at Erdman Hall on Library Place. Finding a body, waiting to be interrogated, waiting to look at the corpse — it was all too much, even if she had not known the person when he was alive. She was exhausted.

And she felt very alone. She had spent two semesters in Princeton before this, but she had been teaching a writing class at Princeton University and was therefore "a member of the university community," with people to turn to in emergencies. And in emergencies, she had dealt with Nick Perry of the Borough police. To be near a murder and without Perry was hard, she thought, and her dearest friend in Princeton, George Bridges, no longer worked at the university. He had jumped at the chance to go with Edgar Battle, former president of the university and George's onetime boss, to Brussels and a job with the European Union. I do miss George, she thought.

McLeod decided to call the only two people she knew at the seminary, Fiona and Angus McKay, who were old friends of hers from Atlanta where they had all grown up. Angus taught medieval church history at the seminary and Fiona did volunteer work with various civic groups.

Fiona's response was quick and warm. "What an awful experience," she said when she heard McLeod's tale on the telephone. "Come on over early — don't wait until dinnertime — and we'll have a cup of tea — or something stronger."

McLeod had forgotten that Fiona had invited her to dinner that night — finding a body had driven it from her mind — and she tried to recover without letting Fiona know. "I'd love to do that, if it won't be too much trouble to have me show up early."

"It will be fine. You can talk to Angus while I slave away in the kitchen."

Delighted, McLeod changed her clothes — she didn't have a big selection with her, but she did have a nice long black wool skirt and a decent-looking sweater. She put her coat back on and walked around the corner to the old house where the McKays lived across the street from the Seminary campus.

Furious barking greeted her when she rang the doorbell, and when the door was opened, Beelzebub and Gabriel greeted her with doggish grins and moans of pleasure. Beelzebub was a black scottie and Gabriel was a suitably angelic wheaten scottie. McLeod, who had met them before, returned their greeting with equal warmth.

The dogs snoozed on the carpet while she and Fiona and Angus had their tea in the library. Fiona even offered homemade scones — "Don't eat too many and spoil your dinner," she warned — and the McKays listened to McLeod. Fiona, a beautiful woman with dark hair streaked with gray and black eyes that were snapping, was outraged that the police had kept her so long.

"And they didn't believe I didn't know the man," McLeod kept saying. "I guess they think I killed him and stuffed him in the garment bag and then called the police."

"It's insane," said Fiona. "There should be an investigation into police brutality."

McLeod was thinking that it really had

not gone that far, and looked at Angus. He was chubbier than he had been when they were all young, but he still had the same angelic smile and the same calm green eyes. When he had decided to go to seminary after college, McLeod's mother had remarked that she had always thought Angus McKay had a call to higher service. And here he was, an ordained Presbyterian minister. He had been the preacher in a little church in a small town in Georgia and then gone to Harvard to get a Ph.D. in religion. He then taught church history at the seminary in Atlanta for years before he and Fiona moved to Princeton two years ago.

"Hmm," said Angus thoughtfully, when Fiona had left for the kitchen. "I guess the lesson we learn from all this is that you let sleeping dogs lie and you leave sleeping bags on the tow path zipped up."

"It was a garment bag," said McLeod, "But I'm sure you're right in principle, Angus. You always are. But you know me. I have to investigate everything."

"I wonder who the corpse is," said Fiona from the kitchen. "No identification, you said?"

"None," said McLeod. "He was naked. Unless he had a tattoo, I can't think how a nude corpse could have identification."

"They'll find out who it is, sooner or later," said Angus. "Somebody will be reported missing and he'll fit the description and the body will be identified."

"I hope it's soon," said McLeod. "And by the way, Angus, you're always into local history. Do you know what the Turning Basin is?"

"It's where the old canal boats could turn around," said Angus. "The barges used to go on the canal from the Pennsylvania coal mines to New York. Some of them would stop here and offload coal for Princeton people. The Turning Basin is just a big round pool they dug where the boats could pull out of the canal and tie up at a dock. Then the empty ones could go back. I understand there was a thriving little business center down there by the canal back then."

"Thanks," said McLeod. "It was driving me crazy. I thought it was something like that, but I'm glad to know."

The doorbell rang — causing great excitement for Beelzebub and Gabriel — and Fiona came out of the kitchen to answer it. Angus and McLeod heard her greeting someone, and a feminine voice replying.

"It's Lucy Summers — you'll like her," said Angus, getting to his feet as Fiona ushered in a nice-looking woman with red hair curling around her face, a face that was wreathed in a warm smile at the world around her. The dogs, having done sentry duty, once again stretched out on the floor.

"Let me take your coat," Fiona said. "Angus can introduce you and fix you a drink."

"Lucy, this is McLeod Dulaney," Angus dutifully said. "We all grew up together in Atlanta. McLeod, this is Lucy Summers. She teaches theology here, too, and she's writing a book about Jael."

"Jail?" asked McLeod. "Prison?"

Lucy laughed uproariously. "No, no. Jael in the Old Testament. She nailed the head of Sisera, an enemy of the Israelites, to the floor. She drove a tent stake right through his head with a hammer. She is such fun to write about."

"Believe it or not, I've actually heard about Jael and Sisera. I'm a Trollope devotee, and in *The Last Chronicle of Barset*, Trollope has the painter, Conrad Dalrymple, paint Miss Van Siever's portrait while she's posing as Jael with a hammer in her hand. He painted himself as Sisera, I think. She was not a passive female, was she?"

"Far from it. I'll have to read *The Last Chronicle of Barset*. I read *Barchester Towers* years ago, but I haven't read anything by Trollope since." Her hazel eyes were sparkling and dimples showed in her cheeks.

"I love him," said McLeod. "Are you doing a whole book on Jael?"

"Oh, no, I'm doing lots of women from all over the Bible. You know the harlot who helped Joshua's spies at Jericho, and Judith —"

"Oh, and the head of Holofernes," interrupted McLeod. "That's been painted a lot, too. Oh, what a bloody bunch they were."

"I knew you two would hit it off," said Angus. "What would you ladies like to drink?"

"Please call us women," said Lucy. "I'd like a martini."

McLeod, who had no objection to being called a lady, said she'd have a martini, too, and Angus went to fetch the drinks.

"Fiona said you were in Princeton to do some research. What are you working on?" Lucy said.

"I'm working on a biography of Elijah P. Lovejoy, and I'm going through the material the seminary library has on him. I also need to find out about the seminary, what it was like when he was here as a student. That sort of thing."

"What a wonderful subject — a genuine, modern martyr," said Lucy. "And you live in Tallahassee?"

"Yes, I'm a newspaper reporter there," said McLeod. "On the *Star of Florida*."

Angus returned carrying a tray with three martinis and a glass of wine on it. "The wine is for Fiona. She says she dares not have a martini when she's cooking," he said, handing around the drinks.

Fiona came in, took her wine, and sat down. "I have a few minutes respite from my terrible labors over the hot stove," she said, dramatically wiping her brow with the back of her hand.

"Can I help?" asked McLeod automatically, as she took the first sip of her martini. "Oh, this is good!"

"Gin helps," said Fiona. "Angus believes in the power of prayer, but I *know* gin helps." They all laughed at that, and then Fiona turned serious. "Lucy, McLeod had a terrible experience today. She found a dead body on the tow path."

"A dead body! Good heavens," said Lucy. "How awful."

"Tell her about it," Fiona urged. "I have to get back to the kitchen. Drink up."

★ ★ ★

Dinner was wonderful. Beelzebub stretched out beside McLeod's chair and Gabriel stuck close to Lucy. "They know we won't feed them at the table," Fiona explained, "but they always think guests can be corrupted." Fiona's chicken pie was made from an old Southern recipe, and although Beelzebub slobbered greedily at her side, McLeod ignored him and ate her dinner with great gusto. She stopped when Lucy and Angus talked about the stir that Rob Hillhouse was causing.

"Who's he?" asked McLeod.

"He's a new member of the faculty," said Angus. "Teaches New Testament. He's very big on the historical Jesus."

"The historical Jesus?" asked McLeod.

"Establishing the historical facts about Jesus' life without including what must have been added by the early church fathers," said Angus.

McLeod must have still looked puzzled, because Lucy added, "You see, fundamentalists, the real conservatives, can't even think about questioning anything that's in the Bible. And emphasizing the historical Jesus, they say, minimizes the eschatological Jesus."

"*What?*" asked McLeod.

"The eschatological Jesus — the Christ who was crucified and rose again from the dead, and will be here at the Second Coming."

"You mean Rob Hillhouse is controversial? Because of that?" asked McLeod.

"Well, he's also very interested in the work of the Jesus Seminar," said Angus.

"What's that?"

"It was a group of Bible scholars from several schools. You know Jesus spoke Aramaic and Hebrew, so the Greek New Testament itself is a translation of his words. The people in the Jesus Seminar studied the oldest texts and then met and discussed each sentence that Jesus was supposed to have said. They voted on which were really said by Jesus and which were added by the early church."

McLeod felt her eyes glaze over the way they always did when people talked about theology or religion for any length of time. "Does it really matter what he said and what was added by the early church?" she asked.

"They think it does. Anyway, the Jesus Seminar came in for terrible criticism from fundamentalists when the Seminar members agreed that Jesus did not say certain things in the Bible. The Bible was written by God, fundamentalists say. You can't tamper with it like that. While Princeton Seminary is not fundamentalist, it has always been rather conservative, and some of the less liberal lights around here are saying Rob Hillhouse has to go. And he just got here. It's too bad — he's a good man."

"And I thought life at a seminary was peaceful and reverent and sweet."

"Ha!" said Fiona.

"People do get excited about things," said Lucy. "For instance, there's this news about the endowment and how it has shrunk."

"No new hires was the latest word today," added Angus. "And we're all very upset about it."

"What happened?" asked McLeod.

"There's the market slump," said Angus, "but the seminary's endowment seems to have taken a harder hit than anybody else's — the university's, for instance."

"It'll recover," said Fiona. "At least nobody's arguing about it the way they do all these other things."

"I know," said Lucy. "Some of my students are still having trouble with inclusive language."

McLeod knew vaguely that "inclusive

language" was something feminist biblical scholars were very interested in. "Inclusive language is where you don't refer to God all the time as 'he,' isn't it?" she asked.

"That's right. For example, you'd read the Twenty-third Psalm as, 'The Lord is my Shepherd. I shall not want.' And instead of saying, 'he leadeth me beside the still waters,' like we did when we were children, you'd say, 'God leads me beside the still waters.' You do that all through the Psalm. And in other places, you refer to 'humankind' instead of 'mankind.' You get the idea."

"That seems harmless enough," said McLeod.

"Lucy's won that campaign here," said Angus. "They use inclusive language in chapel services, and most professors require students to use it in the papers they turn in now."

"No, we haven't won it, not really. Not in the hearts and minds of the conservatives," said Lucy. "And it's certainly still an issue in the church at large. Bible literalists don't want to make the changes at all. Students who come here from fundamentalist backgrounds don't approve. They say God wrote the Bible and you can't change it."

"I should think now that forty percent of

the student body is female that it wouldn't be a problem," McLeod said.

"Oh, a lot of those students who object are women," said Lucy. "They haven't been enlightened — or liberated — yet. Give us time." She smiled at McLeod.

"I never realized a seminary was such a battlefield," said McLeod. "The historical Jesus. Inclusive language. What else?"

"Oh, there's contention about the authority of the Scriptures — that always causes lots of arguments," said Lucy. "It drives people to murderous impulses. Somebody said religion is inherently violent, and I believe it. It's so important to some people that they'd kill for what they believe."

"What's the argument about?" asked McLeod.

"A great many people here believe that a changing culture and new scientific knowledge demand a new interpretation of Scripture," said Lucy. "They say that Jesus never walked on water, never fed thousands from one child's lunch, never made the blind see or the lame walk. This group believes that we should abandon the idea that nobody is saved but through Jesus.

"The other side maintains that Scripture is inspired — 'God-breathed' — and what it says should not be dismissed to accommodate a changing culture. This group believes strongly that Jesus Christ is the 'sole path of salvation for all people.'"

"Does that mean Buddhists or Moslems or Jews will all go to Hell?"

"According to them," said Lucy.

"An outgrowth of the endless disagreement over interpretation of the Bible is the argument over ordination of gay clergy. That and gay marriage are the hottest issues right now."

"The Presbyterians don't ordain gay people, do they?" asked McLeod.

"No, but the United Church of Christ does," said Angus.

"And of course the Unitarians do. The Episcopal church varies from diocese to diocese," said Lucy. "It depends on the bishop."

"We have a good many gay students," said Angus. "They have their own organization and it's very active."

"They face strong opposition from some conservative students, though. They write nasty things on the posters announcing gay student meetings," said Lucy.

"You see, McLeod. The Seminary seethes with discord," said Fiona.

When she and Lucy were leaving, Beelzebub and Gabriel aroused themselves and scampered to the door with them. Angus took down their leashes from a hook by the door and said he would take them for a walk and see the ladies at least partway home. Lucy protested that they needed no escort, but Angus insisted, as McLeod knew he would, and they all set out.

McLeod felt greatly cheered when she got back to Erdman Hall and her tiny room, but she could not forget the body on the tow path. Who was the man? Had he been a poet? A landscape gardener? A stockbroker who commuted to New York? A farmer, perhaps? Although he had looked awfully pale to be a farmer. A handyman? (It seemed to McLeod that handymen were always involved with murders, either as victims or murderers.) Perhaps he had been a spy, or an FBI agent, or a politician. How awful to be robbed of one's identity and stuffed into a garment bag and abandoned on a tow path. McLeod tossed and turned for quite a while before she went to sleep.

Three

On Friday the body in the garment bag was
the talk of Princeton. The *Princeton Packet*
had a story about it in its Friday edition, and
the *Times* of Trenton ran stories speculating
about the identity of the murdered man, re-
porting at length the medical examiner's
findings that the young man had been dead
at least two days when McLeod had found
him on Thursday. McLeod heard little talk
of it in the rather purified air of the seminary — at least no one mentioned it to her.
But nobody here knows me, except Fiona
and Angus, she told herself.

And then at lunch in the cafeteria she
was thinking about the body — was he
somebody who had gambled heavily,
gotten in over his head, and been killed by
his creditors when he couldn't pay them?
Or a drug dealer who tried to cheat and
the gang lords had killed him? But why

Princeton? Why the tow path? These macabre thoughts were interrupted when an older, aristocratic-looking man came to her table and asked if he could join her.

"Of course," said McLeod.

"I'm Henry," he said as he unloaded his tray onto the table. "Henry Fairfield Worthington. I know, it's old-fashioned to use all three names, but I'm an old-fashioned creature. And my mother was a Fairfield and proud of it. She really would have liked it if I had dropped the Henry and become just Fairfield Worthington, but my uncle Henry would have objected to that. So I'm Henry Fairfield Worthington. And you? I'm hoping you're McLeod Dulaney."

"I am," said McLeod, deciding to respond in kind to this nice, white-haired gentleman. "My whole name is Mary McLeod Brannon Dulaney. My mother was a McLeod, Maggie McLeod Brannon, and she loved it when I dropped the Mary. My husband was Holland Dulaney."

"I see," said Henry Fairfield Worthington. "You've handled all this better than I have. If I had married someone in this day and age we would have hyphenated our last names. If her name was Calvin, for instance, I guess I would be Henry Fairfield Worthington-Calvin."

"And you must be a Presbyterian, to even think of Calvin," said McLeod, who was vastly entertained. She liked the look of Henry Fairfield Worthington — white hair, pink cheeks, bright blue eyes — as well as the sound of him.

"Indeed I am," he said. "And I studied Calvin's *Institutes* at seminary. I'll never forget my professor. He loved John Calvin so much that tears sometimes ran down his cheeks when he talked about Calvin on the mystery of God's grace." Henry Fairfield Worthington sighed in affectionate reminiscence. "Oh, how he could go on and on about justification and election and predestination . . ."

Even McLeod's curiosity did not go so far as to make her ask for more information on justification, election, and predestination. "Do you teach here?" she asked.

"I did. I came here to teach speech and I taught for years, and then I was in the administration." McLeod wasn't surprised that he had taught speech — she had noticed that his voice was deep and mellifluous. "I still live in my seminary-owned bachelor apartment, in that house at the corner of Library Place and Mercer Street."

"I love that house," said McLeod. "It's

immense, and so Victorian, with its turrets and porches and gables and bay windows. Do you eat all your meals here at the cafeteria?"

"Oh, no, just lunch from time to time. I like to have a drink with dinner, and alas the seminary dining room is as dry as dust in that regard. If you like the house where I live, you must like Lenox House, the house on the corner of Library Place and Stockton."

"Is that the redbrick one with the steep pitched roof and blue brick trim?"

"Yes. It's another Victorian house. It's where the people work on the Dead Sea Scrolls project."

"Somebody's working on the Dead Sea Scrolls here?"

"Oh, yes, the seminary is publishing new editions of twelve of the scrolls, I believe," said Henry Fairfield Worthington. "Several scholars involved are at other institutions, but the people who are working at it here have their offices in Lenox House. Nobody else wanted Lenox House — but they were glad to get it."

"It's a fascinating house, I'll admit," said McLeod, "but I like yours better. It's more ample, somehow."

"You must come and see my apartment.

It has all sorts of architectural fancies. Come for tea. That's the meal I do best."

"I'd love to," said McLeod. "How did you know I was McLeod Dulaney?"

"My friend Fiona McKay told me you were coming; in fact, she told me you were here, and wanted us to meet. She invited me to dinner last night, and I was extremely sorry that I couldn't come. But I've met you anyway, so I'm somewhat consoled."

"How did you know it was me? Aren't there lots of single women about the seminary?"

"There are, but Fiona described you."

"I know," said McLeod wearily. "She told you I had prematurely white hair . . ."

"That's not all she said," Henry Fairfield Worthington said. "She said you were very attractive and bright and that we'd get along famously. I see she was right, as usual."

"I'm very fond of Fiona," said McLeod. "I've known her since I was in high school in Atlanta. And I was delighted to know she and Angus moved to Princeton not long ago. And they've been very nice to me."

McLeod's curiosity, as usual, surfaced, and she asked Henry Fairfield

Worthington if he had ever thought of the theater. "Oh, no," he said. "But I'm a jack-of-all trades, you see. I majored in science in college and went to seminary, I was trained to be a Presbyterian minister. I learned Greek and Hebrew and all that and I even got called to a church and was ordained. But I was no good as a parish minister. When the seminary offered me a teaching job, I jumped at it. Then I moved to administration and worked in the business office until I retired."

"Hebrew," said McLeod reflectively, seizing on something he said. "Does everybody at the seminary have to learn Hebrew?"

"You have to learn it to be ordained in the Presbyterian church, so all the Presbyterians take it."

"Is it hard to learn?"

"The students complain bitterly that it's harder than Greek. Greek does have a grammatical structure something like western languages. One student told me learning Hebrew was like learning calculus, or a very decorative math. I don't know what that has to do with it."

McLeod reverted to the Dead Sea Scrolls. "I thought all the work on Dead Sea Scrolls was being done in the Middle East somewhere."

"Oh, no. For a while it was done by a small group of scholars, but they were so slow to publish the scrolls that it caused a scandal. Now I think that they've all essentially been published. The seminary will publish new editions of some of these scrolls. The people in Lenox House are all full of themselves — they run off to East Jerusalem all the time and come back with artifacts they've bought from antiquities dealers who got them from Bedouins."

"A lot really goes on at the seminary," said McLeod. "I can't believe it. I had no idea. I thought people just came here and learned to be preachers."

"In the old days, most of the students were Presbyterians and all of them were men. Most of them were young and fresh out of college. Now nearly half the students are women, and a great many students are older and have worked in other fields and decided to become ministers late in life. And many of them are of other denominations."

"What sort of careers did they have before they came here?"

"Everything. Lots of lawyers — apparently wishing to atone for their sins and turning to the church," he said with a laugh. "Many of them were in business.

Women get divorces and come here."

"And what denominations do they come from besides Presbyterian?"

"All of them. Baptist, Methodist, Episcopalian, United Church of Christ, even a few Catholics."

"All one big happy family?"

"Not exactly," said Henry Fairfield Worthington. "Lots of disagreements." He had finished his lunch and stood up. "I'll see you soon, McLeod. You must come to tea. Tomorrow?"

"I'd like to," said McLeod. "What time?"

"Four o'clock. Here's my card with my phone number on it. Lovely to meet you. Thank you for letting me join you."

Four

McLeod had agreed to meet a seminary student named Willy Cameron for dinner in the cafeteria that night. He was a hometown friend of Lyle Cramer, who had been in her first writing class at Princeton University and had told Willy to look her up when she got to the seminary. Willy had duly called McLeod and the date for dinner was the result. When she got to the cafeteria, she found that Willy Cameron had brought along a friend. "I thought you two ought to meet," he said. "McLeod, this is Roscoe Kelly. He's from Two Egg, Tennessee. Roscoe, this is McLeod Dulaney. She's a writer who's doing a book on Elijah P. Lovejoy."

McLeod and Roscoe shook hands. He was a raw-boned young man with red hair and freckles and a smile as wide as a barn door. He towered over Willy Cameron, who was slight and had dark hair and brown eyes. "How do you do, ma'am. I'm pleased to make your acquaintance."

"That's not just an act, McLeod," Willy said. "Roscoe really is a hillbilly from the hills of Tennessee."

Roscoe laughed amiably. "I am what I am," he said.

"I'm from Georgia, so I'm used to that kind of talk," said McLeod. "I like it."

They picked up trays and began to go from station to station, filling them up. McLeod chose creamed chicken and a salad while the young men piled plates high with meat loaf and mashed potatoes.

When they were sitting at a table, Willy and McLeod talked briefly about Lyle Cramer. "I had him in a class at Princeton," she said, explaining that she meant the university, not the seminary. "When they say 'Princeton,' everybody at the university means the university. But when you say 'Princeton' here, everybody means the seminary. It's confusing."

"I know," said Willy Cameron. "And nobody seems to understand there's no longer any connection between the two — except that we use each other's libraries."

"I've learned all about it," said McLeod, telling him about her research on Elijah P. Lovejoy. "Princeton — the university —

46

was founded by Presbyterians — they called themselves New Siders — to educate preachers. They wanted a college more liberal than Harvard or Yale. Then the clergy became upset with the college when it started teaching modern foreign languages like French and German in addition to Greek and Latin and Hebrew, and then the college added science courses. So the Presbyterian General Assembly started a real seminary and this is it, the oldest Presbyterian seminary in the country."

"They're always reminding us that it's the oldest and the richest," said Willy.

They ate without speaking for a few minutes and then Willy, brushing his brown hair back from his eyes, said, "You'll be interested in Roscoe. He keeps rattlesnakes in his room."

"Rattlesnakes?" said McLeod.

"He's a snake handler," said Willy.

McLeod was fascinated. "How did you get started handling snakes?"

"My daddy is a preacher back in Two Egg, and he's a snake handler, and he wanted me to be a preacher. I have to tell you he's very conservative. He wanted me to get a call to be a preacher, but he didn't want me to be what he called a 'seminary preacher.' He said seminary preachers were all brain and no heart. He really didn't want me to go to college. He said he didn't go to college. 'Just listen for your call,' he said. 'You'll hear it.' He can quote Scripture by the hour, and he recited the Bible to me for days, hoping I'd get the call. Mama didn't agree. She wanted me to go to college and so did my high school English teacher. The teacher helped me get a scholarship to Maryville College — that's a little Presbyterian school in the hills of Tennessee, as Willy here puts it."

"Is your father a Presbyterian?" asked McLeod.

"No, ma'am. He started his own church — the Church of the Followers. But Maryville's been around a long time, so he let me go there. And my teachers at Maryville thought I ought to come to seminary if I wanted to be a preacher, or to even see if I really wanted to be a preacher. I liked the idea of coming up north, and so when I got a scholarship, I came. To please my daddy, though, I brought two snakes up here with me. Willy's fascinated. He says he wants to handle them." Roscoe grinned at Willy.

"Do you handle them?" McLeod asked Willy. Willy shook his head. "But *you* handle them?" she asked Roscoe.

"Not really. I just sort of have them," said Roscoe. "My daddy does, though. He really believes in it. He says he doesn't do it to prove his faith. He says it's what God has told him to do."

"Told him personally?" asked McLeod.

"No, it's in Scripture," said Roscoe. "In Mark 16, Jesus says his 'followers will cast out devils, speak in tongues, and take up serpents and not be hurt by them.' "

"Has your father ever been bitten?" asked McLeod.

"A couple of times, but we'd get him to the doctor as quick as we could and he'd be all right."

McLeod thought this over. "Roscoe, are you glad you came to seminary? Do you like it here? Do you want to be a preacher?"

"I'm glad I came. I've met all sorts of new people — like Willy here — and I'm learning lots. I can't tell my daddy any-thing I've learned about the Bible, though. He would tear the house down if I tried to tell him David didn't write the Psalms or that the walls of Jericho didn't fall down when Joshua blew his trumpet. I can't ever tell him what I've learned." For a moment, his wide smile was dimmed, then it broke out again. "But I'm glad I came. Yes, ma'am."

"So you really keep rattlesnakes in your room?" McLeod continued.

"Yes, ma'am. In a cage, though. Everybody comes in to look at them. Willy teases them. I tell him someday they're going to bust out of that cage and come eat him alive."

"What do you feed rattlesnakes?"

"I buy pinkies for them."

"Pinkies?"

"That's what they call little newborn mice. I get them at a pet store out on Route 1 — Willy drives me out there. I don't have a car."

"I may tease those snakes," said Willy, "but I'm their bread and butter. They ought to know it. They better not eat me alive."

"You know, you think it's all foolishness," said Roscoe, "but it just may not be. That's one reason I brought Samson and Delilah — that's their names — up here with me. Mainly to please my daddy, but also I thought, maybe there's something to it. Maybe I need to have my snakes handy in case the seminary turns out to be a crock."

"Are the other students scared of the

rattlesnakes?" asked McLeod.

"You bet they are," said Willy. "They keep their distance."

"I keep my room locked so nobody can come in when I'm not there and fool around with them and maybe get hurt," said Roscoe.

Roscoe and Willy had chosen desserts, but McLeod hadn't. Now, unable to hold out against temptation, she went back and got herself some ice cream. So there, she thought.

When she got back to the table, Roscoe was encouraging Willy. "You'll do fine," he said. "You're smooth. You're polished. I'm not ready to do it, but you are."

McLeod sat down and looked questioningly at them. "We're talking about my sermon," said Willy. "I'm supposed to preach Monday in the chapel."

"That's wonderful," said McLeod. "I'll come hear you."

When they had finished dinner, Willy asked McLeod if she'd like to meet Samson and Delilah. McLeod, ever curious, said she would indeed, and they walked up to Alexander Hall, the oldest building at the seminary, where both young men lived, and up the stairs to Roscoe's room.

Samson and Delilah were in their cage, on a table in Roscoe's austere room. They were coiled and looked huge to McLeod as they opened their mouths and waved their forked tongues around in a menacing way. She shuddered and asked Roscoe if they were safely locked in that cage.

"Yes, ma'am," said Roscoe. "See, it's a double cage. They're locked in that cage in there, and that cage sits inside this bigger cage. That's a precaution. Both cages are locked."

"Good," said McLeod.

Back in Erdman, she got ready for bed and then could not sleep. The corpse haunted her. It seemed to her, from the brief glimpse she had had of him, that the dead man was handsome. Had he been romancing someone's wife, been killed by a jealous husband? In that case, if they could identify the victim, it should be easy to find the murderer. If only he were identified. McLeod tried to think of something else, to create mental images that would be relaxing and soothing — snow-covered mountains, the surf crashing on a beach, a deep blue lake in the north woods. It all seemed menacing — the mountains were dangerous to climb and the air was cold, the surf looked really dangerous, as if an approaching tidal wave might engulf everyone on the coast, and the deep blue lake was a place to drown someone. At last McLeod slept.

Five

On Saturday, George Bridges called Mc-Leod from Brussels. He was bitterly sorry, he said, not to be in town when she was there. How was everything in Princeton?

"Horrible," said McLeod, and gave him a summary of events of the past two days.

"Well, aside from being involved in a murder case," said George, a hint of irony in his voice, "how are things at the seminary?"

"It's very different from the university. It seems narrow to me — everybody teaching religion. At the university you have people teaching English and history and physics and art history and French and engineering and chemistry and biology. Oh, the seminary has different departments, but it's all religion. And you wouldn't believe the wars they wage." She told him a little bit about inclusive language and the furor over gay marriage. "But I have to say, everybody is very sweet to me — the librarians and the staff at Erdman Hall — everybody I deal with. Everybody is just as nice as he or she can be. It's wonderful."

They talked about the body McLeod had found. "I can't stop thinking about him," said McLeod.

"I guess not," said George.

"I don't see how they'll ever identify him," McLeod said. "No clothes. No wallet. No nothing."

"They'll find out who he is," said George. "Someone will report him missing. Or maybe he's a spy who got fingered."

"Actually, I thought of that," said McLeod, though she could see that George was teasing her.

That afternoon, McLeod went, as arranged, to tea at Henry Fairfield Worthington's apartment, a space that she immediately loved, with its bay window, fireplace, book-filled shelves, Oriental carpets, piano, big overstuffed sofa and chairs covered in faded chintz, and many lamps, all lit.

Fiona was there. "Where's Angus?" asked McLeod.

"Oh, he's going to preach at some church up in North Jersey tomorrow and he's working on his sermon. It's like the times when we were in a parish church. Saturdays are shot."

Henry Fairfield Worthington looked splendid in a velvet smoking jacket — the first one McLeod had ever seen off the stage or screen. "Ladies, is Lapsang Soochong all right with you?"

"Lovely," said Fiona, and McLeod nodded. Henry poured them cups of tea and passed plates of tiny cucumber sandwiches. "And there's cake," Henry said.

As soon as McLeod had drunk some tea, she asked the other two if either of them knew Roscoe Kelly. Fiona and Henry shook their heads.

"He's a student," said McLeod. "A second-year student, I think, like my friend Willy Cameron —"

"We call them 'middlers,' " Fiona said, interrupting. McLeod went on undeterred. "Roscoe's from Two Egg, Tennessee, and he's a snake handler. I met his snakes, two rattlers named Samson and Delilah."

Henry Fairfield Worthington looked interested, and Fiona said, "Now that you mention the snakes, I think Angus has talked about him, but I've never met him."

"Did you know about him, Henry?" McLeod asked.

"Yes, I've heard of him, but I've never

met him," said Henry. "We do get some weird ones. I knew the students were getting more conservative, but this is the first snake-cult member I've heard of."

"Roscoe does come from a very conservative background," said McLeod. "He was talking about how his father would hate some of the things he's learned here — things like Moses didn't write the Pentateuch and David didn't write the Psalms."

"Some of them simply cannot handle serious Bible study and criticism of various kinds," said Henry Fairfield Worthington.

"What is 'higher criticism'?" McLeod asked. "I've heard about it all my life."

"Higher criticism involves taking facts from historical sources or archaeological discoveries and applying them to the Bible," said Henry. "Source criticism seeks to identify literary sources of biblical texts. As an example of higher criticism, archaeologists have determined that the walls of Jericho did not fall down when Joshua had seven trumpeters march around the city for seven days and then blow their trumpets. Jericho was destroyed around 1300 BC, and Joshua came along three hundred years later. These conservative students have a hard time coming to terms with things like that."

McLeod was fascinated with what Henry was saying. "The other night, Lucy Summers was telling me about her students who say, 'But the Bible *has* to be right. It's the way God wrote it.' "

"Of course, this has been an issue of debate for some time," said Henry. "I remember my uncle — who was a student at Union Seminary in Richmond right after World War Two — had a wonderful story to tell. Let me explain that at Union back then the dietician was a clergyman's widow who had no pension. She needed the job, but she knew very little about institutional cooking. She served the same thing every week — roast beef on Sunday, hash on Monday, meat loaf on Tuesday, and a repellent dish made of macaroni and tomatoes on Wednesday. The students called it Blood and Guts. And one Wednesday night, this charming middler who had been truly shaken by what he had learned in Old Testament class, sighed and said, "Well, I've found out that Moses didn't write the first five books of the Bible. Isaiah didn't write half of Isaiah, and David didn't write the Psalms. But of one thing I'm sure — if it's Wednesday night, we'll have Blood and Guts."

McLeod laughed. "I love it," she said.

★ ★ ★

A buzzer sounded and Henry went to open the door to a new arrival, who greeted Henry gustily, clapping him on the shoulder and wringing his hand. "It's good of you to have me, old chap," he said.

"This is McLeod Dulaney," Henry said. "She's honoring us with her presence while she does research here on Elijah P. Lovejoy. And you surely know Fiona McKay, wife of our own esteemed Angus."

"Oh, yes," said the newcomer, bowing in turn to McLeod and then Fiona.

"And, ladies, this is Ernst von Kemp. He's our famous biblical archeologist, and he's working on the seminary's Dead Sea Scrolls project."

McLeod was happy to meet von Kemp, a chubby, bald man with a bushy beard and rimless glasses, who looked a little like Santa Claus in mufti. She moved over to sit beside him as soon as he was settled with a cup of tea and a plate of sandwiches at his elbow. "Tell me about the Dead Sea Scrolls," she said abruptly. "I'm afraid I'm totally ignorant. Aren't lots of them still unpublished?"

"The scrolls were found near the Dead Sea," said Ernst von Kemp, beaming happily. "Goat herdsmen found them in caves

59

at Qumran near Jericho, in 1947. The scrolls were stored in tall ceramic jars. One of the goatherds knew enough about antiquities to know they were valuable. They took them to an antiquities dealer in Bethlehem and the scrolls came on the market through that dealer. You're wrong, however" — and his eyes twinkled even more brightly, as though he liked it when he was able to point out when someone was wrong — "about publication. The first ones, found in Cave One, were published fairly quickly. They were intact and well preserved. Then, as hundreds more turned up — mostly in fragments — in other caves, scholars who worked on them in East Jerusalem held on to them and failed to publish for an unconscionably long time. But then the Huntingdon Library, which had a set of microfilms of all the scrolls, opened them to all scholars. Virtually all of them have been published by this time."

"They caused a sensation at the time they were found, didn't they? Didn't Edmund Wilson learn Hebrew just so he could read them?" asked McLeod.

"He did," said von Kemp. "He learned Hebrew right here at Princeton Seminary, didn't he, Henry?" Von Kemp was enjoying himself immensely.

"He did," said Henry. "He came to Princeton to give the Gauss lectures at the university — he went there as an undergraduate, you know — and while he was in town for a semester, he came over to our place and learned Hebrew."

"I wonder if he was a good student," said McLeod.

"Very good, I understand," said Henry Fairfield Worthington. "He wanted to read the Scrolls for himself because he thought they would knock Christianity for a loop. They didn't. Christianity is still alive and well, not looped. But he was a good student and a scholar when he wanted to be."

"The scrolls are really important, aren't they?" asked McLeod.

"They are," said von Kemp, "because they include copies of most of the books of the Old Testament and all of them are at least a thousand years older than any copies we had before they were found. It was tremendous luck that they were as well preserved as they were. Here at the seminary we're working on an edition of twelve of the scrolls that are non-biblical."

"Non-biblical?" asked McLeod.

"Yes, there are several scrolls that aren't in the Bible. These particular ones are concerned with the life of the Essene community."

"The Essenes?"

"The Essenes were a Jewish sect — like Pharisees or Sadducees — and they had a community at Qumran, near the caves where the scrolls were found. One of the non-biblical scrolls is the Rule of the Community — the rules that the Essenes lived by. Another one is called the Temple Scroll — it's all about the Temple, as you might expect. Right now we're working on the Damascus Scroll, as it's called. The first copy of it was found in Egypt, and then other copies were found at Qumran. But the Copper Scroll is the one that fascinates everyone."

"Copper?" asked McLeod. "I thought they would be on papyrus."

"Most of them are on leather, a few on papyrus, but this one was on very thin copper. It was the devil's own work to unroll it. They had to send it to the University of Manchester where they had the technical facilities to get it unrolled. But the Copper Scroll tells where some kind of treasure is hidden. Of course, hordes of people have gone to the sites mentioned to look for the treasure, but nobody's ever found it."

He took a sip of tea.

"Are they all written in Hebrew?" asked McLeod.

"Some are written in Greek and some in Aramaic, but most of them are in Hebrew."

While McLeod talked with von Kemp, Fiona and Henry went over to the piano and began to play a duet.

"I'm so happy to learn something about the scrolls," said McLeod, above the sound of music. "Is it possible that you could discover something among them that has been overlooked?" McLeod asked von Kemp.

"What do you mean?" asked von Kemp.

"Oh, I mean something that would be revolutionary. A new book of the Bible, for instance."

"Oh, no, not among these scrolls," said von Kemp carefully. "They've been picked over too much. I think every fragment is well known by now. Of course, there's always a chance of finding something new. Every time I go to East Jerusalem, antiquarian dealers offer me things. But mostly they're objects, not documents." He paused. "Actually, I think I'm onto something myself right now. I can't talk about it just yet, but it's quite exciting."

"How wonderful. Can you give me a clue?"

"Oh, no. Not yet. But it's the biggest thing I've ever been involved with," said von Kemp.

"So they're still finding caves," said McLeod.

"Oh, this didn't come from a cave." McLeod watched him closely.

"Where did it come from?"

Von Kemp hesitated again. "Well, actually, it came from a tomb. But I'd better not say anything else — even though you're such a good listener."

"You are a good explainer," said McLeod, deciding to lay on a little flattery. "It's all so fascinating."

The piano was suddenly quiet, and Fiona and Henry were laughing heartily. They congratulated each other on finishing the duet at the same time, and the tea party began to break up.

As they were leaving, Fiona turned to McLeod. "We're going out to dinner tonight — at the president's house," said Fiona, making snoring noises to indicate the boredom she expected. "Or I'd have you over. Poor baby."

"Don't worry about me. I'm going to work on my notes. I've practically forgotten poor Elijah P. Lovejoy. And tomorrow, I'll tell you one thing, Fiona

McKay, I'm not going to church. I'm sick of religion."

"I know what you mean. Lots of times I feel the same way, but I have to keep on. Head up and smiling, like a lamb to the slaughter."

"Lambs don't smile on the way to slaughter," said McLeod. "They bleat."

"Baaaa, baaaaa," said Fiona, as they parted on the sidewalk of Library Place.

At least no one had asked her about the body, McLeod thought. That night, tired after two nights of tossing and turning, she felt sure she would go to sleep quickly. But, no, the body in the garment bag kept appearing before her eyes. Was the young man killed by a woman whom he had betrayed, a jealous woman, or maybe a woman he had broken up with? Or had he been the object of a cold-blooded experiment in killing like the one Leopold and Loeb had carried out all those years ago in Chicago? At last she slept.

Six

And so it was on early Sunday morning that McLeod walked down to the railroad station on the university campus and took the Dinky — the shuttle — to Princeton Junction, where she caught a train for New York.

New York was wonderful, as always. As she always did when she rode the Madison Avenue bus uptown, she felt a strong urge to live there. How could I do that? she wondered. Could I get a job up here? Would I really want to leave Tallahassee and the Gulf Coast to come up here? The questions were still unanswered as she walked to Fifth Avenue and climbed the awe-inspiring steps of the Metropolitan Museum of Art.

An exhibition of art from ancient Mesopotamia captured her interest. Were these treasures anything like the things Ernst von Kemp was offered by antiquities dealers in East Jerusalem? Another question she couldn't answer. She moved out of the ancient art galleries and into the ones where the work of the Impressionists blinked and flashed pure light at her. She sighed.

She looked at her watch and shot out of the galleries and away from the pictures' brightness. It was time to meet Harry. Harry was her son, a graduate student at Yale. A perpetual graduate student, she thought sadly. But a darling perpetual graduate student, she added happily to herself, heading toward the sidewalk café across the street from the Met to find Harry already waiting. His hair, she noticed, was even grayer than it had been the last time she saw him. He would be prematurely white, just like his mother.

She hugged him fiercely and they looked at each other. "It's good to see you," they said simultaneously, and then McLeod thanked him for coming down from New Haven to have lunch with her, and they began to catch up. Harry wanted to know how she was getting along with her work on Elijah P. Lovejoy and McLeod explained that she had discovered lots about him at Colby College in Waterville, Maine, where Lovejoy's diary and many of his letters were archived. "When I finish up at Princeton, I

67

can go to St. Louis and Alton, Illinois, and that will be an end to the research. Then back home to Tallahassee and write the damned thing. And how's your dissertation — the writing still going well?"

She felt as though she had been asking this question for several years, and indeed she had.

"Very well," said Harry, as he had been replying for several years.

"Good," she said. The waiter brought menus and they ordered, McLeod a salad and Harry a hamburger.

Harry told her about his teaching — he was a T.A. in the art history department this year and he loved it.

"Any idea when you'll finish your dissertation?" she asked.

"I plan to finish it by the end of this academic year," said Harry. "I'm really sick of it. My adviser kicked it back to me this week, and I've got to work on all the things he suggested."

"I hope you can get it behind you," said McLeod, trying to sound encouraging and not nagging. "I wish you well."

"At least I'm self-supporting," said Harry, who felt somewhat guilty about the amount of time he had spent in graduate school.

"I know you are," said McLeod. "It's wonderful the way you piece together fellowships and teaching and grants to keep yourself afloat. I just think —"

"I know, you think there's a wider world out there," said Harry. "I hear there is. I'll get to it."

"I know you will," said McLeod.

They chatted then about other things — news from Tallahassee and news from Harry's sister Rosie, who worked on a newspaper in Charlotte, North Carolina. It was an amiable, even delightful conversation.

McLeod told him about finding the body, and they discussed this much-less-delightful topic. "The body hasn't been identified yet," said McLeod. "I have no idea who it is. Isn't that weird?"

"It's probably a Princeton professor who drove a graduate student advisee into a murderous frenzy," said Harry.

"I just glimpsed his face, but I don't think he's old enough to be a Princeton professor," said McLeod.

"Maybe it was the graduate student. He was so slow finishing his dissertation that his mother couldn't stand it and killed him and stuffed him in a garment bag," said Harry.

"Be warned," said McLeod.

"You know, Ma, you're lucky to get leave from the paper to come up North as often as you do."

"I know it. But I've worked there so long and so hard and Charlie Campbell knows it. I love to come up here. I'm lucky, and I know it."

Afterward they walked down Fifth Avenue and went into the Frick, where Harry wanted to see the John Singer Sargent exhibition. They walked around the permanent collection and admired the Vermeers. Few things could be grander, thought McLeod, than going to a museum with a son who was a graduate student in art history.

Late that afternoon, when she got off the train at Princeton Junction, she saw Lucy Summers, red hair shining brightly, headed with another woman toward the platform to catch the Dinky. "Have you been away for the weekend?" McLeod asked her, eyeing the suitcase fastened with bungee cords to a little metal cart that Lucy was pulling behind her.

"We went to Chicago to visit an old friend," Lucy said. "McLeod, this is Hester Hardin. She's in the business office at the seminary."

"I've heard so much about you," said Hester Hardin, a pleasant-looking woman with short gray hair. "You're the one who found the body, aren't you?"

"I found the body. Did you go to Chicago on the train?" asked McLeod, quickly changing the subject.

"No, we flew. We just caught the train at Newark Airport. They have a new rail connection, and it's easier to take the train than to drive, especially since we can walk to the Dinky from my house," Lucy said.

They sat together on two facing seats on the Dinky, and Lucy asked McLeod if she, too, had been away.

"I just spent the day in New York," she said. "I went to the Met and then I met my son for lunch and we went to the Frick to say hello to the Vermeers. It was a heavenly day." She did not mention the nagging worry about Harry and his dissertation.

"I'll bet it was a treat to get away from seminary food," said Lucy.

"It was," said McLeod. "And it was a treat to be in New York."

As they walked up the hill toward the seminary, Lucy said, "You're looking at my old cart. I know everybody else has those bags with wheels, but I seem to have so much old luggage and I hate to throw it away. I'm thrifty, you know."

"An admirable habit," said McLeod. "I remember when Rosie, my daughter, was learning to be a Girl Scout and she had to memorize the Scout laws. One of them is, 'A Girl Scout Is Thrifty.' Rosie said to me, 'Mama, what's thrifty? Does that mean you laugh a lot?' "

When they got to Library Place, McLeod prepared to peel off. "You must come to my house for dinner," said Lucy. "I'll call you when we can check our calendars."

"I'd like to very much," said McLeod. "I'm glad I met you, Hester."

Exhausted from all the walking she'd done — to the Dinky and back and all over New York — McLeod went early to bed, where the corpse from the tow path haunted her again. Who was he? What was he doing when he died? Had he perhaps been killed by a business partner who felt he'd been cheated? There was the possibility that kept occurring to McLeod over and over again — he was simply the victim of random violence. Or maybe he was killed in a drunken brawl and stripped and stuffed in the garment bag.

Finally, McLeod slept.

Seven

On Monday morning McLeod went to the Seminary library prepared to buckle down to Elijah P. Lovejoy. In the stacks she found *Discourse on the Alton Outrage*, a book published in 1838 about Lovejoy's murder by a pro-slavery mob the year before. She brought it out to a table in the periodical room because the sunshine flooded in through the tall windows there. She also liked the portraits of long-dead seminary professors that hung on the walls. Among all those dead white men in beards and suits was one African-American woman, Betsey Stockton. "Born in slavery in Princeton," read a small plaque beneath her picture, "she was freed and raised in the family of Ashbel Green, a founder of the seminary. She was educated by Dr. Green and three seminary students and became a missionary teacher in Hawaii."

McLeod pondered this extraordinary biography until she began making notes on her laptop. Just in time, she remembered that Willy was preaching that morning. She left her work to hurry down to the chapel, her favorite seminary building with its yellow walls and white woodwork, including a white rococo carved screen behind the altar.

She liked Willy's sermon. He talked about how second-year students at the seminary all went through a crisis, thinking they had lost their faith when they studied theology and history. The message often seemed lost, but this was wrong. The message was still there, the message of God's power and love, of the need to care for the poor and the aged, to feed the hungry. "The message is one of mystery and wonder and hope . . . How awesome are God's works," he concluded. It was a very different sermon than the one the student had preached the week before. McLeod was impressed.

After the benediction, McLeod went up to congratulate Willy and then hurried back to the library and the *Discourse on the Alton Outrage.*

When she finished with the *Discourse*, she decided to knock off early for lunch. The seminary library was the only library

McLeod had found where you could leave a laptop on a table and expect to find it still there when you got back. She put on her jacket and went outside. Instead of heading across Mercer Street to the dining hall, she detoured by Erdman Hall to see if she had any mail.

When she got to the lobby of Erdman, the young woman behind the desk said, "Ms. Dulaney, there's somebody waiting to see you." She motioned toward a tall man standing by the wall, away from the reception desk. McLeod realized it was Lester Brasher.

"I'd like to have a few words with you," he said.

"Sure," said McLeod. "Let's go into the lounge." The lounge was a very attractive room, with comfortable furniture and many windows that looked out on evergreens — although McLeod thought it was too bad you couldn't see fall foliage.

They sat down and Brasher said, "We've identified the body," he said.

"Oh," said McLeod. "Who is it?"

"He was Daniel Strong, a seminary student," said Brasher. He looked at her.

"A seminary student?" said McLeod.

"Yes, it's quite a coincidence, isn't it?"

"Coincidence?"

"Yes, that he's a student at this seminary where you're working. And you found the body."

"I suppose so," said McLeod. "Why would anybody kill a seminary student?"

"That's what we have to find out," said Brasher. He paused, continued to look at McLeod. "And you're sure you didn't know the victim."

"I'm sure."

"His name was *Daniel Strong*," said Brasher. He waited, ominously, it seemed to McLeod. "Are you sure you didn't know him?" he asked again.

"I'm sure," McLeod said.

"You can level with us," Brasher said. "And tell us how you knew him."

"But I didn't," said McLeod. "Truly, I didn't."

"How long have you been staying here?" asked Brasher, switching gears.

"I got here October first."

"So you've been here ten days and you had never seen Mr. Strong before last Thursday?"

"That's right."

Brasher stood up and stretched to his full height. He was very tall. McLeod thought he had probably played basketball at one time or another. "Ms. Dulaney, you signed the visitor's book at Miller Chapel on the seminary campus last Monday, did you not?"

"Yes, I did," said McLeod. "Someone told me that a student preached every Monday, and I was curious. I wanted to see what a student-led service would be like."

"So you don't deny that you were present?"

"No," said McLeod.

"Daniel Strong was the student preacher for that service, a week ago today." Brasher frowned down at her from a height that seemed like the skies to McLeod, still seated.

"Was he?" she said, somewhat confused.

"Do you still deny that you knew him?"

"I deny that I *knew* him," McLeod said steadily. "I did not know his name. There was no printed order of service, and no one introduced the student preacher. I didn't know who he was. Now, I know the student who preached this morning, but I had met him before."

"And when you discovered Daniel Strong's body, you did not recognize him?"

"I did not," said McLeod. "He was dressed up at the service — he wore a coat and tie. When I saw him — his body — at the canal last Thursday, you know that I said he looked familiar but that I didn't know him. And I didn't. I simply didn't recognize him. It was a very short service and his sermon was extremely odd, I thought, and the chapel is so beautiful that I was looking around at it most of the time. I had never been in it before."

Brasher began to question her about how she had spent her time before last Thursday, and since then. McLeod answered with as much patience as she could muster.

"Ms. Dulaney, we need to search your room. Will you give us permission?"

"Of course."

"And your car?"

"I don't have a car. I didn't drive up here."

Brasher called someone on his cell phone, and another detective appeared so quickly that McLeod decided he must have been right outside Erdman Hall. McLeod took them up to her room and watched while they searched everywhere. It was a small room with no furniture except a desk and chair, a single bed, and a wardrobe, and they combed it carefully. They looked in the bathroom medicine cabinet and in the tiny laundry hamper.

"Thanks very much," said Brasher at last. "We may have to ask you to come to police headquarters, so please don't leave town."

"I won't," she said.

The policemen left. McLeod splashed cold water on her face. It did feel good. She picked up the phone and dialed Fiona McKay's number in order to tell her about the latest "police brutality." When no one answered, she left a message that the police had been to Erdman Hall to question her, and hung up.

She missed Nick Perry. He was one of the nicest policemen she had ever known. But Lester Brasher was a horse of a different color. And for some mad reason he suspected her of murder. McLeod felt a moment of lonely panic.

It was too late to get lunch in the seminary cafeteria, so she walked uptown to the Red Onion and had a Reuben. Back in the library that afternoon, it was a relief to be dealing with Elijah P. Lovejoy. After she finished work, she went back to Erdman, where she found a message from Fiona inviting her to dinner again that night. Thank heavens, McLeod thought, calling immediately to accept. She looked at her clock and decided she had plenty of time to walk up Nassau Street to Bunches, that nice flower shop, and get something for Angus and Fiona. The walk would do her good.

Eight

Promptly at 6:30, McLeod, bearing a huge bunch of fluffy, shaggy, pale-yellow chrysanthemums, rang the doorbell at the McKays' house, and, when the door was opened, returned the enthusiastic greeting from Beelzebub and Gabriel.

Fiona hugged her — chrysanthemums and all — and went to find a vase. She came back with a tall brown pitcher in which the chrysanthemums looked lovely, and took McLeod into the living room, where a small fire was burning. The dogs trotted over to the fireplace and lay down in front of it, as close as they could get to the flames.

"Oh, thank you for having me," said McLeod. "I had a terrible day."

"Let me get us a drink. We won't even wait for Angus. What will you have?"

"I think I'd like a martini."

"Great," said Fiona. "Coming up." She

came back with a tray bearing two martinis and a plate with slices of French bread topped with smoked salmon. "I don't have to worry about dinner tonight," she said. "I put it in the slow cooker this morning and it's all done, all by itself. I'll throw together a salad and that's it."

"Sounds great," said McLeod. "Where's Angus?"

"Oh, he's in his study as usual, doing something about God, I guess." Fiona shrugged.

McLeod thought Fiona's offhand attitude about Angus's work was amusing and wondered if it bothered Angus. How had Fiona been received as a preacher's wife when Angus had his own parish? She would ask Fiona someday, she decided, but not just now. Instead, she told her about the police interview and the search.

"That odious Thrasher," said Fiona, when McLeod had finished her tale of woe. "He is a brute. And then you worked all day on poor old Elijah. All those murdered people. Dan Strong and Elijah P. Lovejoy. Poor baby."

"His name is Brasher," said McLeod. "And I've hardly worked at all today."

"Thrasher's much more appropriate," said Fiona.

"What are people at the seminary saying about the murder?" McLeod asked.

"I don't know," said Fiona, "I spent the day at the university art museum. I'm learning to be a docent. It's enormous fun to take up something new at my age, but nobody there was much interested in a seminary student, I'm afraid. I hear Angus emerging from his study. We'll ask him."

Angus looked at them over his half glasses, and went to get himself a drink. When he came back, Fiona ordered McLeod to retell the story of her day — she did — and then both women asked Angus about the reaction at the seminary to the news that the tow path corpse was Dan Strong.

"Everybody was shocked, of course," said Angus. "And we all talked about Dan Strong. Nobody wanted to speak ill of the dead, but I noticed that some people had a hard time finding something good to say about Dan."

"Did you like him?" asked McLeod.

"He wasn't one of my favorites, to be honest. He was a senior. He was smart, and he worked hard. He always turned his work in on time. He learned his Hebrew and his Greek. But he seemed to have a chip on his shoulder, and he simply wasn't open to new ideas."

"Do you know who identified him?" asked McLeod.

"The dean," said Angus. "He went down to Trenton, where they took the body."

"Why did they call the dean?"

"They didn't. As I understand it, the dean called them. You see, Dan's girlfriend is Sharon Leland. She's a nice girl. Anyway, she told the dean on Sunday that Dan was missing. He didn't show up at the church where he was working, and she was really worried. She told the dean she hadn't seen him since Tuesday."

That was almost a week before, McLeod thought. Quite a time for a student to be missing. "The dean told her to check with Dan's family, and Sharon said his family had been trying to get in touch with him for days, so they certainly didn't know where Dan was. The dean hates any fuss and he hates bad publicity for the seminary, but he did finally call the police and the police asked if he would come down and look at this unidentified body. And the dean did, and it was Dan."

"How was he killed?"

"I don't know," said Angus. "I don't know whether he was shot or stabbed or what."

"It's a strange story," said McLeod.

"It certainly is," said Angus. "And it's really dreadful that you're mixed up in it."

Fiona went to do the salad and soon called them to the dining room. Beelzebub and Gabriel trotted in and sat on either side of McLeod. Fiona put a tureen in front of Angus and asked him to serve the plates. "It's veal stew, and it has cooked the whole livelong day," she said. "It should be good."

And it was good. They all ate hungrily.

"You know, this is bad news for the seminary — a student murdered," Angus said. "The trustees will be horrified. They'll want to hush it up."

"Hush it up?" said McLeod. "You can't hush up a murder."

"No, I know that," said Angus, "but they'll want to."

"But the murder probably has nothing to do with the seminary," said McLeod. "His body wasn't found here or anything. I shouldn't think it would be any kind of reflection on the seminary."

"The trustees are so paranoid that they'll see it that way," said Fiona. "Do you suppose they'll forbid people to talk about it to anybody, the way they did about Cyrus Monroe?"

"Who's Cyrus Monroe?" asked McLeod.

"See what you've done," Angus said crossly. "You shouldn't talk about it yourself."

It took all the willpower McLeod could muster not to keep asking questions. Virtue was rewarded, however, because Fiona was unmoved by Angus's reproof, and told it all. "He was this wonderful, charismatic teacher here," Fiona said. "And a graduate student — a woman — filed a sexual harassment suit against him. The Board clamped down. They made sure that it was settled out of court and they forbade anybody, including Cyrus and the graduate student, to say one word about it. I don't know what power they had over the graduate student, but it was hushed up. Cyrus had to leave."

Angus was quiet until they talked about Dan Strong again. McLeod could contribute nothing except that she had heard him preach in the chapel a week ago. "It was a very odd sermon," she said. "The text was about how the husband is going to punish his wife — strip her naked and punish her with thirst."

"Oh, he used that passage from Hosea, did he?" said Angus. "That's God talking to Israel. That is a very strange text for a student sermon."

"It went on from there about how every-body was going to be stripped," said McLeod.

"Sounds lively," said Fiona. "I should have gone."

Angus took the dogs out as McLeod was leaving and they walked McLeod back to Erdman. In her room, McLeod was again quite cheered after an evening with the McKays. Angus was a good man, and Fiona was good in a different way, and very good for Angus, she thought. If it weren't for Fiona, he might take himself too seriously.

Nine

On Tuesday, McLeod crossed Mercer Street and went to the seminary cafeteria for breakfast. The cafeteria had wonderful muffins and good, very hot water for tea, so she was a happy woman as she took her tray to a table by one of the big south-facing windows. One thing she liked about Princeton Theological Seminary was the prevalence of light. Was it the "Light of the World?" she wondered idly, or "The New Light"? What was the New Light anyway? She kept running across it in her reading about the seminary and Lovejoy. It was some sort of religious revival in the early nineteenth century, and that was all she knew. She had to get it straight because her writing about Elijah P. Lovejoy demanded it.

She read the *New York Times* and then glanced at the Trenton paper, which had a story about the identification of the "tow path corpse." This story also said that the Princeton Township police had not yet determined the cause of death, nor established the place where the murder had taken place.

"Can I join you?" McLeod looked up. Willy Cameron was resting his tray on her table and looking hopeful.

"Sure," she said, "I'll be glad to have company."

As Willy sat down, McLeod admired his very substantial breakfast that included juice, pancakes, sausage, eggs, milk, and coffee. "Lyle told me about the murders you and his class worked on," said Willy.

"Oh, dear," said McLeod.

"Anyway, when the tow path corpse turned out to be Dan Strong, I thought, 'This is providential. McLeod Dulaney is right here when we need her.' "

"I am not going to investigate the murder of Dan Strong," said McLeod. "Believe me."

Willy Cameron looked surprised, bewildered even. "Okay," he said, "but just let me talk to you about him then. Please. You might have some advice for me. I'm desperate."

Looking at her with enormous brown eyes from under the hair that fell on his forehead, he looked very young and vulnerable.

"All right," she said. She was almost ashamed to see that her usual curiosity was rearing its ugly head. "Talk to me." She pushed her tray and newspaper aside, folded her arms on the table, and looked at Willy.

"Dan Strong was a very odd duck. He had been out of college for years — he wasn't as old as some students, he hadn't had a career in the law or anything, but he had worked for the police in his hometown, someplace in Indiana. He was a big conservative, and, like a lot of students from conservative backgrounds, he had problems at the seminary. He was appalled by the way we learn to read the Bible, to do higher criticism and literary criticism. He was one of those who say, 'But it's the Word of God — you can't question it.' He detested the use of inclusive language. He didn't even approve of the ordination of women, and that's been going on for years. He disapproved of a lot of people on the faculty and thought they were far too liberal. He didn't approve of jazz worship services — he wanted only traditional hymns. He thought lots of the students — all of us except his little crowd — were immoral."

"Goodness, he sounds terrible," said McLeod.

"Furthermore, he insisted that homosexuality is a sin, that gay people have made a choice, have chosen to be homosexual, that they could become happily heterosexual if only they'd turn to Christ."

"I think scientific opinion is against him," McLeod said mildly. "Isn't it pretty well understood that homosexuality is innate?"

Willy Cameron took a huge bite of pancake and sausage, and didn't answer until he had chewed and swallowed. "Of course it is," he said. "And there are plenty of gay people at the seminary. I'm one of them, as a matter of fact, and it's not easy." He looked at her, letting this information sink in. When McLeod did not react, he continued. "But Dan wanted to out all of us and get rid of us if we wouldn't renounce our sexuality. He said there was no place for queers at the seminary, that we couldn't be ordained. And shouldn't be ordained."

"Is that true? That gays can't be ordained?" asked McLeod.

"Gay people can't be ordained in the Presbyterian Church," said Willy. "But there are gay students here. There's an organization called BGLASS — that stands for Bisexuals, Gays, Lesbians, and Straight

Seminarians. Whenever we put up notices of a BGLASS meeting, Dan went around and tore them down or wrote on top of them with a Magic Marker. He wrote things like 'HELLFIRE FOR QUEERS' or 'PERVERTS REPENT' or just 'SODO-MITES.' "

"He sounds very uptight — to say the least," said McLeod.

"Oh, he was," said Willy. "And he obviously made no secret of how he felt. He couldn't take people as they are. He wanted everybody to change, to be like him. And then there was his sermon last Monday."

"You know, I heard that sermon. I thought it was odd, but then I figured, he's a student, he's learning."

"It was more than odd, McLeod. It was a threat. That sermon was giving notice that Dan Strong had had enough, that he was going to reveal everyone's sins and get things cleaned up around here."

"I know he quoted Hosea on how the husband is going to punish his wife. A friend of mine said last night that that passage referred to God and Israel."

"Oh, yes, but Dan said that the wife was the seminary. God was going to strip it bare," he said. " 'Strip her naked and make her like a wilderness and turn her into parched land and kill her with thirst,' " he quoted. "Then he said that all her sins would be revealed to the rulers."

"Did everybody see the sermon the same way you did?"

"There wasn't any other way to see it, knowing Dan. The people who were there got the message. Not many faculty members came that day. In fact, not many people at all came. Dan was not the most popular student at the seminary. But the people who were there told the others about it and it got everybody stirred up. And then Dan disappeared. And now we find out he was murdered. There must be a connection."

McLeod thought about this. Could the sermon that a seminary student preached in chapel be his death warrant? "Do all students preach in the chapel?" asked McLeod. "I know students only preach on Monday and that it's the faculty other days, isn't it?"

"The president of the seminary preaches on Tuesday, it's prayer and music on Wednesday, a faculty member on Thursday, and on Friday it's communion with a professor serving and a student doing the meditation. It's good experience," said Willy.

"I see," said McLeod. "And you think the sermon is why Dan disappeared and was killed? I had been thinking that he was killed somewhere away from the seminary — maybe a random attack — but your idea is interesting."

"What do you think we should do about it? I mean, should we tell the police all this, or should we hush it up for the seminary's sake? The dean is already making noises about discretion. The police will be all over the seminary, but the administration is maintaining that Dan was murdered by someone who wasn't connected to the seminary."

"Somebody told me last night that the seminary would try to play it down as much as possible, but, Willy, this is a murder inquiry. I don't think you can play it down. You have to tell the police anything, anything at all, that might be helpful."

"That's what I think, too," said Willy. "But it will be hard for a lot of people — if they talk openly to the police, it will mean coming out for them. And some of them aren't ready for that yet."

"So most gay students are still in the closet."

"I'd say so," said Willy. "The administration doesn't help them any. This seminary is more conservative than lots of others. Last spring, two gay women applied here for married student housing and the seminary turned them down because they weren't married. When they applied as roommates for a suite in Hodge Hall, a dormitory for single students, they were turned down because they weren't 'just roommates.' They rented an apartment off campus. You can't win if you come out."

McLeod nodded sympathetically.

"Some of us — some who are gay — really want to be ordained," Willy went on. "We feel that we're called to be ministers, but the Presbyterian church won't ordain gay people. And if we switch to the United Church of Christ or the Episcopal Church I understand they're so overrun with gay applicants that they can't place them."

"The Episcopalians confirmed an openly gay bishop," said McLeod. "And I thought there was a tremendous shortage of ministers."

"There is and there isn't," said Willy. "I don't think many churches out there are looking for gay ministers."

"I see what you mean," McLeod said. "Willy, are you sure you want to be a minister?"

"It's the only thing I've ever been sure about," said Willy. "I always wanted to be a minister. And it was fine, as long as I didn't realize I was gay. And I didn't, as they say, 'confront my sexuality,' not until I got here. I came to terms with it. I had already been before my Presbytery and they had taken me under care — you have to be under a Presbytery's care to be a candidate for the ministry, as you probably know — and the question didn't come up with them. But it will, I'm sure. I don't know what will happen then. I'm going to finish seminary and see how it goes. I'm not going to lie about it. But I am worried about this police investigation."

"Still, I think everyone has to help in a murder inquiry in any way he can." Conscious of the need for gender-free language, she hastily added, "or *she,* can. Isn't there some way that people can tell the police all this without revealing that they're gay? I mean, you said BGLASS had straight seminarians among its members, didn't you?"

"Yes, but there are still difficulties."

"And the police maybe won't even suspect students or faculty, Willy. Let me say again that the murder may have been a random act of violence. The police probably won't even question you, and if you don't have any information — hard evidence, I mean — then . . . Come on. Cheer up. Have some more coffee while I finish my tea."

"Thanks," said Willy. "You're right. I may be worried for nothing." He took his cup and headed back to the coffee machines. When he came back, he still looked troubled. "I said you're right, but I have a horrible feeling that the police will look on anybody who admits he's gay as a murder suspect."

"Surely not," said McLeod. Each of them silently sipped from a mug.

Ten

After her breakfast with Willy, McLeod went to the library with her laptop to get back to work. She saw a notice on the bulletin board by the reference librarian's desk and, ever curious, stopped to read it. It was a copy of a faculty resolution deploring the defacing of BGLASS posters. Such actions, it said, were a "violation of the values of freedom of expression, of academic excellence, of Christian charity and civil behavior that we seek to embody as an institution." So there, thought McLeod. At least the seminary faculty did not have the attitude that Dan Strong had had.

She went on to the sunny periodical room, nodded to Betsey Stockton's portrait, and opened her laptop. When a woman came up to her table and paused, McLeod looked at her inquiringly — she didn't recognize her as a librarian.

"Excuse me," the woman said. "Are

you McLeod Dulaney?"

"Yes, I am."

"I'm Denise Morrow, Dean Tilley's secretary. He'd like to talk to you very much indeed. I wonder if you could come back with me to his office."

"Me?"

"Yes, he'd like to see you. If you don't mind . . ." The secretary's voice trailed away.

"Certainly," said McLeod, rising. She pulled her jacket from the back of her chair and put it on, smiling at Denise Morrow, who did not smile back.

She followed Denise out of the library and across Mercer Street, past Alexander Hall, across the quadrangle to the administration building. "What does the dean want to talk to me about?" she asked.

"I'll let him tell you," said Denise. For the first time, she smiled at McLeod, but her smile was weak and rather grim.

"All right," said McLeod, trudging along, through the door and across the hall to the dean's office. Denise stuck her head in a door to an inner office and said, "Ms. Dulaney is here, Dean Tilley."

"Oh, you found her?" a male voice, rather high-pitched, replied. "Thank you, Miss Morrow."

"This way, please," said Denise, ushering

McLeod into the dean's office. He did not rise from his desk.

"How do you do?" he asked her. "Ms. Dulaney, is it? Yes. I'm Dean Ted Tilley. Please sit down."

McLeod thought she had never seen a more unattractive man. He reminded her of a turtle, with his reptilian head peeking out from curved shoulders. His face was yellowish, seamed with wrinkles. His hair was thin and brushed across his scalp in an attempt to hide his baldness. His lips were pursed.

"You wanted to see me?" McLeod looked around for a chair, and pulled one up close to the dean's desk and sat.

"Yes, I did want to see you," he said. He made an attempt to be friendly and tried to smile, but did a bad job of it. "Are you enjoying the use of our facilities here at Princeton?" he asked.

"Very much," said McLeod. "And everyone is so helpful and nice. It's a great place to do research here."

"Oh, yes, you're doing research on — just who is it?"

"Lovejoy, Elijah P. Lovejoy."

"Oh, yes. He was a kind of rabble rouser, wasn't he?" said Dean Tilley. "Most unfortunate end."

"I prefer to think of him as a man who wrote editorials from principle, and was prepared to die for those principles," said McLeod. This was the first time she had ever heard Lovejoy called a rabble rouser.

"Of course, of course," said Dean Tilley. He held his little short, fat hands up before him, the fingers spread and the tips of those on one hand touching the tips of the ones on the other, forming a cage that he peered over. "But he caused trouble. And we don't like trouble."

"I'm sure you don't," said McLeod. The dean reminded her of a certain oily old county commissioner in Florida who tried to be ingratiating and succeeded only in being repulsive. Dean Tilley doesn't scare me, she thought.

"Now, you're a stranger here," Tilley went on, "and you found this body down by the canal and the body has turned out to be that of a student at this seminary. A very fine student, you understand. One of our finest. He didn't mind speaking out about corruption — especially licentiousness and sodomy — and he was foursquare behind God and the Bible. And you, the person who found this body, you're staying in our guest house and working in our library. The police think there must be a connection between you and this corpse."

"Well, there's not," said McLeod. "At least as far as I know."

"We want to keep this as quiet as possible," the dean said, his little brown eyes narrowed to a squint.

"It's hard to keep a murder case quiet. And this may not really involve the seminary," said McLeod, who believed very much after her breakfast with Willy that somebody at the seminary was, in fact, involved in the murder of Dan Strong.

"We realize that," said the dean. "But we were wondering if you could, perhaps, wind up your research early, and return to your home."

"You mean you want to get me off the seminary campus?"

"It would perhaps be best for the seminary if one cause of celebrity were removed." The dean blinked his eyes, unaware, McLeod thought, how he had mangled the French phrase. His fingers were still touching before him.

"It would be difficult," McLeod said carefully. "I'm on leave from my newspaper, and I need to finish the work here while I'm still on leave."

"Everyone seems to know that you're the one who found the body, and they talk about it incestuously," Tilley said.

Surely he must mean "incessantly," McLeod thought. Tilley went on: "We feel that if things could quiet down on the seminary campus at least, that the whole thing might get less attention."

McLeod could not see the logic of his position, and replied sharply, "Of course, if the seminary expels me, I'll have to go."

"We wouldn't be expelling you," Tilley said. "Your leaving would remove a source of agitation, for the time being. When this case is settled, perhaps we can negotiate a way for you to come back."

"We'll see," said McLeod. "I'll have to talk to the police and see what they say. They told me not to leave town without their permission."

For the first time, Ted Tilley stood up. He attempted another smile at McLeod, but again failed. "Perhaps I could talk to the police for you," he said. "The seminary is not without influence."

McLeod stood up, too, and faced him. He was so short that she felt that she, not a tall woman, towered over him. This was ridiculous, she thought, and spoke sharply. "I must tell you in all fairness that if I leave, I will talk to the local papers about this. I'm a journalist, like Elijah P. Lovejoy was, and I think this is a good story — a writer forced to stop her research and leave town to help muffle a murder story."

Like most bullies, Ted Tilley crumpled when faced with a spark of opposition.

"Now, now," he said. "Don't be hasty. We're not forcing you. It's all for the good of the seminary, you know. It's the Lord's work. This will all die down, and we can perhaps work something out then."

"Perhaps," said McLeod, turning to leave.

"And you won't go to the press?" said Tilley.

"I *am* the press," said McLeod loftily, and went out, slamming the door behind her. "Good-bye," she said to Denise Morrow in the outer office. Denise looked at her, the expression on her face not changing. What a pair, thought McLeod — a stone face and a turtle.

Eleven

Back at Erdman Hall, McLeod tried to call Lester Brasher at the Township, but he was out. She left word that she wanted to talk to him and that she would be in the seminary library. She was settled once more — she gave a nod to Betsey Stockton — and had started making notes on her laptop when Brasher appeared.

"I got your message," he said.

"Let's go outside," said McLeod. "It's warm enough, I think."

Standing on the little terrace in front of Speer Library, she told Brasher about the dean's request.

"No, you can't leave town," said Brasher. "You're a material witness."

"I'll tell him what you said," McLeod said. "I don't want to go anywhere anyway. I'm working here, as you can see."

"All right. Still sure you didn't know Dan Strong?"

"Still sure," said McLeod.

"You heard him preach," said Brasher.

"I did, but that's all. And when I saw him after he'd been dead for three days and stuffed in a garment bag and carted down to the canal, I didn't recognize him. That's not so strange."

"Calm down," said Brasher. "How do you know he'd been in the garment bag three days?"

"I understand his girlfriend had not seen him since Tuesday, and I found the garment bag on Thursday," said McLeod. "I was speaking loosely when I said three days."

"How did you know his girlfriend said she hadn't seen him since Tuesday?"

"I have friends here. Angus and Fiona McKay. Angus teaches at the seminary. He told us last night," said McLeod.

"How do you know he was carted down to the canal?"

McLeod kept her temper. She knew it was foolish to lose it with a policeman who was interrogating her. If she was anything but humble and sweet, it would just inflame his suspicions. But oh, how she wanted to say to him, "Well, he didn't walk, did he?" Instead, she said as quietly as she could. "I just assumed it."

"Who are these friends of yours you're staying with? And where do they live."

McLeod told him.

Brasher stared at her. She looked back at him, then dropped her gaze. "Can I ask you a couple of questions?" she said.

"Sure," he said.

"How was Dan Strong killed?"

"You tell me," said Brasher. "I think you might know more about this than I do."

McLeod gave up on her resolve to hold her temper. She remembered how the police worked in Florida, and how Nick Perry and the Borough police worked in Princeton. "Have you talked to any of his friends? Any of his teachers?" she asked. "To any of the people he had offended with his criticisms? Why are you so convinced I know something important? Just because I stumbled — literally — on the body? There must be a hundred people right here on the seminary campus who could give you ten times, a hundred times, more vital information than I can."

"That's what they always say," Brasher said. "But that's all for now. Don't leave town." He turned and walked away.

McLeod went back in the library and tried to work. It was no use. She packed up her laptop and went back to her tiny room in Erdman. She tried to call Fiona, but got the answering machine — she left a message that she'd call back. Desperate, she called Nick Perry at the Borough police.

"Where have you been?" he asked her. "I've been trying to find you. I knew you found that body down by the canal, and then this morning Dean Tilley from the seminary came by to see the chief and asked for you to be allowed to leave town. The chief told him it was outside our jurisdiction, that the Township police were handling the murder case. So Tilley left. But I thought I'd better call you. Are those yokels giving you a hard time?"

"I seem to be under suspicion. Lester Brasher is the one who's been hounding me."

"Brasher? He's the biggest yokel of them all," said Nick. "Maybe you'd better talk to a lawyer."

"I guess I'll call Cowboy — he's everybody's lawyer." McLeod had met Cowboy Tarleton when she was in Princeton before.

"He's a good man, McLeod."

"Isn't there some way you can get involved?"

"If it turns out the murder took place in

108

the Borough, we can take over, I think," said Nick.

"I'm going to get busy and find out where that murder took place," said McLeod. "I'm sick of this."

"Be careful," said Nick. "Don't act like Nancy Drew. Leave it to the professionals."

"Even if the professionals are yokels?"

"Even if they're yokels. Let me nose around and see what I can find out. The yokels may be glad to get it off their hands."

Twelve

It was clear to McLeod that she had to find some evidence that would bring the Borough police into the picture. Surely Dan Strong had not been murdered on the tow path. He must have been killed on the seminary campus, or somewhere close by, someplace that was in the Borough. She wished she had asked Willy Cameron more questions at breakfast. Where was he now? It was close to lunchtime. She borrowed a seminary directory from the librarian at the front desk and called his room in Alexander Hall. He answered immediately and agreed to meet her for lunch.

"I've changed my mind a little," McLeod told him when they had filled their trays and found seats at a table by the window. "I'm really interested in this murder. The Township police think I did it for some reason, and Dean Tilley apparently sees me as a troublemaker for the seminary and wants me to leave."

"Dean Tilley! The students call him Toad Tilley. He's awful," said Willy.

"I thought he was awful myself. But the Township police say I can't leave. It's a mess. Can I ask you some questions?"

"I'd love it if you'd ask me some questions," Willy said.

"Well, this sermon that Dan Strong preached. Who exactly was he threatening? Do you know?"

"I think he was threatening all of the gay and lesbian students at the seminary. Not just the ones who are out, but the ones who are still in the closet. And to tell you the truth, there are a good many people in that category. We all got the distinct impression he was going to name names very soon." Willy paused. "And you know there are gay faculty members. A professor died last year of AIDS, and there are others still in the closet. Everybody I've talked to thought that Dan knew some things, and was going to name names sooner or later."

"So it was just gay people he was attacking?"

"Oh, no, he talked about the dangers of serpents and Roscoe — you know Roscoe Kelly — thought he was attacking snake handlers."

"Good heavens! Sweet Roscoe Kelly. Anybody else?"

"Feminists," said Willy. "He raged on about the demeanor of women. And that could mean faculty as well as students. Also, a friend of mine pointed out that when Dan was talking about how the 'keeper of the treasure' was to be stripped, he must have been talking about the people who manage the seminary's endowment, which has shrunk quite a bit recently. And I forget how he phrased it, but he said something that could have referred to anybody who reads the Bible critically and doesn't take it as the literal word of God or accurate history."

"But nobody would kill him because of that, would they? I mean, they still aren't going to teach the Bible without using higher criticism or source criticism or literary criticism," asked McLeod, who was learning fast. "I mean, Dan Strong couldn't stop that, could he, even if he denounced people, as you say?"

"No, but he could cause a lot of trouble," said Willy. "He could have gone to the newspapers. They always want to print stories about how God is dead and how preachers have lost their faith and everything like that. And all Dan's talk about false idols — as somebody said — that could only be Ernst von Kemp, with all that junk he brings back when he goes to the Middle East."

"What kind of junk?" asked McLeod. "I met Mr. von Kemp Saturday afternoon."

"He likes to be called *Doctor* von Kemp. He's one of those people who wants you to use his title. He goes to East Jerusalem on Dead Sea Scrolls business — they're in the Rockefeller Museum there — and he knows these antiquities dealers and they're always trying to sell him things they've bought from the Bedouins. He's brought back jars that held the Dead Sea Scrolls in those caves — they're big pottery jars. And he brings back other things — little figurines that have nothing to do with the Essenes or the Hebrews. They're pagan images — of Baal, I guess. And little cylinder seals."

"It's kind of far-fetched to accuse him of worshipping false images, isn't it?"

"Dan Strong was far-fetched. That's the point."

"But it's far-fetched to think that a man like von Kemp would kill a seminary student who might accuse him of worshipping false idols, isn't it?"

113

"Sure," said Willy. "But this whole thing is unreal."

"I guess you're right." McLeod got out a notebook and wrote down von Kemp's name.

"Put down Lucy Summers," said Willy. "They had an awful argument in class one day. It got downright personal. He said she was corrupting the Bible with her insistence on inclusive language."

"Poor Lucy," said McLeod. "I can't believe she'd kill a student who disagreed with her, though."

"It is hard to imagine," agreed Willy.

"What about you?" she asked him.

"Me?"

"Are you one of those people who were so scared of being denounced by Dan Strong that you would have killed him?"

"No, I didn't worry about him denouncing me. I'm already out of the closet. When I talked to you at breakfast this morning I was afraid that the police might suspect me, but since then I've realized that if you're out, that's sort of an alibi."

"I see what you mean," said McLeod. "Have the police talked to you yet?"

"No, but they did talk to some other students this morning. Maybe like you said before, it could just have been a case of random violence," said Willy. "Maybe Dan was out for a walk and somebody shot him without any reason and then tried to hide the body."

"I'm not sure he was shot. Was he? The police haven't said. Let's start at this another way," said McLeod. "When was Dan last seen? Who are his friends?"

"Sharon Leland was his girlfriend."

"Oh, yes," said McLeod. "Who else?"

"Dan wasn't exactly Mr. Congeniality," said Willy, thinking hard. "But he was the leader of a coterie of sorts."

"Who were they?"

Willy rattled off some names. "I think the police are trying to find out who last saw Dan and when and where."

"It's about time they got around to that," said McLeod. She threw down her pencil. "This is hopeless. I feel utterly helpless. I certainly can't go around interviewing students. Especially the way the police feel about me."

"I'll poke around among the students," said Willy. "Most of Dan's friends are barely civil to me, but I think Sharon Leland is pretty decent. At least she believes in the 'hate the sin, but love the sinner' concept. I'll talk to her as soon as it's possible. I don't know when or where the funeral's going to be, but wherever it is, I'm sure Sharon will be going. He was from the midwest someplace. In the meantime, I'll find out what I can about Dan's movements."

"Great," said McLeod. "I'll — I don't know what I'll do. Talk to my friend Fiona, I guess. She's always been pretty smart."

"I'll find out all I can," said Willy.

"Good luck," said McLeod. "If we can find out *where* he was killed, and if it was on campus, then the Borough police will come in."

"I'll call you," said Willy.

They bussed their trays and walked out into the autumn air together. McLeod shivered, as Willy left her. She walked back to Speer Library, feeling more frustrated and helpless than she ever had before.

Thirteen

McLeod went back to her room and, finding a message from Fiona, called her and told her about Dean Tilley and Brasher.

"McLeod, baby, you have to move over here. You should have stayed with us from the beginning. I'll bring the car around and we'll get you and your stuff. I'll be right there."

McLeod hesitated, but could think of no good reason not to do as Fiona suggested. "Thank you," was all she could manage to get out before she hung up the phone and began to pack.

Beelzebub and Gabriel were in the car when Fiona arrived to pick up McLeod and her baggage at Erdman Hall. They seemed ecstatic when they all got to the house and wagged their tails frantically as they followed McLeod and Fiona through the back door and into the house. With some difficulty they climbed the stairs behind them when Fiona showed McLeod her room. They circled McLeod's suitcase, briefcase, and laptop when she set them on the floor and sniffed at them assiduously. They smiled their doggish smiles and waved their tails and bounced easily down the stairs when everybody went to the library.

"Shall we have tea — or sherry?" asked Fiona.

"Sherry," said McLeod.

"Of course. Sit down. I think I'll light a fire. Don't you think it's turning cold?"

McLeod agreed that it was indeed cool enough for a fire, and Fiona struck a match and lit the newspaper beneath the neatly laid logs and kindling in the library fireplace. It flamed immediately.

"That's wonderful," said McLeod.

"Angus lays the fires," said Fiona. "Isn't he a lamb? He loves fires. I do, too, but he knows I'm too lazy to do anything about it."

When they had settled themselves with glasses of Tio Pepe, Fiona said, "Okay, tell me about all of it."

"Dean Tilley first. He wants me to leave the seminary — he thinks I'm causing too much excitement. And I haven't finished my research, and Brasher says I can't leave, that I'm a material witness."

"This is a horror story," said Fiona. "It really is. That odious Tilley. Even Angus doesn't like Ted Tilley. And somebody has to be really bad for Angus to dislike him. And Brasher is a fright. I've never met him, and even I know that."

"Fiona, I can't thank you enough for taking me in. I didn't know what I was going to do. At least this gives me breathing space." She took a sip of sherry. "But wait a minute. The seminary owns this house, doesn't it? Won't Tilley be mad at you and Angus for harboring me?"

"So what if he is? Foolish old thing."

"But I'm afraid Angus will think we're flouting the administration's authority if I move in here . . ."

"I've been flouting people for years. Angus is used to it. In fact, I think he sort of admires it. Maybe he's a closet flouter himself — you know, wants not to conform, but can't quite bring himself to rebel. He'll certainly understand this flout. More sherry?"

"Just a little," said McLeod. They sipped for a minute, then McLeod spoke, "I'd really like to get this murder solved. Then maybe I wouldn't be a persona non grata here. Have I told you about Willy?"

"Willy who?"

"Willy Cameron. He's a student." She explained how she had come to know Willy, but somehow, she did not feel free to tell Fiona Willy's worries about gays becoming suspects. "Anyway, he's going to talk to some of Dan Strong's friends. Find out what the police are up to and also when the friends last saw Dan. That kind of thing."

"Then you and I must talk to the faculty and staff!" cried Fiona. "We'll be like Nancy Drew and her friend . . . What was her name?"

"She had two. One was named George —"

"No, I meant *girl*friend," said Fiona.

"One girlfriend was George and the other was Bess. Her boyfriend was Ned."

"McLeod, how do you remember things like that? Anyway, you'll be Nancy and I'll be George. I love it. Let's see, who needs to be interrogated?"

The more help she had, the better it would be, McLeod decided. "Well, Willy said I should talk to Lucy —"

"Lucy? Lucy Summers?" said Fiona. "Good heavens! Is she a suspect?"

"Willy said she and Dan Strong had a terrible argument in class about inclusive language. He also mentioned Dr. von Kemp."

"Ernst von Kemp? He'd make a lovely villain, wouldn't he? Who else?"

"I rather liked Dr. von Kemp. He was so jolly and his eyes sparkled when he talked," said McLeod. "Willie said Roscoe Kelly might be a suspect. You know Roscoe's the student who's a snake handler."

"You told me about him," said Fiona. "He's created quite a stir, Angus says. If his rattlesnakes live in his room — I bet he can't keep a roommate."

"He's a nice young man," said McLeod. "And he has a single room."

"Why would he kill Dan Strong? Why is he a suspect?"

"Willy thinks Dan was going to denounce Roscoe," said McLeod.

"But everybody already knew he was a snake handler," said Fiona. "What did he have to fear? No, I like von Kemp as a suspect myself."

"Willy said Dan seemed to be threatening to denounce him for having false idols or something — pagan images he brings back from the Middle East."

"This is all too marvelous," said Fiona. "A seminary student putting the fear of God — or the fear of something — into all these people. Let's question Ernst."

"How can we question him?"

"That's easy. I'll ask him to dinner," said Fiona. "And we'll quiz him relentlessly. Tonight. He'd be a nice beau for you, McLeod. All those trips to the Middle East."

"We met — at Henry Fairfield Worthington's house. Remember?"

"That's right. I'm sure he must have fallen for you —"

"He showed no signs of it," said McLeod. "We talked about the Dead Sea Scrolls."

"I'll ask him to dinner, and you can ask him some more questions."

Then McLeod could hear Fiona in the kitchen, talking on the phone. "He can't come tonight," she said when she came back to the library. "But he's coming tomorrow. You'll be here, won't you?"

"Where else?" said McLeod. "I want to find out more about the big thing he's about to come up with. He talked about it a little Saturday and then clammed up. Listen, Fiona, let me take you and Angus out tonight. We'll go to Lahiere's. I haven't been there since I've been in town this time. And if I'm going to be a houseguest that's the least I can do."

"You know, that's a great idea," said

Fiona. "Angus loves Lahiere's. That will mollify him, just in case he's the least bit upset with me for flouting."

McLeod was upstairs — unaccompanied by dogs this time — unpacking when Angus came home, and she could hear the McKays talking downstairs. When she came downstairs, ready to go out, she found them in the library.

"McLeod, Angus doesn't think I flouted at all. He says I did the right thing."

"Of course you did," said Angus. "McLeod, you're welcome here. Ted Tilley is a jerk if there ever was one. I'm glad Fiona had the sense to get you over here. You should have stayed with us from the beginning."

When they left for Lahiere's the dogs protested violently at being left at home, but quieted when the door was firmly shut in their faces. After McLeod and the McKays had walked downtown and settled in the restaurant, Fiona urged McLeod to tell Angus about Willy Cameron. "She had breakfast and lunch with him today, Angus. Do you think we're keeping her from him tonight?"

"Fiona, he's gay," said Angus.

"And thirty years younger than I am," said McLeod.

"Willy's a great student and a good person, and he has to put up with some flack because he's openly gay. I didn't realize he was a friend of Roscoe Kelly, though."

"I somehow didn't get the idea that they were a couple," said McLeod.

"Probably not," said Angus. "You know, we've told you that the whole issue of gay marriage and gay ordination is the hottest issue on seminary campuses and in the church in general right now."

"How do most people feel about it?" asked McLeod.

"They're all over the place," said Angus. "It varies from Ted Tilley, who's totally antigay, to Rob Hillhouse, who's all for gay marriages."

"I'll never understand it all," said McLeod. "But back to Willy. He thinks that Dan's sermon — that sermon last Monday on Hosea — was very threatening to a number of people. He thought he was attacking gays and threatening to out some closeted ones. He thought Dan was attacking everybody from feminists to financial managers to Ernst von Kemp for possessing artifacts from the Middle East that he referred to as false gods and graven images. There may have been some others on his list — oh, I think everybody who doesn't take the Bible literally and people who insist on inclusive language."

"The only thing is: That list includes nearly everybody at the seminary except for Dan Strong and his friends," said Angus. "But it's an interesting idea."

"It doesn't include Ted Tilley," said Fiona. "I guess he's not a suspect, alas."

McLeod agreed that it was too bad that Dean Tilley would not be suspected and arrested.

"And executed," said Fiona. "Although of course I don't really believe in capital punishment."

"Willy is afraid that the police will hear about Dan's campaign against gays and suspect him — Willy — of the murder," McLeod said.

"I expect it's going to be rather unpleasant around here for a while," said Angus.

Nobody knew how right he was.

Fourteen

The next morning, Wednesday, McLeod dressed and went down to the kitchen to find Angus seated alone — alone, that is, except for Beelzebub and Gabriel — at the table, drinking coffee and reading the *New York Times*. He got up hastily and offered to prepare toast or cereal for McLeod or even cook eggs.

"No, no, thank you, Angus. Let me just get my own breakfast. You all are so kind to take me in — but you don't have to wait on me." Angus sat back down and returned to the paper, and McLeod put water in the kettle to make tea, found orange juice, and put two slices of bread in the toaster.

When she sat down, Angus handed her all of the *Times*, except the first section, which he continued to read as he drank more coffee. Fiona came in wearing a housecoat and yawning widely. "I'm a terrible hostess," she said, patting McLeod's shoulder. "Did you find everything you need?"

"I'm fine," said McLeod. "And Angus offered to fix breakfast for me, but it was easy to find everything my heart desired." Fiona poured herself a cup of coffee.

McLeod finished her breakfast and announced she was going to the library to get some work done for a change. When she came back downstairs with her laptop in her briefcase, Fiona met her at the front door and handed her a house key. Beelzebub and Gabriel clamored to go with McLeod, but Fiona held them back. "You've already been out," she told them, "and I'll take you out again. Do hush. Come back here for lunch," she said to McLeod. "I won't be here — I have to be at the YWCA, but there's tuna salad — you can make a sandwich. And remember, von Kemp is coming to dinner."

"What can I do for you?" said McLeod. "Can I go to the grocery store?"

"We'll go together when I get home," said Fiona.

McLeod left and walked to the kiosk in Palmer Square to buy her own copy of the *New York Times* and a copy of the *Times* of Trenton. Then she hurried to Speer Library where she could sit down and read them. The worst part of being a houseguest, she thought, was having to wait to read the newspaper, but she believed in this case the advantages outweighed the disadvantages.

A story in the Trenton paper said that the Township police had found that the last person to see Dan Strong alive was apparently Sharon Leland, identified as a seminary student and close friend of the victim. "We left the dining hall together last Tuesday," she was quoted as saying, "I went back to my dorm room but Dan said he had to see somebody and he'd talk to me later. I never saw him again." About time they got around to talking to her, thought McLeod.

"The cause of death has not yet been determined," the paper quoted Lester Brasher, "although snakebite is a possibility. It's very complicated, and the pathologists are working on it."

Snakebite? McLeod thought. Did Brasher think Dan Strong had been bitten by a snake on the canal bank and then crawled into a garment bag? It was bizarre. Could snakes be used to murder somebody? She thought of Roscoe Kelly and his rattlesnakes, and gasped.

As if looking for help, she gazed inquiringly at the portrait of Betsey Stockton, but the black woman in the white turban and apron stared back at her enigmatically. McLeod shook her head and tried to read the *New York Times,* and then tried to work. But the murder of Dan Strong in Princeton was on her mind — not the lynching of Elijah P. Lovejoy in Alton, Illinois.

She managed to hang on in the library until almost noon. When she left, she started toward the McKays' house, but turned back and crossed Mercer Street. Instead of going to the McKays' to eat a lonely tuna fish sandwich, she went to the cafeteria in search of Willy, Roscoe, or both.

"I was looking for you at breakfast," said Willy Cameron, appearing at her side as she entered the cafeteria.

"I've moved in with the McKays," said McLeod. "So I had breakfast there. Have you seen this?" She showed him the story in the Trenton paper.

He read it and said, "I found out myself that Sharon was the last person to see Dan, but this snakebite thing — what do you suppose it means?"

"If it's true," said McLeod, "could it

have anything to do with Roscoe?"

"It couldn't," said Willy. "He keeps those snakes under lock and key — always."

"Seems like an awfully strange coincidence," said McLeod.

"Let's see if Roscoe is inside. We need to talk to him."

Willy spotted Roscoe at a large table with some friends and went over to get him. McLeod waited, newspaper in hand. As Roscoe read it, he turned white.

"Can you use a snake to kill somebody?" McLeod asked.

Roscoe looked at her. "I know one man that tried to use a snake to kill somebody," he said. "He was a preacher that lived about thirty miles from us. He was a drunk and no good. But he preached loud and long and handled snakes as well as anybody. He tried to murder his wife — forced her to put her hand in the snake's cage. The snake bit her, but she managed to get out of the house and call her sister to take her to the hospital. They arrested him and tried him and convicted him of attempted murder. It was a big deal."

"But Samson and Delilah haven't been out of their cages, have they?" asked McLeod.

"Not since we got back here this fall," said Roscoe. "But it's worrisome."

"I'm sure it is," said McLeod. "But I don't think the police know you keep snakes."

"Even if they did . . ." said Roscoe, trailing off.

"Oh, somebody will tell them," said Willy.

"Don't worry, Roscoe," said McLeod, feeling motherly.

She and Willy said good-bye and filled their trays and sat down at a table for two. "Have you picked up anything from Dan's friends?" asked McLeod.

"Not much. They had mixed feelings about his sermon. Some of them thought it was good old hellfire and brimstone in the evangelical tradition. Others thought he went too far. Actually most of them thought he went too far for his own good. They thought some of the faculty might get mad at him about it."

"The question is: Where did Dan go after he told Sharon good night? It was fairly early, wasn't it?" said McLeod. "Do you have any ideas?"

"Everybody's speculating about that," said Willy. "I can't find a single student who saw him after that — not in the library, not in the dorm, nowhere. But he had to be somewhere. How about you? What are you finding out?"

"Not much," said McLeod. "Fiona has asked Ernst von Kemp to dinner tonight so we can find out about his false idols or whatever. Maybe we should have Lucy Summers, too."

"Let me know what happens," said Willy.

"I will. Keep in touch."

McLeod used her key to open the McKays' front door and Beelzebub and Gabriel greeted her ecstatically. Fiona was at home and thinking about dinner. "Ernst von Kemp," Fiona said thoughtfully. "What shall we have to eat?"

McLeod's mind went blank.

"I'll make lasagna — that's easy enough," said Fiona. "I think I'll make vegetarian lasagna — everybody seems to be a vegetarian. Have you noticed?"

"I have. If you like, I'll make crab bisque for a first course. Most vegetarians eat seafood. I'll walk up to the fish market and get the crab."

"Oh, good," said Fiona. "Protein. But we'll drive. I'll get everything I need from Wild Oats and you can run across to the seafood place."

The dogs were dying to go with them, so Fiona snapped on their leashes and led them to the car. They climbed into the backseat and stood up to look out the rear window. "They're awfully cute," McLeod said.

"They are," said Fiona. "But they're a pain in the neck. We don't have a fenced yard, so we have to take them out for walks constantly. But we both like them, and they like us. That's so good for our morale."

Back home, they spent a couple of pleasant hours in the kitchen together, while Beelzebub and Gabriel lay on the floor and watched them carefully. "Why is it that cooking is so much more fun when you're not in the kitchen slaving away by yourself?" asked Fiona.

"Many hands make light work — that's part of it, but it's just the company, too. Cooking is lonely a lot of the time, isn't it?"

When Angus came home, he made them a pre-guest drink and McLeod showed them the story in the Trenton paper. "The police don't seem to be making much headway, do they?" said Angus.

"That's why McLeod and I are doing a little detective work," said Fiona.

133

"What are you doing?" asked Angus.

"Well, McLeod is going to quiz Ernst unmercifully tonight at dinner."

"Good luck," said Angus. "He can be a windbag."

"I rather like him," said McLeod.

"So do I," said Angus. "But he's like all of us. He's got his faults."

"What do you think about the snakebike angle?" McLeod asked Angus. "Do you know Roscoe Kelly?"

"Everybody knows Roscoe," said Angus. "Everybody's fascinated with him and his snakes. I think he just keeps them up here to sort of show everybody here — and at home — that he hasn't given up everything from his past since he came to seminary."

"But I've been meaning to ask you about how you explain to students from a fundamentalist background like Roscoe's that the Bible is not always accurate history, that the walls of Jericho, for instance, did not fall down when Joshua blew his trumpet?"

"I tell them that the Bible is a retrospectival document," Angus said. "It's made up of traditional stories and oral tales and long memories. None of it was written down until long after it happened —"

"Look, the paper says that Dan Strong's girlfriend was Sharon Leland," Fiona interrupted heedlessly. "You remember, that nice girl who worked for you when you were trying to finish up the book on Scholasticism."

"I certainly do remember her. She keyboarded all those changes for me. She was wonderful."

"She was nice, too," Fiona said to McLeod. "She was a bit stiff and priggish at first, but she warmed up to us, didn't she? She came here to do the work, McLeod. Angus has thousands of computers in his study."

"I have two, McLeod," said Angus. "A desktop and a laptop. Sharon was so careful," said Angus. "She did a better job than I could have done. Time was short, but she met the deadline, too."

"This is a terrible thing that's happened to her. We should have her over one night," said Fiona.

"Fine with me," said Angus.

McLeod, listening to this, was quite happy. She would love to meet Sharon Leland and talk to her.

"But I guess we shouldn't ask her tonight, with Ernst von Kemp."

"Too late, anyway," said Angus.

135

Fifteen

Right on cue, the doorbell rang. Beelzebub and Gabriel sprang into guard duty, barking fiercely until Ernst von Kemp came in, beaming, eyes twinkling, beard bristling happily. Then the dogs began to prance around him admiringly. He ignored them. "So nice of you to have me," he said. He handed a bottle of red wine over to Angus, who looked at the label and nodded approvingly.

He shook hands with Fiona and McLeod and prepared to enjoy himself.

Dinner was a huge success, although McLeod noted that Beelzebub and Gabriel seemed to realize Ernst von Kemp was not a potential food donor and stuck to her. The conversation centered more or less on the Dead Sea Scrolls ("Oh, yes, you're the lady who asked me all those questions," said von Kemp) and discussion between Angus and Ernst on the state of the seminary's edition of the twelve non-biblical scrolls. Angus pointed out to McLeod that von Kemp was not just an archaeologist, "but a biblical scholar as well, or he wouldn't be doing the Dead Sea Scrolls."

"I see," said McLeod.

It wasn't boring her, but Fiona was getting impatient. "Get on with it," she hissed at McLeod when the two women were in the kitchen dishing up dessert.

"Where did you grow up, Dr. von Kemp?" McLeod dutifully asked when they were all back at the table. She was using her time-honored technique for putting people at ease for a newspaper interview: Ask them simple biographical questions first.

"All over the place," he said. "My father was a Lutheran minister and we moved constantly."

"How did you get interested in archaeology?"

"Arrowheads," he said. "Indian arrowheads when I was a child."

"But that's not classical — I mean biblical archaeology."

"I know," said von Kemp. "But they got me interested in old objects that were lying around the world."

"And religion? When did that become important?"

"Religion was always around, of course. After college I won a fellowship to a German university and got my graduate degree there. And incidentally learned about biblical archaeology — the Germans are really the experts at classical and biblical archaeology. That's where I first got interested in the Scrolls."

"Which German university?" asked McLeod, thinking of Heidelberg and *The Student Prince* and beer steins and dueling scars.

"Tübingen," said von Kemp. "Wonderful place."

The men were having second helpings of dessert when McLeod began again. "Did you happen to hear Dan Strong's sermon a week ago Monday?"

"No, but I heard about it," said von Kemp.

"Did you take offense?"

"Take offense? Why should I?"

"I guess it's silly, but somebody said he was talking about you and your antiquities when he blasted people who keep false idols," said McLeod.

"I didn't think of it that way." Ernst von Kemp was not as jolly as he had been on Saturday, McLeod noted.

"But do you bring home false idols — or

pagan images, I guess I mean?" she asked him.

"I have brought home some very small Mesopotamian fertility images. They're a dime a dozen — not really, of course, but they're plentiful over there — and I've picked up several. But I really can't believe that Dan Strong was attacking me. I thought from what I heard of the sermon that it was just a diatribe against modern ways by an over-enthusiastic student. Youthful ravings, really." McLeod could not tell if he was really as unconcerned about the sermon as he seemed to be.

"I'm so ignorant of the ways of the seminary," she said, turning to the others. "Have students often preached sermons that were that inflammatory?"

"Not really," said Angus. "I didn't hear that one either, of course, but it did excite people, Ernst. Everyone was talking about it."

"And then he was killed," said McLeod.

Ernst von Kemp gave her a sharp look — his eyes weren't twinkling now. "Well, I didn't regard the reports of the sermon as serious enough for me to even remonstrate with Dan — much less kill him. And I personally think Dan Strong was out for a walk and was attacked and then stripped and his body left beside the tow path. I don't think he was killed because of his sermon."

"Fiona, this apple cake is wonderful," said Angus, seeking to steer the conversation to a more pleasant subject.

After everybody else praised the apple cake, McLeod brought up Ernst's latest find. "Can you tell us anything about it yet?" she asked. "I was fascinated to hear you talk about it Saturday."

"What's that, Ernst?" asked Angus.

"I can't talk about it, not yet," said Ernst. "But when I can, I guarantee you will listen, Angus."

"Angus would listen to anything about God, wouldn't you, sweetie?" said Fiona. She smiled at Angus affectionately.

"No," said Angus, "but I'd listen to Ernst."

After Ernst had left, and Angus had gone out with the dogs, Fiona and McLeod conferred briefly. "What next, Nancy Drew?" Fiona asked her.

"I think I want to talk to Lucy Summers," said McLeod.

"Oh, good. Let's see. I have to be at the art museum all day tomorrow. Angus is going off to some dinner meeting. Why don't we take her out for dinner?"

"Good plan."

Sixteen

McLeod spent Thursday morning in the library poring over an account of the riots in Alton that followed the murder of Elijah P. Lovejoy. She stopped for lunch and crossed Mercer Street to get to the main campus of the seminary. Chrysanthemums had replaced the impatiens that had been planted around the stone gate posts, and the air was getting cooler.

Walking past Alexander Hall, the oldest building at the seminary, she wondered why the seminary seemed gloomier than Princeton University a few blocks away. The quadrangle behind Alexander was nice, with the motley collection of buildings lined around it — the new music building, the old, cream, brick chapel with its six white columns, V-shaped Hodge Hall (which had been dubbed the Fertile Crescent when the married students who lived there always seemed to be pregnant), and the gray stone administration building at the foot of the green.

It was all right, she thought, but hanging over it was a somber religious pall, or was it a Calvinist sobriety?

The cafeteria was, as always, more cheerful. It was in the Student Center, a long, low redbrick building and it was always buzzing with activity.

She had just sat down and was eating her lunch — a boring green salad — when once again Henry Fairfield Worthington asked if he could join her. "Please do," said McLeod, who enjoyed him.

He set his plate of country fried steak, mashed potatoes, and string beans on the table. "I had a good time at your tea party Saturday," she said when he had settled down.

"Thanks. Glad you enjoyed it."

"Henry, did you know Dan Strong?" said McLeod, getting right into the fray.

"No, I didn't. I try to meet as many students as I can — I go to hear them preach on Mondays — but I didn't know him."

"Did you hear his sermon last week?"

"I did."

"I did, too. What did you think about it?"

"I thought it was a bloodthirsty sort of

sermon. But they have to learn. Students, I mean, have to learn."

"Did you think he was threatening people?"

"He was threatening lots of people with the judgment of God. Preachers used to do that a lot more than they do now. These days, all too often, it's just about 'me and Jesus.' "

"You mean you thought bloodthirsty was good?"

"I didn't say that. And I don't usually think of a student's sermon as good or bad. I'm afraid I pay a lot of attention to their delivery and the technical details of preaching. I was a speech teacher, remember," said Henry.

They ate in silence, broken after a few moments by McLeod. "Did you hear Willy Cameron's sermon Monday? I liked it."

"I did, too. His delivery is excellent. At first, I thought his voice wasn't strong enough, but he projected very well."

They went on to talk about the acoustics of the seminary's Miller Chapel and about its interior beauty, which still impressed McLeod.

After lunch, McLeod went back to the library and read, to her horror, that the people, Lovejoy's friends, who had tried to defend him when the lynch mob came, were afterward indicted and tried on riot charges. They were not convicted, but then neither were the members of the lynch mob when they were put on trial. Nobody went to prison; nobody received any punishment for the deed.

By five o'clock McLeod was indeed ready for dinner. She and Fiona took Beelzebub and Gabriel for a walk, came back, and prepared to go to dinner with Lucy. She arrived shortly, looking flustered. "Am I late?" she said. "I've had a terrible day." She looked a little rumpled.

"What happened?" said McLeod.

"Oh, one thing and another," said Lucy. "I just never had time to catch up. Well, that's not it. It was just disorganized with unexpected meetings with students and a call from the dean and I couldn't find what I wanted in the library. It just went on and on. But it's over now."

"Was the dean a problem?" asked McLeod, who regarded Dean Tilley as a constant problem.

"Oh, no, not really. In fact, he's inconsequential. But he takes up time."

Fiona was putting on her coat and McLeod took hers off the hook in the hall.

"Are we ready to go?" asked Fiona.

Gabriel and Beelzebub trotted up, obviously ready to go.

"No, no, you've been out. You have to stay here. *By yourselves*. Face up to it," said Fiona.

The dogs were clearly incensed at being left alone, but Fiona held firm. "Hush, hush. We're leaving." The three women slid out the door and walked downtown.

"I do love Princeton," said McLeod, as they walked past little shops, then, across the street, the main gates to the university campus. "Look at this building the jewelry store's in — all Tudor and with beautiful window boxes."

The others murmured agreement. "You're too used to it," she said. But they couldn't kill her enthusiasm. "I love the Annex," she said when they were settled in at the restaurant and she looked around the cozy basement interior. "It's like an English pub."

They ate pasta and shared a carafe of red wine. Fiona kicked McLeod under the table, and McLeod began her "interview." "Lucy, where are you from? Do I hear a Southern accent?"

"What's left of one," said Lucy. "I grew up in Mississippi. Can you believe it?"

"What made you go to a seminary?"

"She means how did you get into this religion racket?" Fiona explained.

Lucy laughed. "Circuitously. I went to college in New Orleans at Sophie Newcomb, as it was then — now it's part of Tulane. I loved Newcomb. I did all sorts of things — I acted in plays and I was on the rifle team. I taught school in Arkansas for a while, and then I went to graduate school in religion, of all things, at Emory and got a Ph.D. Then I decided I wanted to be a minister, so I went to Columbia Seminary — that's where I met Angus and Fiona — and then I actually got called to a church in Alabama and got ordained. But I wanted a more intellectual life, so I snapped at the chance to teach here when it came along."

"So you have a lot of degrees," said McLeod.

"For what they're worth," said Lucy, sipping her wine. "That's enough about me, though." And she asked McLeod about Lovejoy.

As fast as she could, she ran through her Lovejoy project and then changed the subject, asking Lucy about Dan Strong. "That twerp," said Lucy. "I believe in speaking ill of the dead," she explained. "Much better than speaking ill of the living, I always say. And he was a twerp. Do they know who killed him yet? I suppose it was some loner hanging out on the tow path or something. Something random."

"I used to think that," said McLeod. "But lately, I've been wondering if his death isn't more closely connected with the seminary. I understand he could be very annoying," said McLeod. "He was rude to you in class, wasn't he?"

"He was extremely rude to me in class. Many times. And I was rude right back to him in the end."

"Was that about inclusive language?"

"Inclusive language, the rights of women, the ordination of women. Even women wearing pants. He quoted Scripture all the time, and one of the things he shouted at me was a verse from Deuteronomy 22: 'The woman shall not wear that which pertaineth unto a man . . . : for all that do so are an abomination unto the Lord thy God.' Can you believe it?"

"It must have been maddening," said McLeod.

"The accumulation of his criticism was maddening. I get angry all over again just thinking about him."

Fiona kicked McLeod under the table

again. "Do you think anybody at the seminary might have killed him?" McLeod dutifully asked Lucy.

"I don't know of anybody he drove up the wall the way he did me," said Lucy. "And if people went around killing students because they're obnoxious, the enrollment would be cut in half."

"Had you heard about the sermon he preached last Monday?"

"Somebody said something or other about it," said Lucy. "But I think that was just Dan's customary odiousness extended to the pulpit." She shook her head. "Let's talk about something else. How is your friend, Henry Fairfield Worthington, Fiona?"

They chatted about the niceness of Henry Fairfield Worthington for a while and then went on to Rob Hillhouse, whom McLeod had heard of but not met.

"He performed a commitment ceremony for two gay men," said Lucy, "and some people here are incensed about it."

"In Miller Chapel?" asked McLeod.

"Oh, no. It was in New York," said Lucy.

"That was even worse than the Jesus Seminar business," said Fiona.

And then they talked about Hester Hardin, whom McLeod had met briefly.

"You must get to know Hester while you're here," said Lucy. "She works in the business office. She went to seminary but never could find a church, so she hasn't been ordained. It's a crying shame, because she's such a wonderful person."

"What does she do in the business office?" asked McLeod.

"She single-handedly manages the endowment," said Lucy.

McLeod nodded as though she were impressed, but she was thinking of the way seminaries took people who had trained to be ministers but hadn't made the grade for one reason or another and used them in various capacities. Did it work? she wondered, but she did not voice her doubts to Lucy. Instead, she switched subjects: "Lucy, Ernst von Kemp told us he was on to something really big," McLeod said. "What do you think it could be?"

"Who knows? He's always bringing stuff back from the Middle East. I had the idea from something he said that it might be a manuscript and not an artifact. But I don't know."

"If it's a manuscript, what could be so sensational? He already told me it couldn't be a new Dead Sea Scroll."

"Let's see," said Lucy, thinking aloud.

"Maybe it's something about the Davidic empire — you know when David was king. Hmmm. To prove his empire existed just like the Bible says wouldn't be exciting though. It would have to prove it did *not* exist. Now *that* would cause a lot of stir. But it could be almost anything, I suppose."

"How could you prove a kingdom did *not* exist?" asked McLeod. "Would you have to find something written down on papyrus that said, 'Those Israelites are still living as nomads. Won't they *ever* settle down?' "

"I see what you mean," said Lucy. "I'll have to think about this."

"Wait a minute, what would be sensational would be a new gospel," said Fiona. "You know, like the Gospel of Thomas, the one that the Jesus Seminar people quote all the time. It was found in Egypt."

"The Jesus Seminar was pretty interesting stuff," said McLeod.

"I know. The way the process worked itself out was interesting enough," said Lucy. "After each member had gone over the gospels word by word, they voted on the authenticity of each phrase that Jesus uttered, including the Gnostic gospels. They used one color if they were absolutely sure it was authentic, another color for 'maybe,' another for 'maybe not,' and a fourth for 'absolutely not.' "

"It's very controversial," said Fiona. "People at the seminary practically get into fistfights about it."

"I know! I know what it could be!" said Lucy, suddenly very excited. "The new find could be the Q document!"

"Oh, how mysterious! The secret document that is supposed to be the basis of Matthew and Luke," said McLeod. "Even I have heard of it. That *would* be a find, wouldn't it?"

As they were leaving the Annex, McLeod saw Trudy Sergeant, a staunchly feminist English professor she had met on a previous stay at the university, and went over to speak to her.

Trudy, who seemed overjoyed to see her, invited her to a cocktail party at her house the next day. "You know, it's my big fall do," she said. "You must come. Remember it's all catered, so it's bound to be better than if I did any of it."

"You still refuse to cook?" asked McLeod.

"Cooking is part of the conspiracy to enslave women," said Trudy. "And I won't be an enabler for that."

"Hooray for you," said McLeod.

"I'll see you tomorrow," said Trudy. "Five to seven. You remember where I live?"

"I do, and I'll be there," said McLeod.

Seventeen

As they passed the library on their way home from the Annex, they could see several police cars and an ambulance in the back next to Lenox House.

"Wonder what's going on?" said McLeod.

"Maybe somebody tried to steal some of Ernst's artifacts," said Fiona.

"There's so many of them," said McLeod. "I mean so many police cars."

"The Princeton police always seem to turn out in force," said Lucy. "They're a little overzealous."

McLeod kept turning back to peer down Library Place until they got past the corner and could no longer see anything. She and Fiona walked Lucy to her house, and then turned back to the McKays' house, to be greeted enthusiastically by Beelzebub and Gabriel.

Fiona patted the noisy dogs and took off

her coat. McLeod kept hers on. "I know I'm a nut," she said, "but I'm going over to see what the police are doing at Lenox House."

"Once a reporter, always a reporter," said Fiona. "You're like an old fire horse — you smell the smoke and off you go."

"I can't help it," said McLeod.

"I know you can't," said Fiona. "Shall I come with you?"

"That's all right," said McLeod. "It's just around the corner." Fiona started upstairs, and McLeod slipped out the front door.

As she came up to the police tape barrier surrounding Lenox House, she saw that medics were carrying out a covered body on a stretcher. She tried to find somebody to ask who it was, and finally saw Dick Coffey, a reporter from the *Times* of Trenton whom she remembered. He was standing in the midst of a huddle of young people, obviously reporters, who were blocked by the police tape.

"What is it?" she asked Dick. "Did somebody have a heart attack?"

"It's murder," he said.

McLeod's first reaction was, she realized, totally selfish: Thank God, she thought, I didn't find the body. Her second thought was just as selfish: Lenox House was in the Borough of Princeton, so now at least the Borough police would enter the investigative picture.

"Who?" asked McLeod, trying to think who else had offices in Lenox House besides the Dead Sea project people.

"A professor at the seminary," said Coffey.

"Which one?"

Coffey looked at his notes. "Ernst von Kemp," he said.

"Oh, no!" she said. She gasped, relieved to note that she was feeling shock and grief, more appropriate emotions than gratitude that she hadn't been the one to find the body.

"Who did it? Why?" she asked. "I knew him."

"They don't know," said Coffey. "The body was found by the cleaning lady. That's all they'll tell us."

"We were just coming out to look for you," said Fiona cheerfully when McLeod got back to the house and saw them sitting in the library. "What's the matter? You look like you've seen a ghost."

"Ernst von Kemp has been murdered," McLeod said.

"What!" and "No!" they cried. After

McLeod told them the little she knew, they sat and tried to digest it.

"Who would want to murder Ernst?" asked Fiona.

"When we first saw all the police there, you said that somebody must have been after his artifacts. Do you really think somebody would kill for those things?" asked McLeod.

"You never know. If somebody was trying to steal some things and Ernst caught them at it, then the burglar may have panicked and killed him," said Angus. They pondered this silently. "It's a terrible blow for the seminary."

"Angus, it's a terrible blow for Ernst!" said Fiona.

"I know it, but it does seem that the seminary is having an extraordinary run of bad luck."

They talked fruitlessly — What could you say? wondered McLeod — and finally went to bed.

On Friday, when McLeod came downstairs, both Fiona and Angus were in the kitchen, Fiona standing by the counter and Angus reading the *New York Times*. Beelzebub and Gabriel lay on the floor, keeping an eye on the humans.

"Good morning," said Fiona. "I decided to be a good hostess for a change. I stirred up some waffle batter. I thought it might cheer us all up. Waffle?"

"I'd love a waffle," said McLeod. She poured herself some orange juice and put on water for tea. Fiona opened the waffle iron and with a fork, picked up a golden, light brown waffle. It smelled divine, but McLeod refused it when Fiona proffered it to her on a plate. "Give that one to Angus. He was here first."

Fiona grinned. "Okay, but this next one is yours."

"What about yours?"

"I never get up this early. I can wait."

McLeod had just taken the first bite of her waffle, crisp but tender and melting in her mouth with the honey she had put on it, when the telephone rang.

Fiona picked it up. "It's for you, Angus," she said, handing him the phone.

"Yes," said Angus. Then came a long pause. "I heard. It's terrible." Long pause. "It's bad, yes." Long pause. "Great concern. Yes. Yes. Yes, indeed, if I think of anything that would be helpful, I'll let you know."

Angus hung up the phone and turned to them.

"What was that?" asked Fiona.

"Ted Tilley. He's notifying all the senior faculty about Ernst. Ted is very upset. This raises serious problems for him. Naturally he hates to lose a top-flight man like Ernst, and he's distressed about how they'll replace him. He's extremely concerned about how a murder will affect the seminary. Especially as it comes on top of the murder of a seminary student. What a terrible coincidence this is. Poor Ted."

"What a pathetic creature Ted Tilley is," said Fiona. "To be sorry about a man's death for all those selfish reasons and not to express one ounce, one teeny-weeny little bit of grief or sympathy for the bereaved."

"I'm sure Ted Tilley feels appropriate awe and grief in the face of death — but I'd guess he's in shock. Maybe he felt that he could speak frankly to me about his troubles. I don't know."

"Angus, you always see the good in everybody," said Fiona. "It's disgusting."

They brooded gloomily for a minute. "I was going to have another waffle, but somehow I don't think I want it," said Angus. Even the dogs seemed subdued.

Eighteen

After Angus left for his office, Fiona and McLeod settled down at the kitchen table with cups of fresh coffee and tea. Fiona ate a waffle. "Nancy, we've got to do some real detective work now," she said.

"I don't know, George, I think we could retire now. This murder happened in the Borough, so the Borough police will be investigating it."

"Do you think the two murders are connected?"

"I don't know," said McLeod. "A senior professor and a senior student — it doesn't seem likely. But I would like to know if Ernst was bitten by a snake."

"A snake? What are you talking about?" asked Fiona.

McLeod reminded her that Brasher said snakebite was a possible cause of death.

"Then a snakebite would prove a connection between the murders, wouldn't it?"

"If anything ever proves anything anymore," said McLeod.

"Oh, come now, there are verities," said Fiona. "At least Angus says there are. Don't you think we should talk to Mrs. Turner?"

"Who's that?"

"Abigail Turner. She's Ernst von Kemp's assistant. She's a friend of Lucy Summers and Hester Hardin and that crowd. Everybody says Ernst couldn't function without Abigail Turner."

"Can she function without him? Can she take over the Dead Sea Scrolls project?"

"I hadn't thought about that," said Fiona. "Hmmm. Would that be a motive for murder?"

"I don't have any idea," said McLeod.

"I think I'll call Abigail and invite her over. I'll bet she's upset. We can give her some coffee, cosset her. And ask her a few questions while we provide aid and comfort."

"Fiona, I swear you'd make a good detective. You missed your calling."

"I never had a calling," said Fiona. "All I've ever done is raise three children and piddle around with civic work. And look at you — you're a journalist, a teacher, and now you're writing a biography. And you raised two children single-handed."

"Poor children. I couldn't be with them as much as I wanted to. I had to go to work after Holland died. They think I neglected them seriously."

"Well, you didn't," said Fiona firmly. "And I bet they don't think you did. Let's get off this gloomy subject anyway. Let's just play like we were perfect parents and we've both had rich, full lives. Now we go back to detection. What about Abigail Turner?"

"Fine," said McLeod, "if you can reach her."

"I'll try." Fiona did try, and was very firm and persistent with several people on the other end of the line, and finally, putting her hand over the phone, hissed to McLeod, "She's just leaving, but they're going to let her speak to me." Then she spoke into the phone, "This is terrible, Abigail, darling. Wouldn't you like to come over here and have a cup of coffee and pull yourself together?" Fiona was quiet, and McLeod heard a crackle of a voice on the other end of the line. "Good," said Fiona. "Come right over. You know where we are — right around the corner on Mercer Street."

Fiona hung up. "She's coming. She said she'd be delighted to sit down with a sympathetic soul. Isn't it funny how detection and good deeds overlap?"

Fiona was pert, McLeod thought. It was a word that had been used in her childhood to describe a girl who was lively and almost impudent in her outrageousness.

Fiona made another pot of coffee. "I wonder if Abigail would like a waffle," she said.

Abigail Turner greeted Beelzebub and Gabriel with great courtesy when Fiona opened the door. Fiona hung Abigail's coat on a hook in the hall, introduced her to McLeod, led her into the kitchen, and offered her a waffle.

"I haven't had a homemade waffle in years. I'd love one. And I'm glad you called," she said as she sat down with them at the kitchen table. "It was awful at the office, and I dreaded going home." She was an imposing woman, not large, but impressive, with her gray hair in a thick braid twisted on the back of her head. Her voice was deep and strong, almost a baritone. She was obviously troubled, and showed it, looking, as McLeod's great-aunt Nannie would have said, "like she had been pulled through a knothole backwards."

"I think every policeman in the Borough is in my office," she said after she had drunk some coffee.

"We saw the police there last night when we came home from dinner. But at least you didn't find Ernst. McLeod here found Dan Strong on the tow path last week, and she hasn't been the same since."

I haven't? McLeod asked herself.

"But I had to identify him," said Abigail, holding her mug of coffee in one large, capable hand. "I had to look at the body and identify it as Ernst. They said they'd be going through everything in both offices with a fine-toothed comb for days. And the place is a mess. Somebody — the murderer, I suppose — tore everything to pieces. Emptied desk drawers and threw everything in the file cabinets on the floor. It was maniacal."

Fiona served Abigail her waffle, which she lit into with gusto. "This is good, Fiona. I'm a little bit unstrung. Carbohydrates help, don't they? No, darling doggies, not a bite for you. This is all for me. Fiona doesn't like for people to feed you from the table."

"I guess you can't tell if anything is missing from the office, can you?" McLeod asked her.

"Not at this point," said Abigail.

"When was Dr. von Kemp killed? I know it was before ten o'clock last night," McLeod said. "Did they say what time?"

"I don't think they know that yet," said Abigail.

"And the body wasn't identified until you got to work this morning?" asked McLeod. "That's almost twelve hours."

"The police called the seminary security offices when they got here last night, and security called the president. Of course, he's out of town raising money — he always is. So they called the dean, Ted Tilley, and he came over and told them who it was. But he didn't know who the next-of-kin was or anything like that for a formal identification. So they called me at the crack of dawn and asked me to come in early."

"I bet you didn't have any breakfast," said Fiona. "Have another waffle."

"No, thanks," said Abigail, "but that one was awfully good."

Fiona turned from the waffle iron to McLeod and frowned at her, jerking her head toward Abigail, silently urging McLeod to go ahead with questioning.

"I'm sure this is hard for you," McLeod said. "How long have you worked for Professor von Kemp?"

"Ever since he's been here, about twenty years."

"Was he a good boss?"

"The best," said Abigail. "I loved him. He had his faults, but he was a good man, and so brilliant. He knew everything — Latin, Greek, Hebrew, Aramaic, German. He knew the Bible. He knew theology — knew John Calvin's *Institutes* backward and forward, not to mention Karl Barth. And the Dead Sea Scrolls — he was the overall editor for twelve volumes of the Scrolls. That alone was enough to keep one man busy. But he taught Bible. And he knew archaeology. He said biblical archaeology wasn't looking for monuments, but for the way people lived. So any coin or piece of pottery was valuable."

Fiona poured Abigail more coffee, and McLeod got up to make another cup of tea.

"And Ernst brought coins and pottery back from the Middle East?" McLeod picked up the questioning.

"He brought a lot of things back. He wasn't involved in excavating himself, but he picked things up from antiquities dealers and paid for them himself. They were on shelves high up on the walls of our offices, above the books."

"Did anything get broken when the offices were ransacked last night?" asked McLeod.

"I don't think so," said Abigail. "I think they're all still intact and sitting up there. It seemed to be just paper all over the floor. But I may be wrong."

"What was the marauder looking for in the office? Do you have any idea?"

"I'm sure he was looking for Ernst's latest find." Abigail Turner stopped and looked first at Fiona and then back at McLeod. "It's a secret."

"He mentioned it to me," said McLeod. "But he wouldn't say what it was."

"He talked about it a little at dinner here on Wednesday," said Fiona. "He wouldn't tell us what it was, but he told Angus it would make him pay attention!"

"He thought it certainly would make everybody pay attention," said Abigail. Then she was silent again for a minute. "Actually, he didn't tell me what it was either, but I have a pretty good idea. I'd better not say any more."

"Whatever it is, is it still safe, do you think?" asked McLeod. "Not stolen or — smashed, or whatever?"

"I think it's safe," said Abigail.

"Did Ernst have any enemies?" This was McLeod again, feeling terribly persistent.

"He wasn't the kind of man to make enemies. He had a sweet nature, really. I don't know of anybody who would want to harm him, but I guess people envied him. You know he had a national — an international — reputation. And he did all these exciting things. Everybody who accomplishes anything has enemies I suppose, don't they?"

"Somehow, at the seminary, everybody seems nicer and gentler," said McLeod. "Except for Dean Tilley, of course. I hadn't thought about people being jealous of Ernst."

"Ted Tilley is pretty bad," said Abigail. "I agree. Even Ernst didn't like him, but he felt sorry for him, he said. He said Ted Tilley had to be like the assistant principal in a high school, doing all the discipline — dealing out retribution — and getting no glory. But don't you believe that everybody else is sweet and kind around here. There's no battle like a religious battle."

"I told you the seminary was a battle-field," said Fiona. "Remember?"

"I'm sure you're both right," said McLeod. One important question occurred to her, but she was hesitant to ask. "Abigail, how was Ernst killed? Was it by a snakebite?"

"Snakebite?" said Abigail. "No. Someone drove a . . . a . . . tent stake . . . through his head. It went straight down to the floor." She started to cry.

"Like Jael," said McLeod, gasping.

"Lucy?" whispered Fiona. "It couldn't be."

Abigail looked through her tears at first one, and then the other. "Jael? Oh, that's the woman who drove a tent stake through Sisera's head. And Lucy's writing about her, is that it? Oh, it can't be Lucy. Lucy wouldn't have messed up the offices like that."

McLeod wondered if the police would take the same view.

"Who will take over the Dead Sea Scrolls project now? Do you know?" McLeod asked, putting a hand on Abigail's shoulder.

"Victor Lord at Duke would kill to take over the project. That was a slip of the tongue. He wouldn't 'kill' to take it over, I'm sure. But I guess he'll be pleased if he gets it, despite how."

"Couldn't you take over the project?" asked Fiona.

"I could, but I'm sure they'll never let me do it. I have a Ph.D., but it's in history. I have no religious training. I'm afraid it will be Victor Lord, and he'll move the project to Duke."

"Maybe they'll have sense enough to let you do it," said McLeod. Then she switched subjects. "Didn't Ernst have any family?" she asked.

"He had a brother out west," said Abigail Turner.

"And that's all?" said McLeod.

Abigail drank some coffee and added, "As a matter of fact, he had a wife."

"A wife!" Fiona was astounded. "I had my eye on him for McLeod. Wouldn't they have made a nice couple?"

Abigail did not join Fiona in her enthusiasm.

"Where is his wife?" asked McLeod gently. "Not here?"

"No, not here. She's German," said Abigail. "She lives in Germany."

"Do they have children?"

"No, no children," said Abigail. "He met her when he was in Germany," said Abigail. Then she closed her lips firmly. "I've rattled on too much. I really have. I can't remember when I've been so indiscreet." She stood up. "I really must be going. Thank you, Fiona, for the coffee and the waffle and the company."

"You don't have to go," said Fiona,

rising also. "Stay with us. You haven't been indiscreet. McLeod will never breathe a word of anything you've said, will you, McLeod? And as for me, I won't remember it long enough to tell anyone."

Abigail looked at her wonderingly and shook her head as though in disbelief. "Fiona, you could make me believe that black was white. I was going home, but I'm going back over to Lenox House and see if I can get in the office and start cleaning it up."

"I don't think you'll be able to clean it up for days, maybe weeks," said McLeod. "Crime scenes stay out of bounds forever these days."

"I guess you're right," said Abigail. "But I'll just look in and see. The police have taken over the two empty offices on the second floor for an on-site headquarters. You know, there are always empty offices over there. Nobody really likes Lenox House. Except Ernst. He loved it. He said it was so non-institutional-looking, that redbrick, steep-gabled old house."

"He was nice," said McLeod. "I only met him twice, but I liked him very much. He was quirky."

"I know," said Abigail, catching a sob in her throat. "Oh, I know." She grabbed her coat from a hook in the hall and fled out the front door.

"Poor Abigail," said Fiona. "She's wiped out, isn't she?"

"Yes, she is. When she first got here, I thought she was tough and strong, invincible. But then I saw what a blow this has been for her. I sensed something else, too. Was she in love with Ernst?"

"I certainly got that impression," said Fiona. "And I think she'd like to take on the Dead Sea Scrolls."

"I do, too," said McLeod.

They put the mugs in the sink and left the kitchen, trailed by Beelzebub and Gabriel. "I guess I'd better go over to the library and get some work done," McLeod said.

"Don't go," said Fiona. "Let's talk about what to do next."

"You think about what to do next. It was your idea to ask Abigail Turner over, and that turned out to be brilliant."

"But didn't Abigail raise a million more questions than she answered?"

"She did. Where did the murderer get a tent stake, for one."

"That's not so hard. The seminary often has tents up. At graduation and at the opening of the fall term," said Fiona. "On the quadrangle behind Alexander Hall."

"So a tent was out there in front of everybody not long ago?" said McLeod.

"That's right," said Fiona.

"But it's hard to believe somebody pulled up a tent stake and kept it in case he —"

"— or she," interjected Fiona.

"— in case he or she wanted to murder somebody," said McLeod, finishing her sentence.

"You never know," said Fiona.

"And what was the mysterious new thing Ernst had found?" asked McLeod. "That's what I want to know."

"And why didn't Ernst tell anybody about his wife?" said Fiona.

"Enough of this idle speculation," said McLeod. "I've still got to get some work done. You think of what we should do next, Fiona."

"It's not idle speculation. It's hardcore detective work," said Fiona. "All right, go ahead and have fun at the library. I'll do something in the kitchen while I think about what to do next."

The dogs were hot on her heels, but McLeod evaded them and slipped out the front door, laptop in hand.

Nineteen

"How did you find me?" McLeod asked when she looked up and saw Lt. Nick Perry standing beside her table in the library. Absurdly glad to see him, she felt her face widen into an idiotic grin. The sunshine from the big windows sparkled off his very bald head, and his blue eyes looked at her penetratingly.

"I am a detective, after all," said Nick, smiling back. "Can we talk?"

"Does this mean you're investigating this murder?"

"I am," he said. "Can you come over to my temporary office in Lenox House?"

"Sure." She picked up her jacket from the back of her chair and retrieved her small purse. His inevitable blue blazer and gray flannel trousers made her feel dowdy in her red sweater and rumpled pants. "Let's go."

As they walked around to Lenox House,

McLeod asked again, "How did you find me, really? I kept meaning to call you and leave my number where I'm staying — with Angus and Fiona McKay — but I never got around to it."

"It was easy," said Nick. "I went by Erdman Hall and they said you had moved to the McKays', but that you usually spent all day in here. And there you were, in the first room I went into. Come on in. I'm upstairs."

Perry's office was little bigger than a closet and contained only a table and two chairs. "Sit down. I don't have coffee — or tea — I'm sorry."

"That's all right. Nick, I'm so glad you're on this case — I can't tell you how glad I am. Do you think there's a connection between this murder and the body on the tow path?"

"What do you think?"

McLeod realized that Nick was going to be as close-mouthed as usual. "I think there is," she said.

Perry took a tape recorder out of a drawer in the table and put it on the table. "Do you mind if I tape this?"

"What can I say?" asked McLeod.

"Say, 'No,' " suggested Nick Perry.

"Of course, I don't mind," said McLeod.

"I gather you know something about what's going on here. You always do."

"A little."

"Begin by telling me how you found the body on the tow path."

McLeod went through the tale she had told so often to Brasher: spotting the autumn crocus and kicking the tartan garment bag. Opening the bag, calling 911.

"And you didn't know who it was?"

"Not a clue. That was on Thursday, and the body wasn't identified until Monday. As you know, it turned out to be a student named Dan Strong, a student I had heard preach the Monday before his death in Miller Chapel on the seminary campus. But I didn't remember him. I remembered his sermon. And here's the thing about that sermon. I didn't see any hidden significance. It seemed to me like an old-fashioned 'repent of your sins' sermon, rather odd for a young seminarian, but still not off the wall. But then several people have said he was threatening people at the seminary, threatening to expose them."

"Threatening who?" asked Nick Perry.

"A motley crew — gays, people who handle money, uppity women, people that don't take every word of the Bible seriously, people that worship false idols — everybody you can think of."

"Who at the seminary worships false idols?"

"One of the students told me that Dan was referring to the man who got murdered last night — Ernst von Kemp."

"Are you serious?" Nick Perry asked.

"Of course I'm serious. I remembered what Willy — that's the student, Willy Cameron — said about Ernst von Kemp, of course, but since the murder I hadn't actually thought of it until this moment."

"Did von Kemp worship false gods, whatever that even means these days?"

"He went to the Middle East a lot, to East Jerusalem. He was working on the Dead Sea Scrolls and he brought back artifacts he bought from antiquities dealers. Some of the things he brought back were pagan gods, like Baal. But he was a collector, a scholar. He didn't worship the artifacts."

"And what was the student preacher threatening von Kemp with?" asked Perry.

"He was supposedly threatening everybody with exposure," said McLeod.

"Exposure? What harm is there in bringing back a sculpture of Baal?"

"Nick, I'm not sure. Willy explained to me that Dan would go to the newspapers and get them excited because the media always love stories about ministers and theologians who do anything at all odd."

"Who is Willy?"

"Willy Cameron is a friend of a student of mine from a couple of years ago at the university. Willy is a student here. He's nice. You should talk to him."

"I will. Is he the only one who saw Dan Strong's sermon as a threat?" asked Nick.

"No, some faculty members did, too."

"Now, did you know Ernst von Kemp?"

"I did. I met him at tea on Saturday a week ago at Henry Fairfield Worthington's house. I liked him. And then Fiona McKay asked him to dinner at their house the other night."

"So, they knew him, too," said Nick.

"Sure. Everybody knows everybody at the seminary."

"What kind of man was he?"

"He was pleasant. He was a fine scholar, I understand. Well-trained. He had this Dead Sea Scrolls publishing project, which everybody regards as a real plum. He taught. He bounced about. I don't think anybody knew him really well."

"Was he married? Did he have a family?"

McLeod hesitated. She did not want to implicate Abigail Turner in any way. But this was a murder investigation, and she had a duty to tell everything she knew.

"Well, he had a wife, and I think most people here had no idea at all that he was married."

"Where is she?" asked Nick.

"Germany. You talked to his assistant, Abigail Turner. Didn't she tell you?"

"We asked her who the next of kin was and she said von Kemp had a brother somewhere in the midwest and his address would be in von Kemp's Rolodex. We located him and he's flying in. She never said anything about a wife. I've got to ask her more about the brother, and about the wife."

"That's odd. She mentioned the wife this morning."

"Maybe she meant ex-wife," said Nick.

"She didn't say ex-wife. And she said that she felt she had been indiscreet, so if you ask her about it, please don't tell her I'm the one who told you."

"We'll do the best we can," said Nick. "When did you talk to her?"

"This morning. When Fiona heard about the murder, she called her up and invited her to come over and have coffee with us. For support. Fiona's wonderful."

"Yeah. I bet the two of you plied her

with a ton of questions," said Nick.

"As I recall, Fiona did not ask a single question," said McLeod stiffly.

"I bet you asked enough for two," said Nick. "Who else was a friend of Ernst von Kemp?"

"Henry Fairfield Worthington," said McLeod. "He lives in an apartment on the corner of Library Place and Mercer Street. He's retired. He's in the telephone book."

"Anybody else?" asked Nick.

"That's about all the people I know at the seminary. Except Lucy Summers — and the dean, Ted Tilley."

Nick switched off the tape recorder. "I remember Tilley. He's the one that came to headquarters about you."

"That's right. I never did call a lawyer, Nick. I was too busy."

"Too busy investigating, I suppose," said Nick.

"I have this research I'm trying desperately to finish," she said, as coldly as she could.

Nick switched the recorder back on. "Well, who's Lucy Summers?"

"She's a very attractive woman professor, a feminist who believes strongly in inclusive language." Here she had to stop and explain to Nick about how you shouldn't always refer to God as "He."

"Call God 'She'?" asked Nick.

"No, no. Use gender-neutral terms — like just plain God, or The Lord, even. It makes sense to me." Speaking of Lucy made her remember the method von Kemp's murderer had used.

"What is it? You've got a funny look on your face," said Nick.

"I don't see what significance it could possibly have," said McLeod, "but Lucy Summers has done a lot of work on Jael." Again she had to stop, this time to explain to Nick who Jael was. "Jael was pretending to be nice to Sisera, this guy who was an enemy of the Israelites, and when he went to sleep, she drove a tent stake through his head, pinning him to the floor."

"So you know how von Kemp was apparently killed," said Nick. "Who told you?"

"Abigail Turner told us, this morning."

"Well, it will be in the papers tomorrow. Anything else you can tell me?"

"Nothing, but if I think of anything, I'll let you know."

"Please do, McLeod."

"I will. But what's happening with the other murder — the student? Will you take over that investigation?"

Nick sighed gustily. "No, I guess we'll

'cooperate,' and I use the word loosely on that one. The Township doesn't want to give it up, so we'll let them muddle along for a while. The state police are going to help us with crime scene work here. But we're going to interview everybody who knew von Kemp — students, faculty, and so on. We'll see where that takes us."

"There's one thing I'd really like to know," said McLeod. "Was a snakebite involved in Dan Strong's death? The paper said one time the Township hadn't found out the cause of death and it might be a snakebite."

"Are you just curious, or is there a good reason why you want to know?"

"I'm always curious — you know that," said McLeod. "But if a snakebite was involved —" she stopped. She wouldn't tell Nick about Roscoe and his snakes. He wasn't investigating that murder, and there was no need to get Roscoe involved. "Tell me if it was a snakebite."

Nick sighed. "Okay, it wasn't, but somebody apparently jabbed Dan Strong's wrist with something sharp and small, like a serpent's tooth. Jabbed it twice after he was dead, to make it look like a snakebite."

"That's weird," said McLeod. "Very weird."

181

Twenty

"I told him everything, or nearly everything," McLeod said to Fiona, describing her interview with Nick Perry. "I couldn't believe I knew so much."

It was late Friday afternoon, and the two of them were drinking tea in the McKays' library. Small flames sparkled in the fireplace, which seemed to be guarded carefully by Beelzebub and Gabriel.

"Will he interview me?" asked Fiona. "I've never been asked questions by a policeman."

"You never got a speeding ticket?" asked McLeod.

"Well, yes, I have, but what kind of questions are those? 'Where's the fire?' or 'Do you know how fast you were going?' I mean real criminology questions."

"Nick will probably talk to you and Angus both. He said he was going to interview everybody who knew Ernst."

"Of course, I won't know anything you don't. Not as much even. But I'm going to think hard and try to squeeze out something that will knock his socks off," said Fiona.

"Did Lucy Summers know Ernst von Kemp?" McLeod asked.

"I'm sure she did," said Fiona.

"Was there any reason on earth for her to kill him?"

"You mean because of that tent stake?" asked Fiona. "Why do we always think of Lucy when we hear 'tent stake.' Plenty of people — everybody — around here have read the story of Jael."

"I know. But just suppose —" said McLeod. "Okay, she was a member of the rifle team at Sophie Newcomb."

"But Ernst wasn't shot."

"That's right, but it shows that Lucy isn't a fragile little woman. Still, I have to say that I don't see how she could have overpowered Ernst and driven a tent stake through his head."

"That's right. Unless he was asleep, like Sisera," said Fiona.

"And what motive would she have?"

"Unrequited love?" asked Fiona.

"Somehow I don't think so."

"And if she did kill von Kemp, does that

mean she killed Dan Strong, too? Why would she do that? He couldn't expose her as a feminist or a strong exponent of inclusive language. Everybody already knew she was those things."

"Maybe he just drove her mad," said Fiona. "Maybe she's a closet lesbian, and she was afraid Dan was going to expose her."

"Where did she kill him?" asked McLeod.

"At her house. She enticed him there." Fiona paused. "But then how could she get his body down to the tow path?"

"Actually, I know how she could have done that," said McLeod. "She had one of those little metal carts you strap luggage to. She could have bundled him into the garment bag — she told me she has lots of old luggage — and pulled it anywhere."

"There you go," said Fiona. She paused.

"But doesn't she have a pretty good alibi for von Kemp's murder?" said McLeod. "She was with us, wasn't she? What time did the cleaning lady find the body? We have to find that out somehow."

"Lucy could have killed von Kemp and then met us for dinner," said Fiona.

"She certainly looked a little ruffled, didn't she?" said McLeod.

184

"But I don't like it, do you?" Fiona said.

"Of course not. I don't think Lucy Summers is a murderer. Besides, why would she kill von Kemp? Maybe, by the wildest stretch of the imagination, she had a motive for killing Dan Strong, but what motive could she have for killing von Kemp?"

"Maybe she had to kill von Kemp because he knew she killed Dan. You know, that could apply to anybody who's the murderer. First they kill Dan, and then they have to kill von Kemp because he knows something that would incriminate them. A domino effect."

"How would von Kemp know?"

"I don't know," said Fiona. "Maybe he saw something, knew something."

"It's a possibility," said McLeod.

They were both quiet for a moment. Then McLeod said, "I learned something from Nick Perry today."

"What? What? Tell, tell."

"Dan Strong wasn't bitten by a snake, but the murderer tried to make it look as though he had been. After Dan was dead, the killer punched two holes in his wrist to make it look like a snakebite."

"That's odd," said Fiona.

"It's very odd," said McLeod. "But it

gives me another reason to think the two murders are connected. Doesn't it seem as though Dan's murderer made it look like snakebite to implicate Roscoe Kelly? And, at first, you know we both thought of Lucy Summers when Ernst was killed with that tent stake, but isn't it more likely that Ernst's murderer used a tent stake through the head to implicate Lucy?"

"I'm sure you're right. What does that mean about the murderer though? That he tries to get other people blamed?"

"That he — or she — has imagination and ingenuity," said McLeod. "If it was Lucy, it means she was a busy girl, doesn't it? She killed Dan, carted his body down to the tow path, punctured two holes in his arm to make it look like a snakebite, came home, and disposed of his clothes. Then ten days later she kills von Kemp by driving a tent stake through his head to either direct attention to herself, or to make it look like somebody else drove a tent stake through his head to direct attention at her. Almost too clever. Then she dusts her hands and comes to your house so we can go out to dinner. What a woman."

"Murder is labor intensive, isn't it?" said Fiona.

McLeod smiled. "Very," she said. "You

know, I don't know how Dan was actually killed. I forgot to ask. And probably Nick wouldn't have told me anyway. But I'd like to know that."

"I think we need to do some more detecting, Nancy."

"I don't know. I was so eager for the Borough police to get on the job, but now I remember that Nick often goes off on an unproductive tack. Somebody may have to find out things to egg him on in the right direction. What do you have in mind?"

"We should talk to Henry Fairfield Worthington," said Fiona. "He was probably the best friend Ernst von Kemp had here."

"Maybe I can run into him at the cafeteria," said McLeod.

"What about me?" said Fiona. "I want to talk to him, too. Shall I ask him for dinner tonight? Let me look at the calendar." She went back to the kitchen, where she kept her calendar by the phone, and returned, looking disconsolate. "Angus and I have to go out tonight. I forgot. It's too late anyway to ask him for tonight. What about tomorrow? I can't believe we're free on Saturday night."

"Sure, try him," said McLeod.

Fiona left again and returned to say that

it was a done deal. "Now what shall we serve when he comes?"

They discussed this interesting question until Angus appeared — to the delight of Beelzebub and Gabriel — and led them in a switch from tea to sherry.

"We have to go to that dreadful departmental dinner tonight," Fiona reminded him.

"I know it. It's on my calendar at the office. Why do you think I'm drinking sherry?!" said Angus with a smile. "You're welcome to come along, McLeod."

"Thanks," said McLeod. "But I'll stay here. With Beelzebub and Gabriel." The dogs looked up at the mention of their names. "Beelzebub is a devil, right? And Gabriel an angel? It seems to me that both of them are pretty good. Oh, I almost forgot! I have to go to Trudy Sergeant's cocktail party," she said.

"Where does she live?" asked Fiona.

"On Markham Road."

"That's too far to walk. I'll drive you over. Or you can take my car. Then you can come home when you want to."

"Oh, Fiona, surely I can walk to Markham. It's right past Harrison Street."

"Don't be silly. Take my car."

"Fine."

"You have good judgment," said Fiona,

"about the dogs and the departmental dinner. And, sweetie," this to Angus, "Henry Fairfield Worthington is coming to dinner tomorrow night. He was probably Ernst von Kemp's best friend here, and I thought he might need cheering up."

McLeod could only admire Fiona's cunning. She would convince Angus they were doing a good deed, when she really wanted to question Henry Fairfield Worthington. Or wants me to question him, she thought. "Angus, what's the talk on campus about the murder — or murders?" she asked.

"The talk is despair and grief and a kind of fear," said Angus. "The president cut short his fund-raising tour and came back home. Now he just dithers. Ted Tilley is beside himself. He dithers *and* drives everybody mad. The administration has no idea of how to go about filling Ernst's shoes. He was unique, and they know it. The Board of Trustees is having an emergency meeting tomorrow morning. Quite a few people told me they had no intention of ever staying in their offices after five o'clock in the afternoon again. It's total chaos and bedlam. And dithering."

"Did you see Lucy today?" asked Fiona.

"No, I didn't," said Angus.

"Did you hear how Ernst was killed?"

189

Fiona asked him. When Angus shook his head, she said, "It was with a tent stake stuck through his head."

"And you think Lucy — ?"

"Of course not," said Fiona. "I just wondered if she knew."

"I hope she never finds out," said Angus. "Although I'm not sure why we should immediately think of Lucy when we hear about a tent stake rammed through someone's head."

"I don't either," said Fiona, "but I do."

"I always will," said McLeod.

McLeod drove to Trudy Sergeant's house, a place she liked to visit because of the great modern paintings that Trudy owned. When Trudy greeted her at the door, McLeod could hear the cocktail party noise thundering away behind her.

"Come in, come in," said Trudy. "You know a lot of people here, I'm sure. I'll introduce you to one or two." She led McLeod to a group of women and rattled off everybody's name so fast McLeod caught none of them. The women looked at her politely and then looked back at each other and took up their conversation where they had left off. McLeod looked around helplessly and silently moved away to speak to Grady Schuyler, who had been an assistant professor hoping for tenure when McLeod had met him.

He greeted her warmly and told her proudly that he had won tenure the year before and was now an associate professor.

"Congratulations!" said McLeod. "But I remember you were pretty confident."

"I guess I was. I knew Queer Studies was hot."

"I'm sure that's not the only reason," McLeod said.

"What brings you back to Princeton? Are you teaching writing again?"

"No, I'm doing some research at the seminary," said McLeod.

"Oh, then you must know Victor Lord," said Grady, turning to a man standing nearby whom McLeod had not noticed before.

"Victor Lord? I'm afraid I don't. The name sounds familiar."

"Well, this is Victor Lord," said Grady. "McLeod Dulaney."

"You're from Duke!" said McLeod, suddenly remembering why the name was familiar.

"I am," he said. He was a nice-looking man, tall with brown hair and dark brown eyes.

"He's up here for a seminar on the Dead Sea Scrolls tomorrow in Near Eastern Studies," explained Grady.

"What a coincidence," said McLeod. "I just heard your name this morning. Abigail Turner —"

"Oh, yes," said Lord. "She was a secretary for a project with which I'm involved. Her boss has been murdered. Did you know that?" Lord looked from Grady to McLeod and back again. "Ernst von Kemp. He was supposed to be on a panel with me tomorrow." He shook his head sadly.

"Yes, I know," said McLeod.

Grady was shaking his head so Victor Lord said, "He was a professor at the Seminary and was head of the project on the Scrolls that I'm working on. His body was found last night in his office. He had been murdered, I understand."

"McLeod is working at the seminary, and she's an expert on murder," said Grady. "She can tell us all about it."

"That's about all I know," said McLeod, choosing not to reveal what she did know about Ernst — and Abigail. "I did think Abigail was more than a secretary," she said.

"Really?" said Lord. "Of course, she's

not shy and retiring at all."

McLeod could see why Abigail feared that this man would take over the project. And she suspected it would be hard to work for him. Could he be a suspect? "When did you get here?" she asked him.

"Yesterday," he said. "I flew up and got here in time to chat with some of the people in the religion department. Today, I've been with the Near Eastern people, getting ready for the seminar. I'll have to take poor Ernst von Kemp's place, as well as fill my own."

He did not sound very regretful, McLeod thought. "Do you think you'll take over the Dead Sea Scrolls publishing project?" she asked.

"I expect it's in the cards," said Lord.

"That's quite a plum, isn't it?" asked Grady.

"Oh, it would be, but at such a price," said Lord. "Are you interested?"

"Good Lord, no!" said Grady. "Although, come to think about it, there are some interesting hints at queer activity in some of that stuff, aren't there?"

"There's Leviticus," said Lord.

"Oh, no, I mean other passages, like David and Jonathan, not those dreary laws in Leviticus. But that's another story. I hope you get directorship of the project, if that's what you want."

"Thanks," said Lord.

Back home, the house was empty except for Gabriel and Beelzebub. McLeod cooked some fresh pasta Fiona had urged her to use and made herself a salad. She ate heartily, and, since Fiona wasn't here, fed the dogs from her plate. When they had all finished, she cleaned up the kitchen. In bed, she read a book on the history of the seminary to find out what it was like when Elijah P. Lovejoy was a student in 1832 and 1833 and there were less than a hundred students, a few buildings, and a handful of faculty.

She was surprised to discover that the clerics at the seminary were not wholly behind Lovejoy and his abolitionist stance after he graduated. While they didn't go as far as some Presbyterians in other places who tried abolitionists for heresy, they thought the abolition of slavery should be gradual. Distinguished professors, who were all powerful preachers, pointed out that slavery was common in the Old Testament and not mentioned in the New Testament and therefore not necessarily a sin. So Ted Tilley was not the only one who called Elijah P. Lovejoy a mere agitator, but he was surely the only one in modern times.

Anyway, Lovejoy had remained staunch in his belief that slavery was evil — and he died for that belief and for freedom of the press. Impressed again, but yawning, McLeod turned off her light and went to sleep.

Twenty-one

By the time Angus, accompanied by Beel-zebub and Gabriel, came downstairs to make coffee on Saturday, McLeod was about to leave for the library. "Working on Saturday?" he asked her.

"You bet," she said. "How was the din-ner?"

"We talked about murder," said Angus.

"And the food was as bad as the conver-sation," said Fiona, who came in rubbing her eyes.

"I have to go," said McLeod, "but I want to tell you something, George."

"What, Nancy?"

"I met Victor Lord," she said. "He was at Trudy's party. And he was here in town Thursday night."

"What?" said Fiona again.

"You know — Victor Lord. The man from Duke. Abigail said he would probably take over the Dead Sea Scrolls project . . ."

"Oh," said Fiona. "Oh. Do you think he might have murdered Ernst?"

"It's a possibility," said McLeod.

"What's he doing in town? I mean supposedly," said Fiona.

"He's here for a seminar," said McLeod. "I like him as our suspect. If it's Lord, it's nobody we know and love. But then who killed Dan Strong?"

"Questions, questions," said Fiona. "I can't think until I get some coffee."

"Drink, then think," said McLeod. "I'm off to the library."

She went out, detoured uptown, and picked up a Trenton paper, which she opened and read as soon as she sat down in the library. Von Kemp's murder was page-one news. The murder occurred, the story said, sometime between five and nine o'clock on Thursday night. A head wound was inflicted with a tent stake after death had occurred. The medical examiner was still determining the exact cause of death, which was apparently some kind of poison.

On an inside page, where the von Kemp story ran over from the front page, was another story about the "tow path murder." No one seemed to connect the two murders. Not openly anyway. This story said the medical examiner had decided that

Daniel Strong had been killed with a dose of cyanide in a soft drink. "You can buy potassium cyanide on the Internet," the medical examiner was quoted as saying. "Six grams — it will fit onto a thumb-nail — is enough to kill. And it's the one poison that kills instantly."

McLeod tried to imagine Lucy Summers putting cyanide in a Coke and handing it to a student. It was hard to picture.

She buckled down to work, reading about the memorials and monuments to Elijah P. Lovejoy.

When McLeod got home at lunchtime, Nick Perry was talking to Fiona and Angus in the living room. Fiona must have decided that a visit from a policeman was a serious event, since they were in the living room rather than the less formal library. Beelzebub and Gabriel sat up, looking alert.

Nick Perry stood up and smiled at her when she stood in the doorway. "Come in," said Fiona.

"No, let me talk to you two first, and then I'll talk to Ms. Dulaney again," Nick Perry said.

McLeod was in the kitchen drinking tea when Fiona and Angus came in to say

Nick Perry was through with them and ready for her.

Nick was standing up when she went into the living room and he shook her hand warmly. "They're certainly nice people," said Nick.

"They are," agreed McLeod, sitting down.

"And they were very helpful about background information," Nick said.

"I want to know one thing: Are the two murders connected?"

"I can't tell you anything about the investigation. You know that. My personal opinion — and don't quote me — is that they're not. The methods are different. There's no connection between the victims, except that they're affiliated with the same institution."

"Does that make it harder or easier?" asked McLeod.

"Both. It's incredible that we'd have two murders in the Princeton area in such a short time. But it makes it easier for us in a way because the Township is investigating the tow path murder and we're responsible for this one."

"They don't seem to be making much headway," said McLeod.

"No, they don't seem to," said Nick.

"But you don't know how much headway they're actually making."

"True," said McLeod. She thought about the fake snakebite on Dan Strong's arm and wondered again if she should tell Nick about Roscoe and Samson and Delilah. No, she decided.

"Tell me this," she said. "What time did the cleaning lady find Ernst's body?"

"I guess I can tell you that," said Nick. "It was at seven o'clock Thursday night."

"The paper said the murder occurred sometime between five and nine," McLeod said. She wondered if seven o'clock let Lucy out. But what about everybody else — Henry and Willy and Abigail and all the faculty and students?

"I've got to be going, McLeod," said Nick. "I just wanted to check in with you. Thank the McKays for me. Have you picked up anything new — in your usual way?"

"Yes," she said. And she told him about Victor Lord.

Nick was interested, and made notes on everything McLeod could tell him. "You don't know where he's staying, do you?"

"No, I don't, but he's speaking at a seminar today. Ernst von Kemp was supposed to speak, too. Maybe Lord didn't want von

Kemp to speak. Maybe von Kemp was going to reveal some big secret — maybe tell about his big find."

"Where is this seminar?"

"I don't know where it's meeting. And since it's Saturday I don't know who you could call," said McLeod. "Oh, I know, look on the university's web page — it should be listed someplace."

Nick pulled out his cell phone to call someone at the police department to find out about it, but McLeod said, "Wait, we can use Angus's computer," and led him to the kitchen to make sure it was okay with Angus.

"Certainly," said Angus, so they all trooped into the study while Angus called up the web page. After some searching, he found the seminar.

"It's going on in the Friend Center," he said.

"I know where that is," said Nick. "I'll try to find Lord right now. I've got to go." He rushed out.

"What did he ask you?" asked McLeod.

"He wanted to know what we could tell him about Ernst. We couldn't tell him much. He asked us about Dan Strong — had Angus ever had him in a class and that kind of thing. And he asked about Dan's sermon. So I asked him if the two murders were connected and he said he couldn't talk about that."

"I don't think we told him anything he didn't already know," said Angus.

"And I did so want to be a priceless source of information," said Fiona.

Twenty-two

Henry Fairfield Worthington arrived promptly for dinner bringing a bottle of champagne. "In the midst of death, we are in life," he said. "This is the day the Lord has made; let us rejoice and be glad in it."

Beelzebub and Gabriel made a joyful noise over the newcomer and Henry Fairfield Worthington knelt to rub their ears and to speak sweet nothings to them. "I love dogs," he said, getting up. "I used to have a cairn terrier. I miss him terribly."

He looked handsome and fit in a dark pin-striped suit, his white hair carefully brushed. He kissed Fiona on the cheek, shook hands with Angus, and held out both hands to McLeod, then kissed her cheek, too. He has white hair like mine, and he's ten years older, thought McLeod, but he looks younger and fitter.

They drank the champagne right away. "This is lovely. We all need cheering up," said Fiona. Angus's fire was brilliant and dahlias in a tall vase added another festive note.

McLeod went with Fiona to the kitchen and returned to the library with a tray of smoked salmon on small pieces of brown bread with cream cheese.

Later, when Fiona called them to dinner, Henry Fairfield Worthington said, "It's a pity to leave the fire."

"If you're not hungry . . ." said Fiona.

"I'm hungry. Believe me," said Henry Fairfield Worthington. "I do like a fire-place, though. And I don't have one."

When he saw a fire in the dining room fireplace, he was beside himself with joy. "Two working fireplaces!" he said.

"Isn't that fine?" Fiona asked him. "All the fireplaces in this house work. And I think Angus is a latent pyromaniac — he loves to lay fires. And he remembered that you are a fire fan, too."

The dogs, fire fans too, lay down in front of the dining room fireplace.

It was that evening that at last McLeod began to think of their guest as Henry, instead of Henry Fairfield Worthington. He was charming at dinner, even after McLeod asked him endless questions.

"You were Ernst von Kemp's best friend,

weren't you?" she said.

"I guess I was, but at the same time we weren't all that close," said Henry. "I'm not sure he had any really good friends here. But I liked him. Yes, he interested me. He was bright. He knew a lot, but he was odd. He always held something back. He wasn't perfect by any means. But he could be warm and charming."

"Do you know what his latest find was?" asked McLeod.

"No, I don't. But he told me it was very exciting," said Henry.

"He told me that, too," said Angus. "But I have no idea what it was."

"Do you suppose it's another little object?" asked Fiona. "He loved those ancient clay lamps, didn't he? Those little tiny oil lamps."

"He liked it all," said Henry. "I wonder if they were all authentic, to tell you the truth. How could he afford them, if they were? Of course, he had no family to support, and he may have had private means . . ."

"He had a wife," said McLeod.

"No, he wasn't married," said Henry.

"Henry, he was married," said Fiona. "Abigail Turner said so yesterday morning, in my own kitchen. Didn't she, McLeod?"

"Yes, she did. She said his wife was in Germany."

"Did she mean ex-wife?" asked Henry.

"She didn't say ex-wife," said Fiona, "and she certainly seemed to think she'd been indiscreet."

"Do you know where the brother lives?" asked McLeod.

"In the midwest," said Henry. "I think Ernst told me that his brother had dropped the 'von' from his name and was just plain Kemp."

"How long had Ernst been at the seminary?" asked McLeod.

"Twenty years, would it be, Angus?" asked Henry.

"About that," said Angus. "He came here from a small seminary in the midwest, I think it was Lutheran. He already had some sort of connection with the Dead Sea Scrolls — he'd been in East Jerusalem for a time years ago. The seminary was delighted to have him. He suggested the seminary's Dead Sea Scrolls publication project."

"And it's going well?" asked McLeod.

"Actually, I believe it's well behind schedule, but don't most big publishing projects like that run late?"

"Do they?" asked McLeod.

"What did Ernst do with all those artifacts he brought back?" Fiona asked Henry.

"He kept a lot of them, but he also sold some of them to other collectors."

"Maybe he made enough off the ones he sold to keep buying," said Fiona.

"Maybe so. I think he was trying to raise the money to pay for this latest find. I have an idea it hasn't arrived yet," said Henry.

Dessert was apple dumplings, and Henry was as enthusiastic about them as he had been about everything else. "My mother used to make them," he said. "I haven't had any apple dumplings since I was a boy."

"All our mothers used to make them," said Fiona.

Fiona waited until they were having coffee to get back to detecting. "Who do you think could have killed Ernst?" she asked Henry.

"I can't imagine," he said. "He had his faults, as I said, but he didn't have a malicious bone in his body. I can't see why anybody would kill him. Unless it was somebody who thought there were valuable objects in his office."

"Would a thief — somebody from outside the seminary — use a tent stake to kill him?" asked Angus.

"Who knows," said Henry. "The whole thing is weird."

"So is the student's murder," pointed out McLeod. "The Trenton paper said this morning that he was killed with cyanide but that somebody poked two holes in his wrist, to make it look like snakebite."

"These murders are the most outlandish things that have ever happened around here," said Henry.

"Do you think the two murders are connected?" asked McLeod.

They all agreed that it was hard to see how they would be connected, but equally hard to believe they were not connected.

"By the way, Henry, what were you doing Thursday between five and nine?" asked McLeod.

Henry looked startled. "I was at home, alone," he said. "What were you doing?"

"Fiona and I and Lucy went out to dinner at the Annex," said McLeod.

"Did you go at five?" asked Henry Fairfield Worthington. "You see, McLeod, what's sauce for the gander is sauce for the goose."

"Actually, I was at the library in plain sight of many people until five, and then I was with Fiona here every minute until we met Lucy."

"You're lucky," said Henry. "Probably nobody else at the seminary has such a firm alibi."

"Altogether, it was a success," said Fiona as she and McLeod cleaned up the kitchen after Henry Fairfield Worthington had gone home. "The dinner party, I mean."

"It was, indeed," said McLeod. "I like Henry Fairfield Worthington, even when he's acerbic."

Twenty-three

On Sunday morning McLeod was again up before her hosts — or the hosts' dogs — came downstairs, and caught the phone in the kitchen on the first ring. It was George Bridges calling her from Brussels.

"Where are you?" he asked. "I called Erdman Hall yesterday and they said you'd moved out, but they didn't know where you were. I tried again today and somebody there gave me this number."

"I'm with my friends Fiona and Angus McKay," said McLeod. "He's on the faculty at the seminary. He teaches medieval church history. I knew them in high school in Atlanta. Anyway, let me tell you . . ." and she recounted the tale of the tow path corpse's identification, Dean Tilley's suggestion that she leave the seminary, the Township police refusing to let her go . . .

"And now there's been a second murder."

"And you're investigating it. McLeod —"

"Don't worry. Nick Perry is in charge of this investigation. This one happened in the Borough. It was another professor at the seminary."

"Did you find the body?"

"I did not, George."

"Okay. I worry about you, that's all."

"Thanks. How's Brussels?"

"Brussels is fine. I'm going to Germany Monday."

"George, are you going anywhere near Tübingen?"

"No, I'm going to Berlin, and that's all the way across the country from Tübingen. Why?"

"Curiosity," said McLeod. "That's all."

"What did you want to know about Tübingen?"

"It's not about Tübingen per se. I wanted to know about an alumnus of the university there."

"That's easy. We network with all the big European universities. I'm going to the office Monday before I leave for Berlin. Who is the alumnus?"

"Ernst von Kemp," said McLeod.

"Who's he?"

"He's the latest murder victim. He was a big Biblical scholar and involved with the

Dead Sea Scrolls and antiquities. Nice guy. I'm just curious, that's all."

"Why am I encouraging you? But I'll fax them Monday. Spell it."

McLeod spelled it out for him.

The *New York Times* had a story about von Kemp's murder, with a sidebar by its religion editor talking about the precedent for using a tent stake to inflict a mortal head wound. As he gloated over bits of information about Jael and Sisera, he managed to work in quotes from Old Testament scholars from every seminary except Princeton. "It does not necessarily mean that the murderer was a woman," said one.

When Fiona came downstairs, accompanied by Beelzebub and Gabriel, she was eager for more detection work. "Let me just take these pests outside a minute — Angus usually does it, but he's not up yet."

When Fiona was back inside, McLeod had to confess she was momentarily stymied about how to proceed with detection work. She dutifully went to Nassau Presbyterian Church with Fiona and Angus and during the service decided that she was so tired of Presbyterianism that she would become an Episcopalian. But during the interminable pastoral prayer, she had an idea.

"I think we should talk to some students," she told Fiona when they were back at home and had greeted the dogs.

"Students?" said Fiona.

"Seminary students," said McLeod kindly.

"I know *that*," said Fiona. "I was just trying to get used to the idea. How should we do it? What shall we do?"

"We could have some over for supper tonight. Nothing elaborate. I'll bet they'd be glad to get hot dogs on Sunday nights. The cafeteria is closed. I'll do the shopping and the cooking this time."

"Fine," said Fiona. "Who do you think we should ask?"

"Well, Willy and Roscoe, for starters," said McLeod.

"Roscoe! Do you think he'd bring Samson and Delilah?" Fiona was clearly excited.

"I doubt it. You can ask him, though."

"And who else? I know, we can have Sharon Leland."

"Dan Strong's girlfriend?" said McLeod. "The last one to see him alive — except for the murderer, of course. Call her!"

Sharon accepted with pleasure, and so did Willy. Roscoe declined to bring his snakes, but he said that "Mrs. McKay can walk back to Alexander Hall with us and see them in my room."

"I certainly will," said Fiona.

Angus said he'd go along with her and see the snakes himself. "But I don't understand why you're inviting all these students to dinner," he said.

"It's civic work," said Fiona. "We're helping with a criminal investigation."

"Indeed," said Angus. "I'll bet the police are delighted. If we're having students to dinner, we should ask Gretchen Green."

Fiona made a face. "I guess so," she said.

"Who's Gretchen Green?" asked McLeod.

"She's from Atlanta," said Fiona. "We knew her a little bit back there. She worked for an auditing firm, and she advised the seminary down there about auditing their books. When her marriage broke up and she went through a messy divorce, she decided to come to the seminary herself, find a new life. But she came here, instead of staying in Atlanta. A lot of seminary students now are divorced women — it's interesting."

"It certainly is," said McLeod. "By all means ask her. I'd love to meet her."

"I feel guilty every time I see her," said Angus, "because we never ask her over."

"How old is she?" asked McLeod.

"Around forty, I think," said Fiona.

"I wonder if she'll expect something better than hot dogs? Should I revise my menu?"

"She's older, but I don't think she's much of an epicure," said Fiona. "Let's go with hot dogs."

Sharon Leland turned out to be, as proclaimed on every hand, a very nice young woman, with pale brown hair, light blue eyes, and a sweet smile, but she looked tired. She greeted Angus and Fiona warmly and thanked them for the condolences they had sent.

"It's hard," she said. "And school goes on. I can't just give up and mourn, which is what I'd like to do. Dan's parents are inconsolable. Naturally. And they want to have his funeral, but the police haven't released his . . . body yet."

Then she turned her attention to Beelzebub and Gabriel, who were dancing around her feet. "Hey, guys, it's so good to see you again."

Fiona introduced McLeod, who impulsively embraced Sharon. "I'm glad to meet you, but I'm so sorry it's at this difficult time of your life."

Sharon smiled wanly. Willy and Roscoe appeared, and they all moved into the library. The young men were introduced to Gabriel and Beelzebub and everybody had enthusiastically accepted the offer of beer when Gretchen Green arrived.

Gretchen was an unhappy looking woman who never smiled. The world rested heavily on her shoulders, it seemed, and she frowned continually. She ignored the small dogs who had gotten up to investigate the new arrival and were circling her with great interest and energy. They followed her into the living room, but peeled off and sought the floor in front of the fire, where Roscoe came over to pet them.

"How do you do?" Gretchen said when introduced to McLeod. "You're the one who found the body?" she asked, ignoring the presence and sensibilities of Sharon Leland.

"I'm the one who found one body," said McLeod. "The one by the canal. The cleaning lady found the latest body."

"The cleaning lady?" said Gretchen, frowning even more heavily. "I thought it was the assiduous Turner."

"Assiduous?" McLeod said.

"Oh, so hardworking, so thorough, so loyal," said Gretchen. "Loyal to von Kemp, anyway."

"Aren't those qualities to be admired, Gretchen?" Angus asked mildly. "Would you like a beer? We all seem to be drinking beer."

"I don't like beer," said Gretchen flatly. "But if that's what everyone is drinking, I suppose I can drink it, too."

"You don't have to," said Angus. "What would you like? We have everything. Wine? Red or white? A gin and tonic?"

Gretchen finally insisted on having a beer. "I don't know why I said I didn't like it. I'd be happy with a beer."

A self-sacrificial martyr, thought McLeod, as she went into the kitchen for the last-minute chores. What a pill. She's going to drink beer but let everybody know she hates it so everybody will think she's noble.

When they were all seated at the dining table eating hot dogs and potato salad, McLeod could not bring herself to ask questions about Dan with Sharon present. The students tried surreptitiously to feed the dogs bits of hot dogs while they talked in general terms about their internships. All of them were working in churches part-time this year and had spent most of the day in those churches.

Roscoe rode the bus to Trenton to help with the Sunday school in a downtown church. Willy worked at Fifth Avenue Presbyterian in New York City. "I like it," he said. "I like New York."

Gretchen had a part-time job with a chaplain in a hospital in New Brunswick. "It's all right," she said, "but I'm not sure the chaplain knows what he's doing."

Sharon said she quite liked her work with a church in Far Hills — a horsey, upscale community an hour's drive away. "They are just the sweetest people," she said.

"Isn't that where Jacqueline Kennedy kept her horses for a while?" asked McLeod.

"I think so," said Sharon.

"But Sharon doesn't like just rich people. I remember that you worked for a year with Mother Teresa in India and just loved that, too, didn't you, Sharon," said Angus. "And nothing could be more different from Calcutta than Far Hills."

Sharon laughed and blushed and said, "They were sweet, too. I did love India."

Then McLeod turned to Gretchen. "What made you decide to come to seminary?"

"Why does anybody decide to go to seminary?" asked Gretchen. "You mean because I'm so old?"

"I see lots of students around who are your age or older," said McLeod. "It's just a phenomenon that I wasn't familiar with until I saw it for myself. Do you want to be a parish minister or are you interested in teaching?"

"I want to do counseling. I think I can help people sort out their lives. My experience — I've been an accountant and an auditor and I was married for fifteen years — I think that gives me a background that should provide insights that would be helpful to other people."

They talked about Rob Hillhouse and the service of commitment he had held for the gay couple in New York. Sharon thought it was a sin, "downright blasphemous," she said. Willy was delighted with Hillhouse's action. Roscoe reserved judgment. "I don't know what everybody in Two Egg would say about that," he said. Gretchen said Rob Hillhouse was a poseur, but she was glad he'd done the service.

Gretchen left as soon as dinner was over, saying she had to study. Roscoe, Willy, and Sharon stayed on, talking a little about Gretchen.

"She's not happy," said Sharon. "I mean,

I'm not happy but everybody says I'll get over it, and I know I will. She's really basically not happy."

McLeod wondered, since Gretchen was so sour, if she would be good at counseling.

"Oh, I've figured her out," said Willy. "I'll tell you why this outlandish person is here: because the FBI put her here in a witness protection program. She doesn't really belong here, but this is a perfect cover for her."

Everyone liked this hypothesis. Their laughter excited Beelzebub and Gabriel, who began to leap about and bark.

With everybody in such a good humor, McLeod decided to get back to detecting. "I'm asking everybody this," she said, "so don't get on your high horses. Where were you between five and seven on Thursday night? The police will ask eventually, if they haven't already."

"You mean when Dr. von Kemp was killed?" asked Willy. McLeod nodded. "I was in the library until five and then I went to my room and then went to dinner at the cafeteria. Then I guess I was by myself for the rest of the evening."

"People saw you in the library and at the cafeteria?" asked McLeod.

"Oh, yes, I ate with Roscoe and some others."

"That's right," said Roscoe. "I think we can pretty much vouch for each other."

"Good," said McLeod.

Sharon said that she had been with Dan's family from five o'clock on. "They had come the day before, I remember that, and they were here until yesterday. They took me to dinner on that Thursday."

When the seminarians were leaving, with many thanks for the meal, the adults got their coats, too. Fiona and Angus, accompanied by Beelzebub and Gabriel, were going to Alexander Hall to see Roscoe's snakes.

McLeod said that since she had already made the acquaintance of Samson and Delilah, she would walk with Sharon down to Hodge Hall. "I need to stretch my legs just a little," she said.

"And I certainly don't want to see those nasty snakes," said Sharon. "And I don't see how you can touch them, Roscoe."

As they walked, Sharon told McLeod that she detested the idea of snakes and snake handling and she couldn't bring herself to even like Roscoe himself. "It's so creepy," she said.

"But I like Roscoe," McLeod said. She

asked Sharon if she happened to have a copy of Dan's sermon.

"I do, actually," said Sharon.

"Do you think I could see it?" asked McLeod. "Of course I heard it that Monday, but I'd like to read it."

"Of course you can. Oh, I'm so glad I have a copy. Everything in his room is still under seal, but he had asked me to look the sermon over and I did. But I didn't have any suggestions, so I didn't give my copy back to him. And I'm so glad. I hope we can print it in the program for his memorial service."

"I remember that it sounded rather angry," said McLeod. "Do you think it would be suitable?"

"It would show the real true crusading Danny."

"Was he aiming his crusade at people here at the seminary, do you think?"

"In a way he was," said Sharon. "You can have a copy to keep, if you like. I made several copies of my copy. I gave one to his parents. Come up to my room and I'll give it to you."

Sharon's room was as neat as Sharon herself. When Sharon was looking through a file folder, McLeod noticed a rash on her hands.

"You don't have poison ivy do you?" she asked.

"No, not at all," said Sharon. "I'm allergic to dogs and I hate it that I am. I love Beelzebub and Gabriel, I really do, and I can't resist petting them. And then I break out. Every time."

When Sharon had handed the sermon to McLeod, she said, "You know, I know people are saying horrible things about this sermon, but Dan thought we had a wonderful opportunity here at the seminary to change the world and that we were wasting that opportunity. He hated what he called the slipshod faith of so many people here that kept them from being what he called 'steadfast for the Lord.' He thought Roscoe Kelly was typical — clinging to fragments of a primitive past and not at all sure of anything he believed in. I know he made people — even professors — mad. Dan was a very strong man, McLeod. And he was good looking and so nice to me. I loved him so much."

Again, McLeod impulsively hugged Sharon. "I know it's hard," she said. "Did you and Dan have fun together? You didn't spend all your time talking about how bad things were at the seminary, did you?"

"Heavens, no," said Sharon. "We had a

good time. We didn't go to movies much — Dan thought too many of them were silly. We'd go swimming — you know the seminary has a pool out in the West Windsor property they own. And we'd go on picnics. We'd go down to Marquand Park — it's just down the street — or down to Turning Basin Park. We both had cars, so we would ride over to Lambertville or once or twice over to the Jersey shore. It was so great."

They parted, promising to see more of each other.

"That was fun," said Fiona as they loaded the dishwasher later on. "I'm glad you suggested it."

"I'm kind of sorry we had them all at the same time," said McLeod. "I was dying to ask Roscoe who hated him, who would try to implicate him by making a phony snakebite on a corpse. But I didn't feel I could ask him in front of Sharon."

"No, I guess not," said Fiona.

"Did Willy and Roscoe have anything interesting to say when Sharon wasn't there?"

"Only that the police don't seem to be doing much," said Fiona.

"How did you like Samson and Delilah?"

"Well, they're very snaky, aren't they? Beelzebub went wild over them. Gabriel just stared and quivered. Well, she kind of pointed at them. I loved meeting a real snake handler. And isn't Sharon a nice girl?"

"She is indeed. It was a pleasant evening."

"But Gretchen Green is a pain, isn't she?" said Fiona.

"At least she left early."

"And our duty's done to her, for a while."

"We're not making any headway with our investigation," said McLeod. "I wonder if Nick found Victor Lord."

"You know he did, if he's still in town."

Twenty-four

George called early Monday morning when McLeod was the only one downstairs. "I have a report for you," he said.

"How can you have faxed Tübingen and gotten an answer already?" asked McLeod. "It's only eight o'clock in the morning."

"It's almost three o'clock here," said George. "I'm in Berlin. I called Brussels just a minute ago and they said a fax had come in from Tübingen and read it to me. It was so interesting I thought I'd better call you right away."

"What did it say?"

"The gist of it is that they had had no student named Ernst von Kemp in the past hundred years but that an Ernest Kemp from the United States had been briefly enrolled in the sixties but had been awarded no degree."

Staggered, McLeod said nothing.

"Did you hear me?" asked George.

"I heard you. I'm stunned. Thank you so much. I can't tell you how much I appreciate it."

"Glad to do it. I'll call you later in the week when I'm back in Brussels."

"Please do."

"Be careful, McLeod. This looks like tricky ground."

As McLeod hung up the phone, Angus came in, followed by Fiona. Each carried a dog under one arm and set it down. Beelzebub ran to drink water from his bowl; Gabriel greeted McLeod. "You are the sweetest dog," said McLeod, rubbing her ears.

"She likes you, McLeod," said Fiona. "Did you get the phone? We figured it was for you and you answered it," Fiona said. "Was it your friend in Brussels?"

"Yes, but he's in Berlin right now. He did a little investigating for me, and guess what? Ernst von Kemp did not get a degree at the University of Tübingen — he was there just for a little while. And his name was Ernest Kemp, not Ernst von Kemp."

Fiona gaped. "Tell me again. I'm slow. I haven't had any coffee."

"I'm making coffee, I'm making it," Angus reassured her. "I was running water so I didn't hear what you said. Tell us again, McLeod."

McLeod did.

Angus shook his head slowly.

"How could he get a job here without an advanced degree?" asked McLeod.

"I don't suppose they actually check up on an applicant's degrees, especially if the person is well known and a published scholar," said Angus. "Ernst had taught somewhere before he came here, and he had published. He had a reputation. But it's hard to imagine somebody with the nerve to say he had a degree from Tübingen when he didn't. Oh, well, an actual degree's not everything."

"But the name," said McLeod. "Somebody said his brother dropped the 'von' but it looks like Ernst added the 'von' himself."

"And he had a wife he said nothing about," Fiona reminded them.

"He had a wife and said he didn't, and he said he had a degree and didn't have it," said McLeod. "Was he a total fraud?"

"We have to get busy," said Fiona.

"I guess I'd better pass this on to Nick Perry," McLeod said.

As soon as she finished breakfast, Mc-

228

Leod told Fiona, Gabriel, and Beelzebub good-bye and started for the library, detouring by way of Lenox House.

A policeman guarding the door of Lenox House let her in when she said she wanted to see Nick Perry. Nick was busy, so McLeod left word with the officer next door that she had information for him. When she came back downstairs, Abigail Turner was coming out of one of the doors that wasn't sealed off with yellow police tape.

After cordial greetings, McLeod said, "So you're back in your office?"

"Not really. They're letting me use another one, though," said Abigail. "They helped me move some of the things from my office to the temporary one, so I can at least get on with handling things concerned with Ernst's death."

"Can I talk to you a minute?" said McLeod.

"Sure. Come on in here. Our offices are still a mess, and, as you can see, still sealed." Abigail motioned her into a bare office containing only a desk, two chairs, a computer, and a file cabinet. "The desk was in here," said Abigail. "But it's my computer, I mean the one I used. I think they copied everything off the hard drive but at least they didn't take it away like they did Ernst's. Have a seat. We have a part-time secretary but she won't be in for a few days while the police are here. Would you like some coffee?"

"No, thanks. I don't drink coffee and anyway I just drank a gallon of tea with breakfast." She paused while Abigail sat down in her desk chair and swiveled around to face McLeod.

"Abigail, I hate to bring this up . . ." she began, then stumbled. She started again, and finally repeated what George Bridges had told her.

Abigail looked at her piteously. It seemed to McLeod that she aged twenty years before her eyes, wrinkles deepening in her face, which lost color, and then turned a bilious yellow. She swiveled back to face her desk and put her head down on her arms and wept.

McLeod sat there, not knowing what to say or do. Finally, Abigail raised her head, reached for a Kleenex, and swiveled back around to face McLeod.

"I'm sorry." She looked no better than she had a moment ago.

"I'm sorry to upset you like that," said McLeod. "I'll be on my way."

"No, no. You might as well hear the

whole story. It will be a relief to talk to somebody about it."

"If you're sure," said McLeod.

"I'm sure. I told you Ernst had his faults. And he did. And deception was one of them. It started so simply. He grew up in the midwest where his father was a Lutheran minister, a hard, conservative sort of man. Ernst went to this little Lutheran college and did wonderfully well. Somehow, one of his professors helped him get a fellowship to Tübingen. It was a very small fellowship. Only enough for a few months, but Ernst thought he could make it last a whole year, and his father was supposed to send more money in a year.

"Ernst loved Tübingen. I don't think he'd ever been out of Minnesota before and he loved Germany, the whole Teutonic thing. He loved the faculty, the theologians. He had studied German in college and he was smart, you know, and his German got better and better. He met this girl. His money ran out. His father didn't send any more money. He tried to make enough to stay at least another semester. Finally, this girl, Lise, said she'd support him and help him stay in the country if he'd marry her. It turned out she was pregnant with another man's child and didn't

231

know what to do. So there was Ernst in a foreign country, suddenly with a new wife who was carrying a child who was not his. And of course his 'wife' could not support a child and a student."

"It's unbelievable," said McLeod. "I mean it's unbelievably tragic."

"It was very tragic. He tried to attend classes when he could. He stayed on — and found all sorts of off the record jobs that helped hold body and soul together. The child was born and Ernst was trapped. He stayed a few years, and he went to the university when he could, but of course he wasn't registered. He said he managed to read a lot and learn a lot on his own. He was good at languages and taught himself Greek and Hebrew. Ernst was rather fond of the child, but he wanted to get on with his life and he felt that Lise had tricked him. So as soon as he could save up the fare to the United States, he came back home."

"He just left his wife and child . . . ?"

"Yes," said Abigail, who was looking somewhat better. "It wasn't his child, you know. You have to remember that."

"I remember you said he didn't have any children," McLeod said.

Abigail looked nonplussed, then went

232

on. "He came back to this country and went to visit his old college and the professor who had encouraged him to go to Tübingen just assumed he had gotten his Ph.D."

"And Ernst let him assume it?"

"I guess he did. He told me he was so overwhelmed by all that had happened that he didn't tell the professor any of it."

"What about his family?" asked McLeod. "Did he tell them about the wife? Or the child?"

"No, I guess not. I think by then his father was dead and he and his brother have never been close."

"So what did Ernst do next?"

"I don't know what he did next. At some point he got a job at that seminary in the midwest. I don't suppose they checked his resume. He was smart, you know; and he knew a lot, an awful lot. He was a good teacher, and as time passed, he wrote books about the Old Testament — books that were very well regarded."

"Do you know how he got interested in the Dead Sea Scrolls?"

"It was when he was in Germany," said Abigail. "That was where everything began for him. He was a natural, you see. He knew the Old Testament so thoroughly,

233

and he knew Hebrew. I don't know, but I think I'd say it was inevitable that he get interested in them, with his Biblical knowledge and his archaeological experience. He worked on them in East Jerusalem some of the time, you know. That was quite a plum."

"And that's where he began picking up artifacts?"

"That's right. He'd visit the antiquities dealers — or they'd stop him on the street — and he'd pick up little fertility figures or occasionally a cuneiform tablet or a vase. Occasionally he'd sell them. He had money problems for a while. He sent money to Lise in Germany. He told her it did not mean he conceded that the child was his, but that he wanted to help her. McLeod, he was a good man — unusual, but basically good. I know that."

"I'm sure you're right," said McLeod. "He was indeed a remarkable man. I wish I'd known him better."

"I was lucky," said Abigail. "I knew him well. I guess I knew him better than anybody did." She stood up and stretched. "I'll miss him."

"Abigail, are you all right? Do you live alone? Do you need company?"

"I'm fine. Thanks. I live alone, but I

have friends. And I have an enormous amount of work to do here, and that will keep me from going crazy." She sat down again and managed to smile at McLeod.

"Who is Ernst's next of kin?" asked McLeod.

"I suppose it would be his brother. He never actually divorced Lise. He lost touch with her, but he didn't want to marry m" — McLeod was sure she was about to say "marry me," but Abigail went on after only the smallest of bobbles — "marry until he could get a divorce. But I don't know where she is. So I suppose his brother is the next of kin."

"His name is Gerald Kemp, right?" said McLeod. "Ernst's name was originally Kemp, too, wasn't it?"

"Well, yes, actually it was. He just fell in love with all things German when he went to Germany and he added von to his name. He told me he knew it was silly, but he published his first articles under the name Ernst von Kemp, and he couldn't turn back."

"Did it bother him that he was living under false pretenses?"

"Well, he didn't think of it as false pretenses. He knew he was well qualified without a degree for both the scholarly work and the teaching. The name change he regarded as a youthful peccadillo that everybody should forgive."

"The wife? The child?" asked McLeod.

"Another youthful mistake, and besides, he was tricked."

"The child — was it a girl or a boy? — was legally his, wasn't it, if they were married when it was born?"

"It's a legalistic point, I suppose," said Abigail. "The child was a boy. Man, now, of course. A handsome man."

"You've seen him?" said McLeod, stunned.

"Oh, yes," said Abigail. "He came here not long ago to see Ernst. He wanted to see his 'father,' he said."

"Abigail, wouldn't he be the next of kin?"

"For all practical purposes, no. Ernst had nothing to do with him, except for that one visit. I think it knocked him for a loop."

"I bet it did," said McLeod. "What was he like? What did Ernst say to him? What's his name?"

"His name is Johann von Kemp, but he calls himself John Kemp —" She stopped when McLeod laughed.

"I'm sorry. I shouldn't laugh," said

McLeod. "But it's like father, like son." Abigail looked bewildered. "Ernst Germanized his name and his son Americanized his," she said. Abigail smiled thinly. "Go on, Abigail. What did Ernst feel about him? Did he introduce him to anybody?"

"He was handsome and very polite," said Abigail. "Ernst certainly didn't introduce him to anybody. He didn't stay long, Ernst didn't encourage him to stay, and anyway Johann wanted to see Hollywood and Washington."

"Was he angry with Ernst, bitter about being deserted when he was a small child?"

"He didn't seem to be. Why should he be? I told you Ernst is not his father," said Abigail.

"He was his surrogate father for several years," said McLeod. "It seems to me that any child would be angry with the man who abandoned him and his mother."

"He didn't seem to be angry," said Abigail.

"Has the seminary, or have the police, talked to Gerald Kemp?" asked McLeod.

"Oh, yes," said Abigail. "He flew in Saturday and talked to the police and to the dean. You know I couldn't give them his name Friday — I couldn't remember it. But they found it."

"They're pretty good at finding information," said McLeod.

"You know, they came to my apartment yesterday and asked me question after question about Ernst. I told them about Lise. I had already told you and Fiona. They didn't seem surprised."

McLeod felt no need to let Abigail know that she had told the police about Ernst's wife. "Did you tell them about Johann?"

"No, I didn't."

"Or about the degree — or non-degree — from Tübingen?" asked McLeod.

"No, I didn't." She stood up. "You ask a lot of questions," she said.

"I know I do," said McLeod, standing up herself. "I'm sorry if they upset you. But I can't help myself — I was trained as a journalist and I simply have to ask questions. And when my friend told me about Ernst at Tübingen, I had to ask you about it."

"Are you going to tell the police?"

"I was going to," said McLeod. "That's why I came over here, but Lieutenant Perry was busy. I'm glad I saw you. It would be better if you told the police everything about Ernst yourself."

"I don't know. I talked to them for hours yesterday and they're going to ask me over and over why I didn't tell them everything yesterday. But it just didn't come up. They kept asking me about enemies Ernst might have or love affairs and they were interested in the artifacts, too. No, I've kept Ernst's secrets all these years. I can't stop now."

"Abigail, it's bound to come out."

"I guess so," said Abigail. "But then one shouldn't speak ill of the dead. Should one?"

"Why not?" asked McLeod. "Lucy Summers was talking about Dan Strong the other night and she said she thought it was much better to speak ill of the dead than the living."

Abigail smiled wanly.

"And besides," McLeod plowed on, "you're not speaking ill of Ernst. You understand him and his foibles, you forgive his little deceptions. But if you tell the police everything, it might help them to find his murderer, and you'd like that, wouldn't you?" asked McLeod.

"I guess so," said Abigail.

McLeod was surprised at her lack of fervor.

"What's done is done, isn't it?" asked Abigail. "It can't bring him back."

"Yes, but you don't want a murderer

walking around the seminary, do you?"

Abigail said nothing. Was she protecting somebody? McLeod wondered. "Do you have any idea who killed him?" McLeod asked.

"Not really. I'm still in a daze," said Abigail. "It's so bizarre. I told you and Fiona on Friday that it must have been somebody who was jealous — but I've thought about it, and professional jealousy is not a very good motive for murder, is it? It's a puzzle. The police kept asking me who would want to kill him and I told them that Ernst was basically a sweet man. I cannot imagine why anybody would want to murder him."

"What about all the stuff he had in his office — was there anything anybody would kill for?"

"I think the intruder — the murderer — came looking for Ernst's latest find, and killed Ernst in the process. That's all I can think of. But there was nothing in the office of any great financial value."

"None of those artifacts? Not even his latest find? He kept telling everybody how sensational it was."

"I think," said Abigail carefully, "that he may have meant that it would be more of an intellectual sensation than a financial bonanza. I really don't want to talk about this yet. There's one thing I want to get settled before I discuss it." She shut her mouth firmly, and turned her head so that she was gazing out the narrow window.

"Abigail, I hate to bring this up, but what time did you leave the office on Thursday?"

"I left about six, I guess," said Abigail. "Ernst said '*Auf weidersehen, liebchen.*'" Abigail wiped her eyes.

"Abigail, did you know Victor Lord was in town last week?"

"Victor Lord? Oh, yes. He was."

"Were you here when he came to see Ernst?"

"Oh, yes, he was here when I left," said Abigail. "That was the last time I saw Ernst — with Victor Lord." She burst into tears.

McLeod was aghast. She stood up and helplessly patted Abigail's shoulder. "Let me know — or let Fiona know — if there's anything we can do, Abigail," she said.

"I'll be all right," she said. "Thank you, though."

McLeod left.

Twenty-five

Leaving Abigail's temporary office, McLeod saw Dean Tilley, who was just coming down the stairs.

"Hello," she said. Although she detested him, she spoke cordially enough. "What brings you to Lenox House? The police, I guess."

The dean stopped and twisted his sallow little face into a tortured smile. "And how are you, Ms. Dulaney? Still with us, I see. Yes, I said I'd come over here, although of course the police at first offered to talk to me in my office. We all want to do everything we can to help get to the bottom of this awful affair. I want to help in any way I can."

"I'm sure we all want to," said McLeod. "In fact, I think I'll go upstairs and talk to Lieutenant Perry myself."

"I'm afraid he has someone else with him at the moment," said Dean Tilley.

"The president himself walked over here with me and he insisted that I go in for an interview first." He smiled loftily and, like a tubby little tugboat, puffed past her out the door.

McLeod plowed on to the library, and left her laptop on a table in the sunny periodical room. She waved at Betsey Stockton's portrait and went uptown to buy the Trenton paper. On the way, she noticed that the leaves were less brilliantly colored than they had been. They were beginning to turn brown and fall — it would be winter soon.

Back at the library, she read the newspaper story about the murder, which said that Ernst von Kemp had died from cyanide and the tent stake wound had occurred after death.

So there was a connection between the two murders, she thought. The use of cyanide in both murders made that plain. She immediately thought of Lucy Summers. Was it logical that she would somehow give cyanide to Ernst von Kemp, then after he fell dead, drive a tent stake through his head? No, it wasn't logical — it was pure decoration. But was murder ever logical?

It was hard to settle down to work while

she was stewing over all this. She gazed at Betsey Stockton, and asked her mentally, "What shall I do?"

It seemed to her that Betsey replied, "Investigate," so she left the library and crossed Library Place to the huge Victorian house where Henry Fairfield Worthington had his apartment. She buzzed Henry's door, and she decided that Betsey was a good advisor when Henry Fairfield Worthington greeted her enthusiastically.

"Come in," he said. "I'm very glad to see you. Would you like some coffee? Or tea?"

"Tea, please," McLeod said.

"Sit down," said Henry. "I'll make us both some tea."

"Your apartment is so clean," McLeod called after him. "How do you do it?"

"The cleaning lady was here earlier," said Henry. "Not only do I have to tidy up before she gets here, she cleans it beautifully. I could never do it without her. I'll be right back."

While he was gone, McLeod looked around the living room, with its bay window, deep sofas, beautiful rugs, and handsome lamps.

Henry returned with a tray bearing a pot and two cups and saucers. "I can't get used to mugs," he said. "I always use cups."

"Lovely," said McLeod. "What's new? Have you heard anything about the murder?"

"No, I'm rather isolated these days," said Henry. "I mean isolated from the prevailing wisdom. I don't hear much. What about you? You seem to have a gift for finding things out."

"It's my white hair," said McLeod. "People do tend to tell me things."

"I have white hair, but nobody tells me anything," Henry said.

"I bet they do," said McLeod. "Didn't Ernst tell you things?"

"Some things," said Henry cautiously.

"You said he didn't tell you about his wife, as I recall."

"No, he didn't tell me that. Ever."

"And he didn't tell you about not getting a degree at the University of Tübingen? Or about the child of his in Germany?"

"No!" said Henry.

"Well, he didn't get a degree. He was only enrolled a short time. He got married and had a child, a son. The child was not really his, he claimed. He said that he was tricked by the woman he married."

"I did not know one thing about this. I

find it hard to believe. Who told you this?"

"Abigail Turner," said McLeod.

"You've talked to her again?"

"That's right. This morning."

"Ernst really trusted her. I'm not only surprised to find out all these things, I find them literally incredible. I can't believe it's true."

"Abigail didn't make it up," said McLeod.

"Can you be sure?" asked Henry.

She told him about her query to George and his reply.

"You've been as busy as a beaver this morning, haven't you?" said Henry, with an edge of hostility.

"I can't help myself, Henry. I get curious and I find out things. When I asked Abigail about Tübingen, she confirmed what George had told me and then she told me about the child."

They sipped tea in silence for a few minutes. Then Henry, seeming to regret his earlier brusqueness, pointed out it was almost noon and asked her to have some lunch. "I'll make us an omelet," he said.

"Henry, that's too much trouble," said McLeod. "We can walk over to the cafeteria."

"It's no trouble," said Henry. "I go to

the cafeteria when I'm lonely. I'm not lonely when I have a visitor."

"I'd love an omelet," said McLeod. "Can I help?"

"Come in the kitchen and talk to me while I make it," said Henry.

In the kitchen, which was quite modern for such an old house, Henry busied himself beating eggs. While he waited for the skillet to heat, he deftly made a green salad. In minutes, lunch was ready. Henry filled two plates, and they took them to the table in the bay window, where Henry had put two place mats down and laid the silver.

"How do you do it so quickly and efficiently?" McLeod asked him.

"Long years of experience," said Henry.

"It takes a certain skill, as well as experience," said McLeod. "Henry, this omelet is divine."

She took another bite. "I remember in one of the Rex Stout books, Nero Wolfe made an omelet, and it took him hours. You were much faster and I'll bet you'd be faster at detecting, too."

"That may be," said Henry, "but Nero Wolfe scrambled eggs. He told Lucy Valdon it would take him forty minutes. It was in *The Mother Hunt*."

"How on earth do you remember that?" asked McLeod.

Henry shrugged. "I remember because I always wondered how it could take forty minutes to scramble eggs. I thought of everything you could possibly do, and I just couldn't figure it out."

McLeod changed the subject. "Have you talked to Lieutenant Perry?" she asked.

"No, I talked to another policeman, Sergeant Caldwell. He asked me questions about Ernst, but nothing about Tübingen — or a child."

"I don't think the police know about it yet," said McLeod, "but Abigail said this morning that she was going to tell them." She switched subjects. "And you don't know what Ernst's latest find was?"

"He didn't tell me, but since Saturday night I've been thinking a lot, and I continue to believe that it was not just an artifact. But who knows? The secret may have died with him."

"Not an artifact?"

"Something else, possibly a manuscript of some kind."

"I asked him the first time I met him if it would be possible to find a Dead Sea Scroll that nobody knew about," said McLeod. "He said it would be impossible."

"I think that's right," said Henry.

"Manuscript? Hmmm . . ." said McLeod.

"Frankly, I'm thunderstruck," said Henry. "By the news about his degree and his child. I don't think I can believe it until I have some verification."

"Abigail said the child, a son, a grown man, came to see Ernst not too long ago," said McLeod.

"I certainly didn't meet him," said Henry. "I didn't realize Abigail would be the repository of so many secrets. I find this very disturbing, McLeod. It makes me wonder about other things."

"Other things?"

"Ernst's trading in antiquities, for one thing. I have heard whispers that he wasn't too careful about the provenance of some of the things he brought back."

"You mean they might be stolen?"

"You put it baldly," said Henry. "Or maybe they even came from a looted museum in Iraq. No, I can't believe Ernst would deliberately do that. He really was such a kind person that he was a natural victim. I don't think he suspected anybody else of anything — ever. Enough of this. Would you like coffee?"

"No, thanks."

"I don't want any either," said Henry.

"You know I guess we all have secrets, don't we?"

"I suppose so," said McLeod.

"I hope you don't start prying into *my* past," said Henry.

"Of course not," said McLeod. "Your present is too interesting."

"Thanks," said Henry. "I hate the murder. This mess is awful. But I don't share your zest for detection. I want it to just go away."

"It will go away eventually," said McLeod, although she felt that murder never really "went away."

"Even if doesn't, I am going away," said Henry. "I'm going to Rome in two weeks."

"Business or pleasure?" asked McLeod.

"Pure pleasure," said Henry. "I don't have business anymore, thank goodness."

They talked about Rome and Italy for a while, and Henry said he tried to go to Europe every autumn. "I want to travel while I can," he said. "Pretty soon, I'll be too old. So I go now when I can."

"Oh, you're not going to get too old for anything," said McLeod optimistically.

"You mean you think God will make an exception in my case?" asked Henry.

"That's right," said McLeod. After a while, she left. "Thanks for the tea and the lunch, Henry," she said.

"Thanks for coming by," he said. "Do it often."

"I shall," said McLeod.

As she walked from Henry's apartment to the library, McLeod reflected that he had a nice life with his beautiful apartment, his cleaning lady, and an annual trip to Europe. A nice life for a retired seminary professor of speech.

Twenty-six

Late that afternoon, when McLeod was back at the McKays' house and trying to respond with suitable fervor to affectionate greetings from Beelzebub and Gabriel, Nick Perry called her.

"I hear you have some information for me," he said.

"I do, but you may already have it. Have you talked to Abigail Turner today?"

"No, not today."

"Okay, I'll come over to Lenox House right away. It's important."

"Hold on. I'll come over there, if that's all right. I haven't been out of this room all day. I need a breath of fresh air."

McLeod had no time to report on her day to Fiona before Nick Perry was there. Beelzebub and Gabriel made a great fuss over him, and he eyed them with something like bewilderment. "They look like that advertisement for

Black and White Scotch," he said.

"Fiona says that's what everybody says," said McLeod. As though they were bored with this categorization, the dogs lost interest and padded back to the kitchen and Fiona. McLeod ushered Nick into the library and offered him a drink. Although he looked like a man who could use a stiff drink, he asked if there was coffee. "I'll get it," said McLeod.

In the kitchen, Fiona said she'd make fresh coffee and added, "Invite him to dinner. I spent the day at the museum, but I can work miracles, you know."

"I'm sure he's too busy," said McLeod, "but I'll ask." Back in the library she told Nick that Fiona would bring in coffee, and sat down across from him. "How is the investigation coming? The two murders are linked, aren't they? I mean, since both victims were killed with cyanide."

"It looks that way," said Nick. "At first I thought it might be that von Kemp's murderer was imitating Strong's murder — I thought it was stupid of the medical examiner to tell the press that you can get cyanide on the Internet, and stupid of the press to print it. It gives people ideas."

"People already have ideas," said McLeod, who, having worked for newspapers all her adult life, nearly always rose to the defense of the press.

"Of course they have ideas, but you don't have to encourage them, do you? Anyway, I realized the newspapers didn't print the fact that cyanide killed Dan Strong until Friday morning, and von Kemp was already dead by then."

Fiona brought in the coffee and poured a cup for Nick, offered one to McLeod, who, as usual, refused it. "Would you like some tea, McLeod?" she asked.

"Fiona, I'd love tea, but I can't let you wait on me anymore."

"You can wait on me. I love it," said Nick Perry, smiling his most winning smile, the one that crinkled the lids of his blue eyes. Fiona smiled back and disappeared, waving at McLeod to dismiss her scruples.

"How will it affect the investigation if they are connected?" asked McLeod. "I mean, about the Township police."

"We finally sat down together and talked about the cases. We had a long meeting last night — our chief, their chief, me, Brasher and half a dozen others. We're going to try to cooperate, while the Township concentrates on Strong and the Borough concentrates on von Kemp. We're supposed to pool all information now, and I mean *all*. It just means more paperwork. Or more e-mail work." He sighed, and his smile was gone.

Fiona brought in McLeod's tea and looked at Nick beseechingly — she clearly wanted to join them, but Nick merely waited until she was gone.

"Enough questions for me," he said. "What information do you have for me?"

"Well, this morning, George called me," she began. She told him what George had said about von Kemp and not getting a degree from Tübingen. "So I went over to Lenox House to tell you, and when I couldn't see you, I stopped by Abigail's office and asked her about it. She not only confirmed it, but she told me that von Kemp and this German woman had a son. And the son has been here in Princeton not long ago to see von Kemp."

"Abigail Turner always tells you a lot more than she tells us. We questioned her yesterday and — well, I can't talk about it. But I appreciate your telling me this. I really do. I feel more encouraged — well, I can't say how I feel. How did George know about von Kemp and Tübingen?"

"I asked him to find out for me," said McLeod.

"What made you ask him about it?"

"I don't know, Nick. I just had a feeling about it."

"You can't help asking questions, can you?"

"No, I guess I can't," said McLeod.

"It can be very dangerous to ask questions during a murder investigation. And then you went to talk to Abigail Turner about it."

"I told you I tried to talk to you first. And she promised me she would tell you all about it," said McLeod. "But you're hard to catch."

Nick was frowning. "Not that hard. And there are other detectives on the case. Well, I'm glad you told me."

"Listen, if you're working on the Strong murder, there's some stuff I have to tell you. I don't want another interview with Brasher, but if I can tell you some things, I will."

"I'll do my best to keep Brasher away from you," said Nick. "What is it?"

"Well, you know, I told you that Dan Strong preached a student sermon on the Monday morning before he was killed. And that sermon was interpreted by various people as being a threat to them."

"I've been a policeman for twenty-five

256

years and I never heard of a sermon causing somebody's murder," said Nick. "Boring somebody to death, maybe, but not leading someone to violent action. And I thought the seminary was the most peaceful place in town."

"Somebody here is working on a book about how religion is inherently violent," said McLeod. "And when you think of the Middle East and Ireland and India, you can understand."

"I'll have to think this over. But thanks for reminding me."

"Dan was a very conservative student, and he was so fired up about people he considered too liberal that he made everybody angry. I don't think the Township police ever really talked to students or faculty about that."

Nick was making notes. He looked at her expectantly. "Anything else?" he asked.

"Well, there's that fake snakebite on Dan Strong's arm. You know there's a student here who keeps snakes in his room — his family belongs to some snake-handling cult down in Tennessee. I think the snakebite was a stupid effort to incriminate the student, frame him for the murder."

"Who is this snake-handling student?"

"His name is Roscoe Kelly, and he's the

sweetest young man you'll ever know. I think he'd be the last person to murder somebody, but I thought I'd better tell you." She went on to describe Roscoe and Samson and Delilah. "He keeps those snakes under lock and key — religiously," said McLeod.

"Everybody around here does things religiously, don't they? But I'm glad you told me."

"Again, I don't think the Township police ever talked to Roscoe, or to anybody about him," said McLeod.

"But examination showed rather quickly that it wasn't a real snakebite and not the cause of death," said Nick Perry. "I suppose I can tell you that. It was made by two quick jabs with an ice pick or something, and it wasn't red and swollen like a real snakebite would have been. So it wouldn't have seemed important enough to inquire about."

"Well, I thought it was interesting, and you know about the tent stake weapon and Lucy Summers and her interest in Jael."

"Oh, yes, we did question Lucy Summers. But it didn't lead anywhere. I see what you mean. Anything else? Any other little nuggets for me to chew on?"

"Oh, have you found out what it was

that Ernst von Kemp had brought home that was so valuable?" she asked him.

"I don't know what you mean," said Nick.

"Nobody told you von Kemp said he had stumbled on something in the Middle East that would be a bombshell?" asked McLeod. "Didn't Angus tell you? Or Henry Fairfield Worthington?"

"No," said Nick. "We have to pull information out of these religion people like we were pulling teeth — no, like pulling off toenails. They spout theology to me like geysers, but they are short on facts. I don't understand it."

"Well, I tell you everything, eventually."

"Eventually is not soon enough," said Nick. "Anything else before I go light a fire under Abigail Turner?"

"That's it for now," said McLeod. "Tell me, did you find Victor Lord?"

"I did. He said he went by the Dead Sea Scrolls office Thursday afternoon — as soon as he got here. He said that von Kemp was very much alive when he left — that was about four o'clock, he said."

"Where was he staying?"

"At the Nassau Inn."

"He could have gone back to Lenox House, couldn't he?"

"He could have," said Nick.

"Abigail says he was still there when she left the office at six," said McLeod.

"Really? Lord says he was with people from the religion department at the university from five o'clock on. We're going to uncover a few lies before this is over, I imagine."

He stood up and was clearly about to leave, when Fiona appeared in the door, followed by Beelzebub and Gabriel. "Angus is on the way home," she said. "Can't you stay for a drink, or dinner, Mr. Perry? You have to eat somewhere."

"You have too rosy a view of the policeman's life," said Nick. "I can't take time for anything but takeout at my desk. If I get that, I'm lucky. The press is hounding us for progress, and we haven't made any to speak of. I have to run. I took the time to come interview my favorite witness in person, but that was a luxury. But thanks anyway."

"Thank you, Nick," said McLeod. "I'm glad I'm a luxury."

Twenty-seven

Angus came in as soon as Nick had left. Beelzebub and Gabriel jumped up on him and wagged their tails. Angus abstractedly patted them and murmured, "Down, down."

"You missed the detective," Fiona told him.

"What did he want?" asked Angus.

"Yes, what did he want?" asked Fiona, turning to McLeod.

"I told him I wanted to give him information — you know, what George said in his call this morning," said McLeod. "I left a message at his office this morning and he just now got back to me."

"I'll get some drinks," said Angus. "Wait one minute, McLeod."

Angus came back with white wine for everyone and then lit a fire. Beelzebub and Gabriel nestled down by the fireplace. "Okay, proceed, McLeod," Angus said.

"I told Nick about what Abigail told me

this morning," began McLeod.

"You talked to Abigail again?" asked Fiona.

"Yes, she was in her office when I went to Lenox House to see Nick. So I went in and told her what George had said, and she confirmed it, sadly. Plus, she told me Ernst von Kemp had had a son in Germany. She said his wife tricked him, that it wasn't really his child. But of course it was born after they were married so he was legally responsible. He left them anyway and came back to this country, and the son came to Princeton not long ago. Did you know that?"

"Of course not," said Fiona. "We didn't even know he was married until Abigail told us Friday morning."

"Nick Perry loved it when I told him about the son," said McLeod. "He seemed galvanized. I guess the son will be the chief suspect. And that's stupid."

"Why so?" asked Angus.

"Because he wouldn't have killed Dan Strong."

"Maybe he did," said Fiona. "Maybe he heard the sermon and wanted to protect his father."

"And then killed his father?" asked McLeod.

"I see what you mean," said Fiona.

Everyone sat in quiet gloom for a few minutes. Then McLeod said, "After I talked to Abigail, I wanted to talk to somebody, and you were gone, Fiona, so I went to see Henry Fairfield Worthington. And he didn't know any of this either. He said at first that Abigail was lying, but I told him about George. But I was really trying to find out about Ernst's new discovery. He claims he doesn't know what it is. Abigail said it was really valuable and that whoever broke in and trashed the office might have been looking for it. But she said it was safe."

"She'll tell us eventually," said Fiona. "She's spilled everything else."

"True," said McLeod. "I wonder how long it will take for her to unload it?"

"I can't get over Ernst von Kemp," said Angus. "How could he practice such deception?"

"At a seminary, of all places," said McLeod. "I would never have dreamed it."

"You must have realized by now that people at the seminary are prey to human weakness, just like people everywhere," said Angus.

"I guess so," said McLeod. She gulped her wine and set her glass down. "I just had an idea," she said. "Do you suppose Dan Strong knew about all this German stuff? Was that one of the things he alluded to in that sermon?"

"How could he?" asked Angus. "If none of us knew. Apparently, neither the dean nor the president knew. So how could a middler know?"

"You know, let me get that copy of the sermon. We can do an exegesis of it," said McLeod. "I forgot I had it. I haven't really looked at it since Sharon gave it to me last night."

She ran upstairs and returned with the sermon and handed it to Fiona, who read a page at a time, passing each one to Angus when she had finished. Angus read it and handed it back to McLeod.

"He actually talks about homosexual practices three times," said Angus. "That seems to be a real hangup for him."

"Let's read Hosea," said McLeod.

Angus reached to the nearest shelf and pulled out a Bible. "Bibles all over the place in this house," he pointed out. He found the place and began to read. " 'It is you, priest, that I denounce . . . Old wine and new wine addle their wits . . . Whoring leads them astray . . . they burn incense under oak and poplar . . . "cultic objects" . . . sacrifice to bulls, make a treaty with Assyria . . . People with no understanding . . . Thief breaks into the house . . . Whoring makes them hot as ovens . . . I shall bring them down like birds in the sky . . . I shall be like ringworm for Ephraim and like gangrene for the House of Judah.' "

"It's worse than the sermon, isn't it?" asked McLeod.

"Sure is, but the sermon's pretty bad. Bad in two ways. It's a badly put-together sermon, and it's really all hellfire and damnation, no salvation. It's a student's worst effort," said Angus.

"Can you see how it would drive anybody to murder him?" asked McLeod.

"I don't know," said Angus. "You never know what secrets people may be harboring."

"How did everybody get the idea that he was going to reveal secrets?" Fiona asked.

"He must have ad-libbed something that's not in the script," said McLeod. "No, wait a minute, it's right here in the sermon: 'All this will be revealed, made known like the sins of Judah to Hosea. It is you that I denounce!' I remember now when he said that — he pointed out at the audience — I mean the congregation."

"It's quite a sermon," said Fiona. "I'm glad we've seen it — and we've had our Bible study for the day, haven't we?"

Twenty-eight

McLeod tossed and turned that night and finally went to sleep just before dawn. She woke up late on Tuesday, and got up feeling tired. By the time she managed to get downstairs, Fiona was sitting in the kitchen drinking coffee. Beelzebub and Gabriel lay at her feet.

"Are you all right?" asked Fiona.

"Are *you* all right?" asked McLeod. "You don't often get up before me. Or is it because I'm slow this morning? I'm sorry I'm not dressed yet. Where's Angus?"

"He left for class," said Fiona. "Don't worry — I'm always still in my bathrobe this time of day. I must be corrupting you."

"It's fun being corrupted," said McLeod. "I've done almost everything about Elijah P. Lovejoy I can do in the library here. I'm going to take it easy today." She put on water to make tea and got some orange juice out of the refrigerator.

"I think it's really nippy outside," Fiona was saying when the doorbell rang. She went to answer it, and, although the dogs were at the door barking fiercely, McLeod heard a man's voice and then Fiona saying, "How do you do, Sergeant Brasher? It's very early, and I'm not dressed. Neither is Ms. Dulaney."

"Sorry, but I need to talk to her," rumbled Brasher.

"Come in," said Fiona. "Have a seat in the library. I'll get her."

By the time Fiona got to the kitchen, McLeod was upstairs. She had decided that she could not face Brasher in her nightgown and bathrobe and had dashed up the back stairs and headed for the shower. A quick — very quick — shower and she was struggling into blue jeans and a sweater. She could hear Fiona calling her plaintively from downstairs, then from upstairs. Just as she knocked at the door, McLeod gave her white hair a quick brush and emerged.

"Okay, I'm ready," she said.

Fiona ran down the front stairs ahead of her and called into the library, "I found her. Here she is."

"Hello, Sergeant. Sorry to keep you

268

waiting, but I was in the shower."

Brasher looked sourly at her. "I need some answers to some questions," he said.

"Yes, sir," said McLeod.

Brasher shot her a look that seemed to say, *Don't get smart with me.*

"Let's sit down," said McLeod. "Would you like some coffee?"

Brasher looked tempted, but refused. "Why didn't you tell us about the student who handles snakes?"

"You didn't ask me," said McLeod. "I mean you didn't ask me about other students. I didn't know about Roscoe and his snakes until after I had found the body. I didn't know there was a snakebite, or what looked like a snakebite on the body until almost a week later. I haven't seen you since then, as a matter of fact."

"Why didn't you tell us about the sermon that the victim preached?"

"I just didn't think to tell you," said McLeod. "I was never sure it was of any significance in the murder. If it was significant, I guess I figured that your investigation would bring it to your attention. You were always so anxious to prove I knew Dan Strong that I could hardly think of anything else." She stood up.

Brasher stood up, too, looking startled.

"You told the Borough police about it —" he began.

"I've known Nick Perry for years," said McLeod. "And he wasn't accusing me of murder."

"You know, there's such a thing as obstruction of justice," Brasher said.

"If you're going to threaten me, I think I need a lawyer before I answer any more questions," said McLeod.

"That's all for now," Brasher said. "Just don't leave town."

"I won't," said McLeod. As she showed Brasher out the front door, she was happy to see Beelzebub and Gabriel trot out of the kitchen and growl fiercely at him as he left.

"I heard all that," said Fiona, coming to the hall. "He *is* awful, McLeod. Come on back to the kitchen and eat your breakfast."

McLeod sat down at the table with her tea and toast and glared at Fiona.

"Don't scowl at me like that," said Fiona.

"I'm not scowling at you. I'm frowning in concentration. Fiona, I think we'd better get busy. Police depend on all these scientific tests, and all this forensic stuff takes forever. The Township police are barely beginning to get a clue about what's going on, and that's only because Nick Perry is talking to them. And Nick seems to be spinning his wheels. I think Brasher's still out to get my hide. I can see that we've got to solve these murders, or at least move the investigation in the right direction. Now think."

"All right," said Fiona. "I can frown in concentration, too."

Fiona succeeded so admirably in looking fierce that Gabriel, always sympathetic, came over and leaned against her calf and looked up at her with great concern.

"Seriously," said McLeod. "Nobody's seeing these murders clearly. I believe they're connected. Let's take a straightforward approach: I think somebody killed Dan Strong because the threats in his sermon scared them."

"I don't know what I think," said Fiona. "If you say so . . . I'll think it, too."

"Did Ernst von Kemp kill Dan Strong because Dan was going to tell the world about his wife and son? About his antiquities? And then did somebody else kill Ernst. If they did, why did they do it?"

"That doesn't make much sense," said Fiona. "Does it?"

"Not much. But let's get back to the

murders. Dan Strong's murderer puts a fake snakebite on the victim's arm. Nick Perry says it was so patently fake that it doesn't mean anything. I think it means something. Surely it was meant to point to Roscoe Kelly or to implicate him in some way."

"Well, but why?"

"That's what we have to find out," said McLeod. "Then there's the murder of Ernst von Kemp. Why was he murdered? Had he killed Dan Strong? Or was he a danger to the real murderer? And why was the tent stake used as a diversion? To point to Lucy Summers and implicate her in some way? The answer could be important in indicating something about the murderer, how his mind works. The murderer wanted to confuse things if he — or she — could. Or spread blame, even if it were just confusing things temporarily."

"I have no idea what the answers to those questions are," said Fiona.

"Neither do I, actually," said McLeod. "But we need to find out. How can we find out? How? Who can we talk to? I've had good luck in the past telling people I was working on a freelance article about such and such and use that as an excuse for asking a lot of questions. But what kind of article can I work on?"

"Could you do one about the Dead Sea Scrolls and go back to Abigail and get her to tell you what Ernst's great new find is?"

McLeod looked at Fiona. "I think I could, actually," she said. "And you know, I think I can talk to Sharon again, maybe not use the article ploy, but I think I want to ask her more about Dan. I really liked her, and she seems very sensible, as well as nice."

"I'd love to go with you to interrogate people," said Fiona wistfully, "but I think it's better if you do it alone."

"I guess so. You know, it seems to me we've had this conversation before, maybe several times before. We've got to have some new ideas. You have an original mind. Keep thinking."

"Sure," said Fiona doubtfully. "I'll do my best."

The phone shrilled. Fiona answered it and handed it to McLeod, who held the phone out from her ear so Fiona could hear the angry female voice on the other end berating McLeod.

"What have you done! What have you done! That policeman was just here and it was awful." The noise from the telephone was so raucous that Gabriel and Beelzebub stirred and looked up.

"Abigail, Abigail," McLeod interrupted her. "I just had a policeman here, too. It certainly can be awful, I agree. But I urged you in good faith to tell Nick Perry everything yourself. Did you?"

Abigail's voice became less shrill and not as loud. McLeod held it closer to her ear and Fiona looked disappointed.

"No, I didn't. But he was here — at my house — first thing this morning," Abigail said. "And he is really on fire about Ernst's son. He wanted every shred of information I have about him. They're going to comb through all of Ernst's papers at Lenox House for anything else they can find. They've been through them once but they didn't find anything. And they're going through his desk and everything at his apartment. I hate to think of everything being desecrated this way. Ernst would *die* if he knew."

And she went on deploring the situation. McLeod made sympathetic noises, and listened. Fiona got bored with watching her and started putting the breakfast dishes in the dishwasher. She stopped when McLeod screamed, "WHAT?" and stared at her.

McLeod listened some more. "That does

seem excessive," she said. "I agree. Yes, it's too bad, Abigail. I sympathize totally. Look, I want to talk to you again." She was quiet as Abigail shrieked at her that she had talked to her enough.

"No, I can help you, Abigail, I think. Don't be so angry at me. All this had to come out."

They talked some more — pointlessly, it seemed to McLeod — and finally she was able to hang up, with Abigail mollified somewhat, but only somewhat.

"What was that all about?" Fiona asked.

"It was Abigail —"

"I know that," said Fiona. "I'd have to be deaf as a post not to know that."

"Now I don't think I can go to her and ask her about Ernst's great new find, that's for sure. She's very upset with me because I told Nick Perry about Ernst's son. I *told* her to tell Nick herself. But he went to her house at the crack of dawn today. She kept saying to me, 'I asked you and Fiona to be discreet, and you promised you would.' "

"I have been discreet," said Fiona. "I haven't told anybody anything, have I?"

"No, *you* haven't. Maybe you should be the one to talk to her again. Go around and tell her what an awful friend I am, sympathize with her over my treachery and go from there."

"You must be joking."

"I'm joking."

"What was she saying?" Fiona persisted.

"She said that she had talked to you and me, and then to me alone, with the understanding that we would be discreet, and on the contrary, we had betrayed her. Or I had betrayed her. I couldn't get through to her. She says that Nick Perry is convinced that Johann von Kemp, or John Kemp, whatever his name is, killed his father."

"But as you say, where does that leave Dan Strong's killer?" Fiona asked.

"Oh, I've seen Nick Perry go off on these wild-goose chases before," said McLeod. They were both quiet for a while.

"But I wonder if Johann/John is still in this country," said McLeod. "When was he here?"

"We don't know that," said Fiona.

"I'm just curious. I don't think he's the murderer, but now I'd like to talk to him to hear his side of the story. Just out of simple interest in human affairs."

"Sure," said Fiona. "But if he didn't do the murder, shouldn't you be concentrating on other people?"

"You're probably right. Okay, I'm going

to call Sharon Leland, and believe it or not, I'm going to call Abigail Turner back. There must be a connection between Kemp and Strong. Something we don't know about."

Twenty-nine

McLeod thought Sharon sounded glad to hear from her. Thank heavens, she thought, even if Sharon is just naturally sweet and glad to hear from anybody. I bet I don't get the same reception from Abigail.

Glancing at the clock and seeing that it was after eleven, McLeod asked Sharon if she could have lunch with her.

Fiona tore a sheet off the memo pad on the table, scrawled a note on it, and poked it over in front of McLeod.

ASK HER TO LUNCH, HERE, the note said. McLeod nodded, and listened to Sharon a minute, then proffered the invitation. "Oh, great," McLeod said. "I'll walk down to meet you."

"What'll I have for lunch?" muttered Fiona. "I don't have time to run to the store. I know — I have that —"

"Open a can of soup," said McLeod.

"I don't have to stoop that low," said

Fiona. "I have homemade carrot ginger soup and that good leftover meat loaf. Splendid."

"Great," said McLeod, who went to get her coat from a hook in the hall. "Shall I take the dogs?" she called to Fiona.

"They'd love it," said Fiona, coming out in the hall to help with the leashes. Gabriel and Beelzebub were so excited that it was hard to get them tethered properly. "We're off," said McLeod. "Back in a second."

She met Sharon, in jacket and pants, outside Hodge Hall.

"It was good of you to call," she said to McLeod. "And you brought the dogs. Lovely." She knelt down to rub each canine head.

"Don't forget your allergy," said McLeod. "How's your rash?"

"It was clearing up, and I guess now it will flare up again," said Sharon. "Oh, dear."

"I shouldn't have brought them," said McLeod. She reverted to motherly mode. "Let me see your hands."

"They're fine," said Sharon, putting them in her coat pockets. "It's so nice of you to ask me to lunch."

"I'm glad I caught you at a free time,"

said McLeod. "Fiona's pleased you're coming to lunch. How are things going? Is it getting any easier?"

"Not really. I'll be glad when we can have the funeral. It's been just two weeks today since I last saw Dan, but it seems like ten years."

"I'm sure it does. I'm sure it does. Any news about when the funeral will be?"

"Nobody tells me anything," said Sharon. "Not the police, not Dan's parents. I don't know when the police will release the body." Her voice trembled as she said this, but she went on to add, "I want the funeral service to be here, but Dan's parents want to have it in his hometown."

"Where do they live?" asked McLeod.

"In Indiana — Columbus, Indiana."

"You said they'd been here."

"Oh, yes, they came on the Wednesday after Danny was identified, and they left on Saturday," said Sharon. "This has been a terrible blow for them."

"You know," said McLeod, "it would be simple to have the funeral service and burial in Indiana and have a memorial service in the chapel here. Would that work?"

"I think it would. I don't see how the Strongs could object to that, do you?" said Sharon.

"No, I should think they'd like it very much."

"I suppose the two services would be hard for them, I don't know. I think they'll have to come here anyway to pack up Dan's things as soon as the police give permission."

"Perhaps the seminary would pack his things and ship them to them," said McLeod.

"Maybe. Oh, I don't know. I suppose it will all work out," said Sharon.

"I'm sure it will," said McLeod. "Well, here we are." Inside the front door, she unleashed the dogs, who ran back to the kitchen to report to Fiona on their excursion and to drink vast quantities of water. Fiona came out to meet McLeod and Sharon.

"Let's sit down in the library," said Fiona. "Is that all right? Maybe have a glass of wine before we eat? Here, Sharon, let me take your jacket and hang it up."

"No wine for me, thanks," said Sharon. "Not at lunch. And I have a class at two o'clock."

"I suppose in that case we'd better move along. It's a very simple lunch. I set the table in the dining room. McLeod and I have been sitting in the kitchen so much I thought we needed a change."

"Fiona, you are a wonder," said McLeod. "In ten minutes you've worked a miracle. The table looks lovely. The chrysanthemums are heavenly. I love them with the stems cut short and massed like that."

"Nothing to it," said Fiona modestly. "You sit here Sharon, and you here, McLeod. I'll bring in the soup."

McLeod helped her and they all sat down. Fiona asked Sharon how she was doing and Sharon answered her as she had answered McLeod, and they all agreed again that it would be better when the funeral was over.

They ate their soup; McLeod cleared the soup bowls and Fiona brought in cold plates that contained slices of meat loaf, beet and orange slices, and French bread.

McLeod raved about the meat loaf. "It's better cold than it was hot," she said.

"I know," said Fiona. "I served it cold once to Hester Hardin, and she said she had not had anything like it since she spent a year in France. I was quite flattered."

"And beets and oranges — that's a wonderful combination. I've got to learn to cook," said Sharon. Then, after a minute's thought, she said, "No, I don't. I won't be getting married, will I?"

"Of course, you will," said McLeod. "Just not right away. It's inevitable that somebody as nice as you will get married. Were you and Dan planning on marrying before you graduated from seminary?"

"The wedding was going to be next June, in the chapel here, as soon as Dan graduated. Dean Tilley was going to perform the ceremony." Her blue eyes filled with tears.

"My dear —" said McLeod, getting up and standing behind Sharon, encircling her in her arms.

"Oh, Sharon, it's terrible, I know," said Fiona.

"I'm all right," said Sharon. "I really am. Don't pay any attention to me. Really. I'm *all right*." She began to eat in a determined way.

"We're sorry," said Fiona, as McLeod sat down.

"I know you are," said Sharon. "Don't feel bad. I'm getting over it. I really am. Dan had a brief life but he had a good one."

"I really want to find out who killed Dan," said McLeod. "And I don't think that it was an act of random violence anymore. I think it was somebody here, at the seminary, somebody who wanted to kill

Dan. Can I ask you a few questions?"

"Certainly," said Sharon. "I want to find out who killed him, too. I don't want vengeance," she said. " 'Vengeance is mine, saith the Lord.' I just want to get it clear in my mind so I can go forward."

"That's an admirable attitude," said McLeod. "We talked a little bit about Dan's sermon. Tell me about Dan and von Kemp. Were they friends? Did they know each other?"

"Dan had mixed feelings about Dr. von Kemp," said Sharon. "He admired him for being a go-getter — he liked that — at least at first, when he had a class with him. But Dan thought Dr. von Kemp got too interested in making money off the artifacts he brought back."

"Did he sell many?" asked McLeod.

"He sold a lot of them. Dan helped him bring some to New York one time. And he hated it. Those little fat statues of Baal — he said it was disgusting."

"Did Dan know anything about von Kemp's background, his family or anything?"

"I'm sure he did," said Sharon. "He had ways of finding things out, through the web and all, and he was good at checking people's credit ratings and things like that.

He'd been a policeman, you know."

"I had no idea," said McLeod. McLeod was beginning to detest Dan Strong. How had Sharon tolerated him? She exchanged a glance with Fiona and then plowed on. "Did he ever say anything to you about von Kemp's family?"

Sharon thought a minute. "One time he was talking about Professor von Kemp and his assistant — you know, Ms. Turner. He thought they were committing adultery. And I said, if neither one of them is married, it's not adultery. And he said, oh, but the professor is married. He didn't say anything else. And something came up and I didn't ask him any more questions about it."

"Sharon, who were his friends here, besides you? Who did he like?"

"He liked Dean Tilley — or he used to. He used to say the dean was a good conservative and a true Christian. Dan liked the other conservative members of the faculty — Dr. Rush and Dr. Lancaster. He just had such high standards he didn't approve of most of the students. I don't know how he put up with me."

"Sharon, anybody could put up with you," said McLeod. "Don't be silly." She did not add that she could not see how or why Sharon had put up with Dan Strong. "What do you mean when you say Dan 'used to' like Dean Tilley?"

"I'm not sure what Dan was feeling about Dean Tilley. He just told me that he'd had a revelation about him. He was shocked, he said."

It sounded to McLeod that Dan Strong had not really liked anybody — with the possible exception of Sharon. "That sermon — I know we've talked about it before —"

"I've been thinking about that sermon." Sharon interrupted McLeod. "And I've realized that that sermon came out of a true disillusionment Dan felt about the seminary and about everyone here. I read it again, and you're right — it was angry. A diatribe, I guess."

McLeod pushed on. "But the reference to thieves. Do you know if that applied to the seminary, too? As I've said, this seems to me to be the most thief-free place I've ever seen."

Sharon gave a little gasp. Her hand flew to her face. "Oh, you know what that was? Oh, that was terrible. I don't understand it. You know how the seminary's not doing any new hiring or anything and how funding for the library has been cut back?"

Fiona nodded. "It's hard times at the ranch," she said.

Sharon went on, "Well, Dan thought that somebody had been fiddling with the endowment."

This time McLeod and Fiona gasped. They looked at each other and back at Sharon. Fiona spoke first. "But that would involve Hester Hardin, wouldn't it?"

"I don't know," said Sharon. "I don't know anything about it."

McLeod let it go. "Sharon, did you feel the same way Dan did about homosexuals and inclusive language and the ordination of women and higher criticism?"

"I did," Sharon said carefully. "I do honestly believe that homosexuality is against God's law. Willy Cameron has tried to tell me it's not, but I refuse to listen to him on that subject. I asked one student if she couldn't change, you know, have therapy and change. And she tried to convince me that you couldn't change, that it's inbred. Oh, I've tried to see their side, but I don't. These are complex issues. Inclusive language makes sense, in a way, doesn't it? But all that criticism is nonsense. God wrote the Bible and that's that. And the ordination of women — I'd like to be ordained — I guess, but then I suppose I'll be content to be a director of Christian education or a counselor or something."

"What about Professor von Kemp and his false idols?"

"Oh, I don't know what I believe!" wailed Sharon. "I truly loved Dan. He was such a strong personality, such a powerful person, that he swept me off my feet. I believed everything he said. I don't know how I'll feel now that he's gone. I really don't. I don't want to talk about it anymore."

"Of course you don't," said McLeod soothingly. "I'm sorry if I've upset you. I'm just trying to get a fix on Dan. I want to find out who killed him. You told me you did, too, and that's why I'm asking all these questions."

"You know, I didn't mean to let you think that Dan didn't have any friends among the students. He did. He was a good man. All anybody can think about is his sermon, as if he were some kind of Savonarola burning books and that kind of thing."

McLeod had a strange feeling: She's lucky he died, she thought, and then mentally flogged herself for the thought.

"One more thing," McLeod said. "I want to check something. The last time you saw Dan was Tuesday, two weeks ago, at supper time?"

"That's right. We finished supper and we were leaving the cafeteria, and he said he'd see me in the morning. 'You're not coming back to the dorm?' I asked him, and he said, 'No, I've got to see somebody. I may be late.' And he kissed me on the cheek and went on his way. And I went back to the dorm."

"He just said, 'I've got to see somebody'? He didn't say 'meet a man,' or give you any hint about who it might be?"

"No, he didn't," said Sharon. "The police asked me that over and over again."

"Was it somebody on the seminary campus?"

"I just don't know. I've just told you."

"Who do you think it could have been?"

"I don't know. I don't know."

"Sharon, you've been wonderful," McLeod said. "I mean it."

"Thanks," said Sharon. "I don't know what you think I've been wonderful about."

"Every little bit helps," said McLeod. They were silent.

"Let me get coffee, and a small dessert," said Fiona.

"I try not to eat desserts at lunch," said

McLeod, getting up to clear the table. She brought dessert plates from the kitchen and came back with a platter of assorted cookies. "I'm afraid I'll have to eat a meringue, though. At least they don't have any fat."

Fiona returned with the coffee tray, and McLeod ate a single fat-free meringue and watched gloomily as Sharon ate one of everything on the platter. Oh, the metabolism of the young! She thought ruefully.

After they'd finished coffee, Sharon rose to go. "This was good. Thank you for having me, Mrs. McKay. And McLeod, I wish you luck. I really do. Let me know if I can help. I mean it."

McLeod and Fiona saw her out the front door, as did Beelzebub and Gabriel. "We like her, don't we, guys?" Fiona said to the dogs.

"She's wonderful. Think she could have killed Dan Strong, though?" asked McLeod after Sharon was out of earshot.

"McLeod! One minute you're saying how wonderful she is, and the next you're saying she's a murderer."

"Not 'saying,'" said McLeod. "*Asking.* You have to consider all possibilities. And you know how the police always say the murderer is always a spouse or a close family member. She may be the world's best actress, for all we know. What do you think?"

"I'm trying to adjust to this new wrinkle in your thinking. The problem is, as I'm sure you're aware, is if she killed Dan Strong, who killed Ernst von Kemp? I grant you she might have, *might*, mind you, have gotten so disgusted with Dan Strong that she killed him. Anybody else would have wiped him out long ago."

"And remember, she had access to him and could have slipped him some cyanide. With more ease than anybody else could have," said McLeod. "Maybe he was accusing her of some dreadful wrongdoing — like wearing makeup, or something and she finally got fed up with him."

"I think it is amazing Dan Strong wasn't killed sooner, isn't it?" asked Fiona.

"Yes, it is. He probably lived this long because he came to seminary — which is, in spite of all you say about it being a battlefield, a pretty peaceable place."

"Maybe so," said Fiona. "But if Sharon killed him, how did she get his body down to the tow path?"

"She might have one of those old luggage carts like Lucy has," said McLeod. "And I guess there's always a way for a healthy young person to haul a body a half a mile."

"I see what you mean," said Fiona.

"One thing Sharon said was sensational, Fiona."

"What's that?"

"The endowment. Hester Hardin does manage it, doesn't she?"

"She's supposed to," said Fiona.

"What's her background in financial management?" asked McLeod.

"No idea," said Fiona. "Princeton has the largest endowment of any of the Presbyterian seminaries. I thought it pretty much stayed the same. Do you suppose Hester Hardin was buying and selling stocks and bonds, really trading?"

"I suppose so," said McLeod. "Isn't that what money managers do? But think about it. What if she was really mismanaging it? Would that be thievery? Would that arouse Dan Strong's outrage?"

"You don't suppose Hester was *stealing* from the endowment, do you?" said Fiona.

"How would I know? I met her once — at the train station. She was with Lucy."

"And Lucy had the luggage cart," said Fiona thoughtfully. "Maybe they did the murder together."

"This is getting really far-fetched," said

McLeod, getting up. "Let me put the dishes in the dishwasher and then I'll go try to see Abigail."

"Go on," said Fiona. "I'll do the dishes. You go do the detecting. I'll think deep thoughts while I load the dishwasher and come up with our next noble course of action."

Thirty

Instead of calling Abigail to arrange a visit, McLeod simply set out to look for her. "If she's not over at Lenox House then I'll go to her house," she told Fiona as she was leaving. Beelzebub and Gabriel pleaded for a walk, but McLeod patted them and assured them she would take them out later.

Abigail was in her temporary office when McLeod stuck her head in the door. She frowned at McLeod, but McLeod smiled widely, feeling faintly idiotic, and walked in.

"I am sorry, Abigail, that I've upset you. But I told you the police had to know all of it. And Nick Perry was more excited by the news of Ernst's son than he was by anything I've told him yet."

"Yes, he asked me a great many questions about Johann," Abigail said. "I suppose every detail is important information." Abigail might have been angry with McLeod, but she looked better, less ravaged, than she had appeared before. "He really seems to think Johann murdered his father. He's hot on Johann's trail. Wanted to know how long Johann was going to be in the United States, where he stayed when he was here, where he is now, and on and on."

"Did you know any of these things?" McLeod asked.

"Not really. I know he stayed one night at the Peacock Inn and then moved in with Ernst for a few nights. He went into New York a lot while he was here — sightseeing, I think. Then he went to California. And of course he came back here last week."

"Last week! You mean he was here last Thursday?"

"He certainly was, and I told your policeman he was," said Abigail.

"See, it's all coming out, and it's not so bad, is it?" asked McLeod.

"It's terrible," said Abigail. "After all, he claimed to be Ernst's son. I feel as though I'd betrayed Ernst. Ernst, of all people! But I guess Johann has to deal with the police like the rest of us do."

"Is he still in town now?" asked McLeod.

"Yes," said Abigail flatly.

"Where is he staying?"

"I don't know," said Abigail. "He doesn't confide in me."

"I guess the police found him," said McLeod. "But don't you see it's better to tell the police what you know?"

"I'm not so sure," said Abigail. "The trouble is, I can keep things back from the police, but I can't keep anything back from you. I simply seem to spill my guts to you."

"No, you don't," said McLeod. "And it's better to talk to somebody, don't you think?"

"It would be better to talk to somebody who didn't run to the police with everything I tell them." Abigail took the sting out of what she said when she smiled ruefully at McLeod as she spoke.

"The field is getting bigger and bigger," said McLeod. "The suspects, I mean. Victor Lord — the police have questioned him and they're checking his alibi. And now there's Johann. He's a good villain — he's a German."

Abigail smiled at this. "Victor would be a good villain. It would be just like him to kill Ernst," she said. "I really believe he could do it."

Immensely relieved to see the turn Abigail's talk was taking, McLeod asked another question. "Abigail, there's one thing I really want to know. It's important. How well did Ernst know Dan Strong?"

"He had him in a class last year and I know Dan came over here a couple of times to see Ernst."

"Did they get along? Did Ernst like Dan?"

"I think Ernst was interested in Dan. Dan had worked as a policeman, you know, and Ernst was intrigued. He said he wondered if a policeman's mind-set would work in the ministry. Dan became thoroughly disillusioned with the seminary and the people here. Ernst thought it was more than the usual student's disenchantment. He tried to talk to Dan about it."

"Do you know if Dan threatened Ernst?"

"What do you mean?"

"Dan's girlfriend Sharon says that Dan knew about Lise and Johann." McLeod hesitated, and Abigail broke in.

"I don't believe it," Abigail said. "I don't see how he knew. I was the only one who knew, I'm sure." She looked shattered again.

McLeod still hesitated, then plunged in: "And Sharon said that Dan knew about you and Ernst."

"What about me and Ernst?" asked Abigail. Her voice was weak.

McLeod said nothing.

"Are you going to tell the police what Sharon told you?" said Abigail. "You told them what I told you." She looked at McLeod accusingly.

"I haven't," said McLeod. "If it turns out that it's important, I guess I'll tell the police. I'll tell Nick Perry. You complain about him — well, you ought to have to deal with Sergeant Brasher."

When Abigail looked puzzled, McLeod explained about the Township and the Borough police. "Sharon told me because I asked her about the connection between Dan and Ernst. That's why I was asking you about the two of them. Dan was like a prosecutor. He saw something wrong in everything anybody did. And I think that's why he was murdered. But then why was Ernst murdered? I'm trying to figure that out. It's very puzzling."

"I see," said Abigail. "I'm actually beginning to see where you're coming from — and where you're headed. But what's in it for you? Why are you doing this?"

"I'm always curious. I'm basically a journalist, a researcher. I like to dig into things. I've been involved in murder investigations before. And this time, I'm actually a suspect. The Township police think for some reason that because I found the body I must have known Dan and know lots more that could help them. I don't, but then I don't help myself when I relay some information to Nick Perry at the Borough police, whom I've known for years. The Township detective demands to know why I didn't give *him* the information. It's just so stupid — it's because I like Nick Perry and trust him and he knows me. And now I've badgered you and Sharon both until you're both impatient with me. And I still can't figure it out."

"You need a cup of tea," said Abigail. She got up, picked up the hot pot, and started out of the door with it. "I'll go get some water."

"Thanks," said McLeod. "I'd love a cup of tea."

The tea was soon ready, and as the two women held their mugs and breathed in the steam, anticipating the hot drink, Abigail said, "I'm trying to think what to do, and I don't know. I don't get the connection between the two murders myself. I didn't think there was anything between Dan Strong and Ernst especially. I still don't think there was. But I don't know whether he would have told me if Dan had threatened him in any way."

McLeod mentioned Dan's sermon, and asked if Ernst had mentioned it to her. "No, he didn't," said Abigail. "Do you think Dan was planning to blackmail people with his knowledge of their wrong-doing?"

"I hadn't thought of blackmail," confessed McLeod. "I think he was just planning to denounce everyone publicly, unless of course they confessed and changed their ways. But what could Ernst do about a wife and a 'son' who's a grown man? I guess Dan would have wanted him to live with Lise."

"And to renounce me," said Abigail. "Yes, we were lovers. Ernst and I. I'm proud of it. I don't know why I've been afraid to admit it to you or to anybody else before now. Of course, while Ernst was alive, we thought we ought to be very discreet because, since no one knew Ernst was married, they would have thought we could get married. Oh, it's so complicated. And it rather suited me to have an affair instead of a marriage. And Ernst, too. We're both so set in our ways. We *were* set in our ways, I should say, or he *was* and I *am*." Abigail burst into tears.

McLeod drank her tea, tried to murmur

words of comfort, failed, and finally stood up.

"You're leaving?" asked Abigail. "I'll see you again soon, no doubt. You've got your teeth in this, haven't you? Ernst would approve of you, you know."

"Thanks, Abigail. That's a whale of a compliment."

"Don't go. Stay for one minute. I've told you Ernst was a sweet man, in spite of his faults. None of us is perfect, you know. But he did countless things to help people."

"I met Ernst, remember?" said McLeod, reflecting that everybody seemed to reveal terrible things that Ernst had done but then everybody added, "But he's a terrific guy." "I liked him," she said to Abigail. "Who wouldn't? Nobody's out to 'get' Ernst, or despoil his memory."

"I guess not. Oh, what a mess."

"Murder is a mess," agreed McLeod.

This was a real muddle, she thought trudging back to the McKays' house.

Thirty-one

McLeod found Fiona lying on the sofa in the library with the two Scotties embedded with her.

"Look at you three," said McLeod.

"They'd jump down to greet you but they're afraid I wouldn't let them get back up here with me if somebody's here," said Fiona. "Did you talk to Abigail?"

"I did," said McLeod. "And she talked to me. Did she ever talk to me. She said out loud that she and Ernst were having an affair. And she did love him, as we both thought she did. And Ernst knew Dan Strong — he was worried about Dan's police-like activities and his judgmental attitudes toward people at the seminary. Whether Dan threatened Ernst or not, I do not know. And Abigail continues to insist that Ernst was a good, sweet man who meant no one any harm — in spite of deceiving people about his degree, his marriage, his son, and trading in dubious antiquities."

"Well, Ernst was certainly an entertaining guy!" said Fiona. "And I've always been interested in Abigail. Still waters run deep, you know, and banked fires smoulder inside."

"Mixed metaphors," said McLeod. "But she is complicated. I've driven her mad with questions, but she always rallies and answers everything and tells me even more. But the more I learn from her the more confused I get. I even wonder if she might have killed Ernst herself."

"We talked about that once," said Fiona. "We thought she could have done it because she wanted to do the Dead Sea Scrolls herself. But now it might be she's simmering with fury and frustration at not being married to him?"

"I guess she's not a good suspect, really," said McLeod. "And besides, every time I talk to her I feel like I know less about the murder of Dan Strong. And I still think his murder is connected to von Kemp's."

"I've given up on detection," said Fiona. "Do you want a drink? If you do, get me one, too."

"No, I need some exercise. I'm going for a long walk. Want to go?"

"No thanks," said Fiona. "Indolence is my key note."

"Shall I take the dogs?"

"They'd love it," said Fiona.

"I'll get you a drink before I go," said McLeod. "What'll it be?"

"Oh, I'll get it myself," said Fiona, getting up. "I'll leash up these babies for you." Beelzebub and Gabriel looked sulky when Fiona got up but when they heard their leashes jingle, they perked up and leaped down from the sofa. McLeod prepared to leave.

"Are you going back to the tow path?"

"Yes, but I'll walk the opposite way, toward Washington Road, not toward the golf course."

Walking with two Scotties was strenuous, McLeod found, but rather fun. She had to stop a lot to let one or both of them explore with loud sniffs what were apparently exquisite smells. And sometimes they rushed along so that she had to trot to keep up with them. But it was exercise and it felt good to be outdoors for a long time.

Colors in the leaves on the trees along the tow path were duller than they had been two weeks ago. She shuffled through more brown leaves that had fallen on the ground. The Scotties loved the dry leaves and crashed through them with high spirits.

McLeod thought, as she did almost constantly, about the murders. An obnoxious seminarian and a mysterious faculty member, two people who seemed to have had only a tenuous, casual connection. Who could have killed them? Lots of people were annoyed by, or even frightened of, Dan Strong. But who would want to kill Ernst von Kemp? She ran over the possibilities for the thousandth time — his son, his assistant, a thief or would-be thief interested in his antiquities? What was the connecting link? She gave up and turned Beelzebub and Gabriel around.

At last she and the dogs were climbing slowly up the hill on Alexander Street, headed home. When she got to the McKays' house, Beelzebub and Gabriel pretended they couldn't make it up the front steps. "Oh, stop it," she said. "I've seen you bound up these steps at fifty miles an hour." They turned away from her and grudgingly climbed up. Inside, they drank copious amounts of water and then flopped down in their beds in the kitchen, while McLeod hung her jacket up in the hall.

"They're exhausted and so am I," McLeod said loudly and cheerfully as she got to the library. To her surprise, Fiona was no longer alone. Angus was there, and so was Gretchen Green. The three of them were silent, as they turned and looked blankly at McLeod.

"I'm sorry," said McLeod. "I didn't realize you had company." She turned to leave.

"Don't be silly," said Fiona, getting up. "Come join us. You remember Gretchen."

"I sure do," said McLeod.

"I should be leaving anyway," said Gretchen, also getting up. Angus stood, too.

"Don't go, Gretchen," said Fiona. "Sit down. Let's have a drink. Tell McLeod what you've told us. She's got a lot of sense."

"I shouldn't spread it around," said Gretchen. "I just wanted to get Angus's advice on how to handle it. And Fiona's advice, too, of course. And I did. I think I did."

"You knew what to do," said Angus. "You didn't need advice. Sit down, Gretchen, and have a drink. You can have anything you like — if I don't have it, I'll run to the liquor store and get it. You deserve the drink of your choice."

"Thanks, Angus. You know what I'd like? A double bourbon. With just a little water."

"Coming up," said Angus. "I've got that."

"Let me go get us some crackers or something," said Fiona. "Sit down, Mc-Leod, and entertain Gretchen."

McLeod had noticed that Gretchen, while not the most cheerful person in the world, seemed more relaxed and less angry than she had on Sunday night. They sat down.

"Gretchen, what —" began McLeod.

"McLeod, what brings you to Princeton?" Gretchen got her question in first.

McLeod explained about Elijah P. Lovejoy. "I've almost finished all the research I can do on him," she said, "but now the Township police won't let me leave because I found the body on the tow path."

"I see," said Gretchen. "That's too bad."

"Did you know Dan Strong?" asked McLeod.

"A little. I detested him. And that goody two-shoes sweetness-and-light girlfriend of his, too."

"I don't think I would have liked Dan either," said McLeod, "but I like Sharon

Leland. She was in love with Dan, and I think he pulled the wool over her eyes."

"Maybe so. She actually didn't seem so bad Sunday night, I have to say," conceded Gretchen.

Angus and Fiona returned bearing, respectively, a tray of drinks and a plate of crackers. "The dogs are exhausted," said Fiona. "How far did you walk?"

"Too far," said McLeod after a sip of sherry. "All the way up to the Harrison Street bridge and back."

"Gretchen, tell McLeod what you told us," said Fiona. "She's a good sort."

"Oh, all right. I guess it will all come out anyway. You see, I was an accountant before I came to seminary. We did a lot of audits for Atlanta nonprofits. And so this fall, the seminary hired me part-time to go over the endowment books and make sure everything was ready for the outside auditors. So I said, sure. I've been working on them since the term started. But last week I made this hideous discovery."

She paused to take a gulp of bourbon. She knows how to tell a story, McLeod thought. Employ the dramatic pause.

"You have to check all the not-for-profit entities that the endowment supports — scholarship funds, and that kind of thing — and make sure they are indeed nonprofits. Make sure that the proper papers have been filed with Internal Revenue and all that. And I discovered one was a mess."

"Wait a minute," said McLeod. "This isn't the great endowment shrinkage that Sharon said Dan knew about, is it? The reason the seminary can't hire anybody new?"

"This is nothing like that. The endowment has shrunk because the stock market has shrunk," said Gretchen. "This is small potatoes — not such small potatoes, actually. There is a fund called the Discretionary Fund that the dean and the president can use, mostly in emergencies, to help out a student or a faculty member who is caught in a temporary tight spot. The students call it the Dizzy fund. It's quite sizable, and the seminary puts money into it and donors make memorial gifts to it and that kind of thing. I gather nobody has paid much attention to it for a long time. The dean and the president funnel money out of it and the seminary and donors pour it in there.

"But I decided to look at it closely this time, and sure enough somebody has been pillaging it. Checks have been written for years to cash. I was shocked. I asked a few discreet questions and I found out that it had to be Henry Fairfield Worthington who did it. He was managing the endowment then — and nobody else was. It went on for years and nobody caught it. And I like old Worthington. He's one of the few people I like at the seminary, to tell you the truth. When I got here and they said I needed a diction coach, he worked with me. He was wonderful. And if this comes out, it will cause a terrible stink."

"And it comes on top of two murders," said Angus.

"Worthington could go to jail for this," said Gretchen. "Not to mention the disgrace for him. I didn't know what to do — whether to tell the financial manager what I'd found or just to let it go. It hasn't been caught before and it probably wouldn't be caught by an outside auditor. But then I thought about auditors who turned a blind eye to corporate bookkeeping shenanigans — like Enron's auditors. And this was worse — it was the *seminary*, the church. I usually know exactly what to do, but this time I was confused. I was beside myself. That's why I was in such a bad temper Sunday night, Angus. I was worried about this. And finally, today, I decided

I'd come talk to you about it."

"McLeod, I told her there was only one thing to do," Angus said. "That was to pursue it as she would if she didn't know the perpetrator."

"I'm sure you're right, Angus. You always are. But it seems hard," McLeod said. It sounded as though Henry had been very bold indeed. Was that because he was so sure he would not be caught, or because he thought he was doing nothing wrong? "Gretchen, are you going to speak to Henry about it before you tell the financial manager what you've found?" she asked.

"I haven't gotten that far," said Gretchen. "Up until the time I came over here I was still debating whether to just let it go or not. It went on for a long time, you know. And I thought perhaps we could just let it go for a while longer. I don't know whether anybody caught it before — and let it go — or not."

Gretchen and Angus discussed the advisability of Gretchen's going to Henry Fairfield Worthington, or Angus's going to him, or sending some emissary. But they could reach no conclusion.

"The minute you tell the financial manager, does that mean there's no turning back?" asked McLeod. "Is there a chance that the seminary would prefer to hush it up?"

"I would say ordinarily there would be no turning back," said Angus. "But at this time, with two murders on the table, who knows what the powers that be would decide?"

"Wait a minute," said McLeod. "Is the seminary breaking a law if they don't prosecute? Nobody's stealing anything now, are they? It happened a few years ago. Couldn't you just wait until the statute of limitations runs out?"

"I don't know that I'd feel comfortable with that," said Gretchen. "My stomach would get tied up in knots again."

"I see what you're saying, McLeod," said Angus thoughtfully.

"There's not really much money involved, is there?" said McLeod.

Gretchen looked at her and scowled. "About a quarter of a million dollars."

"Oh!" said McLeod, stunned.

She thought about Henry and the lavish furniture in his apartment, his annual trip to Europe, his good champagne, his lovely clothes. He knows how to spend it, she thought.

Gretchen said, "I've got to get this off my chest. I'm going to talk to Hester

Hardin tomorrow. Then I'll write my report. But I'll let Hester decide what to do next."

"I think you're doing the right thing, Gretchen," Angus said. "But I knew you'd reach the right conclusion."

"I guess it's right. It's not exactly a win-win situation, is it?"

"No, it's not. But we'll pray that it all works out for the best, for the good of those who love the Lord," said Angus.

Fiona and McLeod looked at each other and rolled their eyes. As Angus went to see Gretchen out the front door, Fiona said, "He really does believe all that stuff, you know."

"I know," said McLeod. "But Fiona, Gretchen Green is really not the most pleasant person in the world. I get the idea she's kind of enjoying this."

"I think you're right."

"But what a dilemma she's in," said Angus, who returned in time to hear this. "Be charitable."

"Be charitable!" said Fiona. "Why didn't you advise Gretchen to be charitable and let it drop?" McLeod knew Fiona was wrong, but secretly she agreed with her.

Thirty-two

"It's time I took you two to dinner again," said McLeod. "It's been a week since I did, and I'm eating you out of house and home. Come on, it's off to Lahiere's."

The McKays gladly agreed and there was a little flurry of preparation, which raised false hopes in the Scotties. "Too bad, guys," said Fiona. "We're going off without you, but you've had lots of walks today."

"I've retired from detection," said Fiona when they had settled down at a table at Lahiere's. "And in light of what Gretchen told us, I'm glad I have retired. I don't think crime should be detected. It should be overlooked."

"And what about the perpetrator?" asked Angus. "Should he go free?"

"Absolutely," said Fiona. "Scot-free. Especially when the perp is a friend of mine."

"I see what you mean," said Angus. "But —"

"Ever since we've been married, you've said that — 'I see what you mean, but — ' Why do you always have to add that 'but'?"

Angus sighed heavily and said nothing.

"I almost agree with you," said McLeod. "But my curiosity always wins out. I have to keep on until I find out what really happened. And you do realize what this revelation of Gretchen's means, don't you?"

"Sure, it means Henry Fairfield Worthington will be disgraced in the community where he's lived all his adult life," said Fiona.

"And it means he might be prosecuted," said Angus.

"Aside from that," said McLeod, "it means he had a really terrific motive for murdering Dan Strong."

Fiona and Angus thought about this. "Oh, you mean because Dan was talking about somebody stealing money?" said Fiona. "Lord have mercy!"

Angus shook his head gloomily.

"That's right," said McLeod.

When they got home, Dean Tilley was waiting on the front porch, sitting in a wicker chair.

"Good evening, good evening," he said,

getting up. "I do hope I'm not disturbing you. You're all from the South, so I know you don't mind pop-in calls, do you?"

"Not at all, Ted," said Angus. "Come in."

"Thank you," said Tilley. "After you, ladies," he said, bowing. "Been to the movies?"

"No, we went out to dinner," said Angus. "Did you want to talk to me, Ted? Let's go in the library."

"No, my friend, not you, I want to talk to this little lady here," he gestured toward McLeod. "But anywhere will do. Our business is not necessarily private."

"Use the library," said Angus. He ushered them in and lit the fire in the library fireplace. "I hope a fire cheers you up, Ted. You know, don't you, that McLeod is an old friend of ours, that she grew up with Fiona and me in Atlanta. We are so happy her research on Lovejoy brought her here. Would you like a brandy, Ted? McLeod?" They both declined, and Angus left.

McLeod said nothing, but waited. Tilley sat down and began fussily dusting off his chest with his handkerchief. He wore a three-piece suit — the first McLeod had seen in years — and he seemed to think something was despoiling the vest. "Sit down," he said, looking up at McLeod, who still stood.

"I'll stand," she said.

Discomfited, Tilley, too, stood up. "Now, young lady, I see you've completely disregarded my wishes," Tilley said.

"I disregarded nothing that you said to me," said McLeod. "On the contrary, I weighed everything you said very carefully."

"Thank you," said Tilley, his mouth curved in the shape of a smile, but his small eyes were hard. "I appreciate that. But you're still here."

"Believe me, I want to be gone as much as you want me to go away. I'm virtually through with my research here and I have a job in Tallahassee that I need to get back to. But I'm still here because the police forbade me to leave town."

"Oh, is that right?" said Tilley.

"Yes, it's quite correct, Dean. I did leave Erdman Hall, where you seemed to think I should not be, so I'm staying here."

"This house is seminary property, you know."

"I'm aware of that," said McLeod.

"The seminary is getting more and more unfavorable publicity," said Tilley.

"That's hardly my fault," said McLeod.

"I wonder," said Tilley. He made a real effort to smile at her. Apparently his greatest wish in life was to be known as an affable, likable man, but he had never gotten the hang of it. "I understand you are no longer confining your research to Elijah P. Lovejoy."

"Oh?" She noticed that Dean Tilley was scratching his wrist. He seemed to have a bad rash.

"Is that poison ivy?" she asked him.

"What?" he said.

"Do you have poison ivy on that hand?"

"Well, yes, I do. But, never mind that right now. I'm told that you're asking a great many questions of a great many people. I can't help but think that your activities are harmful to the seminary."

McLeod smiled at Tilley and said, "Baking soda baths are good for poison ivy, but the cortisone ointments you can get over the counter are even better."

"I came to ask you to stop your questioning," said Tilley, obviously enraged.

McLeod nodded.

"And I expect you to honor my request."

McLeod added a smile this time, as she nodded again, but remained silent.

"Cat got your tongue?" shouted Tilley. Obviously maddened by her silence and, no doubt, his poison ivy, he was no longer trying to be civil.

McLeod smiled as Tilley turned and walked out. McLeod sank into a chair by the fire. She heard Angus tell Tilley good night and show him out the front door.

"I heard him, McLeod," Angus said as he came into the library. "He was really ugly. I tried to head him off at the very first when I reminded him that you were an old friend of ours. But it had no effect."

Fiona came in and the two of them sat down on the sofa. "What's his problem?" Fiona asked.

"I can only say in his defense that he is tried beyond endurance by everything that's going on at the seminary," Angus said. "And pretty soon he'll have to deal with somebody fiddling with the endowment."

"But I can't be too sympathetic," said McLeod. "And he has poison ivy — and there was a huge patch of it right beside that garment bag on the tow path."

Fiona let that go right past her. "What a day you've had," she said. She was standing up, taking the pins out of her long black hair with its streak of white. "It began with Sergeant Brasher and ended with Dean Tilley."

"And in between we got the news about Henry Fairfield Worthington," said McLeod.

"Not a good day," said Fiona.

Gabriel and Beelzebub yawned and seemed to nod in agreement.

Thirty-three

On Wednesday morning, Fiona came downstairs with a clatter and greeted everyone — husband, friend, dogs — with gusto. "And McLeod, after we went to bed last night, I thought of something you should have done."

"What?"

"You should have asked Dean Tilley what he was doing last Thursday between six and eight."

McLeod gazed at her with admiration. "If I had thought of it, I certainly would have." She laughed. "What a hoot that would have been."

"You two," said Angus, shaking his head sadly. "McLeod, you encourage her."

"I encourage her, too," said Fiona. "Don't I, McLeod?"

"You certainly do. When I need it most."

"I meant that she eggs you on," said Angus.

"We'll behave," said Fiona. "I promise you, sweetie."

Later that morning, McLeod was in the seminary library cleaning up the last little chores of her research when Willy Cameron came in.

"I was looking for you. I called the McKays' house and Mrs. McKay said you were here," he said.

"Here I am," agreed McLeod, smiling at him. "What can I do for you?"

"Can you come have a cup of coffee?"

"Sure," said McLeod. "Where?"

"The cafeteria," said Willy.

McLeod rose and put on her jacket. "Do you know I'm almost through here?" she asked as they walked across Mercer Street and down to the cafeteria.

"That's good," said Willy. "I don't mean it's good that you'll be leaving, but it's good to finish something, anything, isn't it?"

"That's right. Now I can move on out to Alton, Illinois, as soon as the police say I can leave," said McLeod. "Although I'd hate to leave without seeing how all this turns out."

When they had sat down with coffee for Willy and tea for McLeod, Willy said,

"The Township police had me in for questioning last night. And Roscoe's over there this morning." Willy, she noted, was certainly not his usual ebullient self. He looked downright distraught.

"Has something new turned up?" asked McLeod. She felt a moment of horrible remorse for having told Nick Perry about Roscoe and his snakes. But you had to level with the police in a murder case, she told herself. And it had taken her long enough to do her duty.

"Not really. They finally heard about Roscoe's snakes, so they wanted to talk to him."

"And you?" asked McLeod. "What brought you to their attention?"

"Like I told you it would be at the very first," said Willy. "Remember what I said? Somebody told them about Dan's campaign against BGLASS and they're questioning all the members."

"Don't you think you need a lawyer?" asked McLeod. "This is serious business."

"I know it's serious business," said Willy. "It's my worst nightmare come true. I guess I'd better get in touch with a lawyer — in case they haul me back in."

McLeod told him about Cowboy Tarleton and Willy said he'd call him.

"How were the police?" asked McLeod.

"Well, they weren't gushing over me, that's for sure. But they were civil. They didn't hit me or torture me or anything like that. They asked me a lot of questions about my relationship with Dan. And I said I didn't have one. I remembered something you said to me when we talked about it — it seems as though it was a year ago and it was just a week ago yesterday. You said that since I was openly gay, not closeted, I had nothing to fear from anything Dan could do. So I pointed that out to them. They wanted to know who my partner was and kept asking me if it was Roscoe. I said, no, that Roscoe was straight, but I don't think they believed me. I told them I wasn't in a permanent relationship and they said, 'So you just pick up men,' and I said, no, I didn't, any more than a straight seminarian picked up women. It was nasty."

"It sounds like you handled it very well," said McLeod. "I'm proud of you."

"It's scary. That first time around they were much were more casual. You know, 'When did you last see the deceased?' and that kind of thing. I mean, they interviewed practically every student. But this was different; this was serious. They kept asking me for the names of other people who were gay but weren't out yet."

"Did you give them any names?"

"Of course not," said Willy. "Although, some of them would astonish folks. Dean Tilley, for instance, and several faculty members, men and women, not to mention a great number of students."

"They may all be suspects. Can you tell me their names?" She brought out a notebook and wrote them down as Willy recited them. "As I said, people who have come out — like you — don't have near as good a motive as people who have managed to keep their sexual preferences a secret." She stopped a minute, letting what he had said sink in. "Did you say Dean Tilley?"

"That's right," said Willy.

"But he's such a homophobe. He told me he admired Dan Strong, said he was the 'finest type of student' or something like that. He even praised Dan to me for being so firm about gays. This is astonishing."

"It may astonish you, but it's a fact. He comes on to students now and then, and it's really awful. But mostly I think he limits his activities to the bars in Chelsea, in New York."

"He wouldn't have dared make a pass at Dan, would he? And if he did and got turned down, boy, wouldn't he have the most magnificent motive for murder? What would happen to him if this came out? He'd have to leave the seminary, wouldn't he?"

"I would think so," said Willy. "As long as they have the current administration and Board of Trustees, anyway. I mean if Cy Monroe had to leave because he 'harassed' a female student, what could they do about a dean who 'harasses' male students?"

"Willy, it would almost be a public service to out him."

Willy laughed, but not heartily. "I see what you mean," he said, "but I hate to be the one to name names to the police, even Toad Tilley's name."

"I can understand that, but think about it. Maybe you should. Anyway call Cowboy in case you have to go back." She sighed. "I hate this. It's the nastiest murder case I've ever seen."

"Yeah. It's the only one I've ever seen up close, and it's not something I'd like to see again. And Roscoe's out there at police headquarters now. I don't think he's ever *seen* a policeman before. He was certainly

326

never hauled in for questioning in Two Egg."

"They probably don't even have a policeman in Two Egg," said McLeod. "There would be a sheriff somewhere in the county seat, but I bet they never see him out in Two Egg. But, hey, maybe this is a rite of passage for a hillbilly boy at seminary, or even a sophisticated upstate man like you."

"I guess," said Willy doubtfully. "Well, thanks —"

"I don't know what you have to thank me for," interrupted McLeod.

"Thanks for listening, for giving me the name of a lawyer. His name is really Cowboy Tarleton?"

"It's William Tarleton, but everybody calls him Cowboy. He may even be in the phone book under Cowboy."

"Okay," said Willy. "Look, how are you? I've been so wrapped up in my own troubles, I forgot to ask. Have the police or anybody been bothering you?"

"Oh, Brasher came by the McKays' house first thing yesterday — he was furious that I hadn't told them about Dan's sermon." She refrained from telling Willy that she had told Nick Perry about the sermon. "And then I guess he started asking questions about who Dan was talking about in the sermon. I wonder who he asked."

"I think he talks a lot to Dean Tilley," said Willy.

"Really?"

"Yeah. The Toad is very concerned about the case and he wants it solved. So he keeps in close touch with Sergeant Brasher."

"You know, don't you, that Dean Tilley really wants me out of the way," said McLeod. "He came by to see me last night. He thinks I'm stirring up trouble with all my questions."

"All your questions?" asked Willy.

"You know me. I can't help asking questions. Mostly Abigail Turner and Sharon Leland. And Henry Fairfield Worthington. And I've asked a lot of people what they were doing last Thursday night — you know, when von Kemp was killed. But I don't seem to be getting anywhere. I'm not much of an investigator anymore — if I ever was."

"McLeod, who do you honestly think did the murder, or murders?"

"I don't know," she said. "I just hope it's nobody I've come to like. With that in mind, Tilley would be ideal as the murderer."

"I see what you mean, and I agree with your general low opinion of Toad Tilley," said Willy. "But I just want them to find out who did it so they can leave me alone. And he is a good suspect."

"Call Cowboy."

"I will," said Willy. "Well, thanks again. I'm sorry I dragged you out of the library."

"Oh, Willy, I'm glad you dragged me out of the library. I am always truly glad to see you. Keep in touch. Come by the McKays' house and let us know how Roscoe got along and what happens next. And be of good cheer. As Angus McKay would say, 'All things work together for the good of those who love the Lord.' And as Fiona would say, 'He really believes that stuff.' "

"So did I — once," said Willy, managing a weak smile.

Thirty-four

McLeod felt gloomy after she parted with Willy in front of the cafeteria and set out to return to the library. "It's cold," she said to herself. "Cold and dreary and I want to go home where it's warm." She was surprised at herself. Was she depressed? She had never been homesick for Tallahassee before when she was in Princeton. But this situation was pretty bad — it could hardly be worse, she thought. Her young friends were being interrogated by the police; her older friend was going to be charged with embezzling from the endowment; she herself was officially no longer welcome at Princeton Theological Seminary; she was doubtless a burden on her childhood friends, the McKays. How had everything come to such a pretty pass?

After she crossed Mercer Street, she veered to the left and walked around to Lenox House. If Nick Perry was in his temporary office, she could talk to him about Willy and Roscoe, intercede, perhaps, get Nick to get Brasher off their backs, or at least see that he was fair and reasonable.

Nick was not in, but the uniformed policeman, whose name, McLeod thought, was Bowen, said he'd tell him that Ms. Dulaney had come by. "Thanks," said McLeod.

"He's got that German guy over at headquarters," said Bowen. "Oh, you know, I don't think we'll keep this office much longer, Ms. Dulaney."

"I see," said McLeod, but she didn't see. She wondered if this was an indication that the case was nearly solved. She inferred that the Borough police were sure that Johann von Kemp, or John Kemp, whatever his name was, had murdered his father.

As McLeod came down the stairs, Abigail Turner stuck her head out of her temporary office. "Come on in," she said.

"How are you doing, Abigail?"

"I'm fine. Jim Collins, Ernst's lawyer, just called and said that Ernst left me everything he had. I don't know what to think."

"Think grateful," said McLeod. "That's what to think."

"Do you suppose people will have to know?"

"What do you mean?" asked McLeod.

"Here I go again. I tell you everything. Everything. I don't know why. But I had just as soon not have everybody know it."

"I think people will find out," said McLeod. "It will be in the papers when the lawyer files the will for probate."

"Oh, my God," said Abigail. "Oh, well."

"Do you know how much money is involved?"

"I think it will be about half a million dollars."

"Wow!" said McLeod.

"I know," said Abigail. "Actually, I'm ecstatic."

"And Johann can't — or won't — contest the will, can he?"

"I don't know about that," said Abigail. Her face fell. "He may never know about it, but then he may. He's still in this country, I understand."

"I suppose he'll find out about it," said McLeod. "Oh, but don't even think about his contesting it. I don't know why I brought it up. It's just that things seem to be going wrong all over the place — but I don't think this will go wrong."

"I hope not," said Abigail.

"It's good news," said McLeod. "A legacy is a wonderful thing. And you'll be the proud owner of Ernst's latest find, that mysterious world-shaking object, whatever it is." She hoped Abigail would reveal what she knew about the discovery.

Abigail did not take the bait. Instead she clapped her hand over her mouth. "I forgot about that. For heaven's sake. I certainly will, won't I? But I don't know where it is or what it is. I've searched everywhere high and low for it. Not a trace."

"It will turn up," said McLeod. "And let me know what it is when you find it." She thought that Abigail looked like a different person today. McLeod remembered the first time she had seen her, the morning almost a week ago when Abigail had come to work to find that her boss — and lover — had been brutally murdered. McLeod had thought then what a strong woman she was, but a woman wounded. Now Abigail did not look so wounded and she looked very happy about her inheritance. Money — even the prospect of money — did cheer people up, McLeod thought.

"Come have lunch with me," said McLeod impulsively. "We'll celebrate. I'll treat. We'll go uptown."

Abigail started to get up, then sat back down again. "What am I thinking of?" she said. "Ernst not even in his grave, and I'm going out to celebrate? No, McLeod, I understand your impulse. And I appreciate the offer, but I don't think I'd better go out to 'celebrate.'"

"Just as you say," said McLeod. "I thought it might help."

"It probably would," said Abigail, who was really in a good mood, "but let's just have a cup of tea here. Would that be all right?"

"Sure," said McLeod.

Abigail made the tea. "Sugar? Milk?"

"Nothing for me," said McLeod. Abigail doctored her own. When they were holding their mugs, McLeod asked Abigail where she had grown up. "It sounds like you have a Boston accent," she said.

"I grew up in Boston," Abigail said. "I was raised a Catholic — but I gave that up in college. Don't get me started on the Catholic church."

"And you trained as a historian?"

"That's right. I went to Boston College, but then I got my Ph.D. at Columbia."

"How did you end up here in Princeton?"

"When I finished graduate school, I

couldn't get a job teaching, so I did adjunct teaching all over the place and then took a job as an administrator, an assistant dean at Rutgers. I fell in love with Princeton and answered an advertisement for a research assistant at the seminary. Ernst had just landed the Dead Sea Scrolls project and needed an assistant. I had to do some secretarial work for a while, but that was all right. Ernst captivated me — I can't tell you how charming he was. And it was a good job for me. I guess it became my life. Now I guess I won't have a life."

"Sure you will," said McLeod. "And you'll have a more comfortable life."

Abigail abruptly changed the subject. "Do you think the police will ever find out who killed Ernst?"

"Sure," said McLeod. "But this is a tough one. It seems that the Borough is working on Ernst's murder and the Township is trying to solve Dan Strong's killing. Apparently, Nick Perry passes everything he learns about Dan's murder to the Township; and I suppose the Township, if it learns anything about Ernst, would pass it on to the Borough."

"It doesn't seem like the most efficient way to operate a detective operation, does it?"

"Maybe it has advantages," said McLeod. "I don't know. We'll see." She started to ask Abigail about Ernst's latest discovery, but before she could form the words, Abigail jumped up and said she had an appointment with the dean.

"I have to fly," she said. "I forgot all about it. It's a good thing I didn't go out to lunch with you. Forgive me —" And she shot out the door, not pausing to get a jacket.

McLeod stood up, looked around, tempted to do a little exploring to see what she could find out about Ernst's latest — it was becoming an obsession, she decided. If the police couldn't find anything, how could she? She left Lenox House and started to go into the library's back door, but changed her mind and went straight to Mercer Street.

Thirty-five

At the pedestrian crossing in front of the library, McLeod met Gretchen Green.

"Hey, Gretchen," she said, "you look more cheerful today than you did last night."

"I am more cheerful," she said. "I talked to Hester Hardin this morning and got that over with."

"How did she react?"

"She was shocked, of course," said Gretchen. "But she knows Henry and likes him and she thought that the seminary might not press charges. If Henry can make restitution, repay most of the money, or even some of it, it will be better."

"You mean the seminary might just let it go?" asked McLeod. "That would be wonderful."

"Well, it depends on the president and the trustees," said Gretchen. "Hester is seeing the president this afternoon. I've still got to write my formal report, but right now I've got to catch up on some of my class work."

"Have you had lunch?" asked McLeod.

"Well, no, but I was headed to the library," said Gretchen.

"Let's go uptown and get a sandwich," said McLeod. "The cafeteria's closed."

Gretchen looked at her watch, and hesitated.

"You can practice being a counselor," said McLeod.

"I don't know how good a counselor I'd be, but I'll come if you need help," said Gretchen.

So that was the way to get people at the seminary to go to lunch, McLeod reflected. You told them you needed help. They went to the Red Onion, where McLeod thought the sandwiches, especially the Reubens, were very good, and sat in a dark corner.

"Now, what's your problem?" asked Gretchen with a very professional manner.

"I've got lots," said McLeod. "But I'm worried about Willy Cameron. You met him at the McKays' house Sunday night."

"Sure, I know Willy. He's a big wheel in BGLASS."

"So he is, and that's what he's worried about. The police are questioning gays at the seminary because of Dan's veiled

338

promise to expose them in his sermon. The Township police questioned him for a long time last night."

"That's so ridiculous," said Gretchen. "Utterly foolish. People are being so dumb about the whole gay issue. They're much better about this at Berkeley than they are here."

"But Willy is *here*, not in Berkeley, and he's worried," said McLeod. "So I can't help but worry about him. It does seem to me too much is made of it here. After all, the Episcopalians have a gay bishop."

"I just don't think Willy has anything to worry about, unless he did kill Dan Strong, which I don't believe he did for a minute."

"Neither do I," said McLeod. "Well, you make me feel somewhat better. The police had Roscoe Kelly in this morning. Do you know of other students who are being questioned?"

"No, I don't. I didn't know about those two until you told me," said Gretchen. "I'll keep an eye out, though. I should think anybody being questioned by the police in a murder case would need a lawyer, wouldn't you?"

"It depends," said McLeod. "I certainly advised Willy to get a lawyer, in case they called him back for more questions — he expects they will want to talk to him again.

I thought he ought to have somebody with him, since my opinion of Sergeant Brasher is not very high."

"That's bad news," said Gretchen.

"I wonder if they'll start talking to Lucy Summers and the other feminists at the seminary, because Dan certainly went after them in that sermon."

"I wonder," said Gretchen. "I'm trying to think if I've been a standout women's rights crusader myself. I don't think I have. I'll keep my ear to the ground and try to find out if they talked to any more students. I'll let you know."

"Thanks. But back to Henry Fairfield Worthington. Is there any way you could be mistaken? Is there any chance he did not embezzle money from the endowment?"

"I don't think there's a chance in the world," said Gretchen. "If it wasn't Henry, it was somebody on his watch. And Hester says there isn't anybody she can think of who could have done it but Henry."

"But there's a chance it was somebody else? It's not a done deal that it was Henry?"

"I think we can be pretty sure it was Henry," said Gretchen. "Although no one's confronted him yet."

"Does he know about your audit?" asked Mcleod.

"I don't see how he could know about it — unless you or Angus or Fiona or now Hester has told him. Nobody else knows about it."

"You talk about worried," said McLeod. "I'm worried about Willy, as I said, but I'm much more worried about Henry Fairfield Worthington. I just want him to have a friend around."

"Henry's a grown man. He'll have to face up to the consequences of his actions." Gretchen shrugged.

McLeod was shocked at Gretchen's coldness. "Of course he will," said McLeod. "But I hope his friends will rally around him." She finished up her Reuben and took the last sip of her Diet Coke.

"I'll be glad when the whole business is over," said Gretchen. "It's been terrible for me. This audit is a lot different from the ones I used to do in Atlanta — there we went into somebody's books and it was impersonal. I never knew the people involved and religion never entered into it. We did do the seminary's books, but everything was straightforward."

"I realize this is much harder," said McLeod. "It's hard for everybody concerned, isn't it?" She thought of Henry and wondered how this could affect a motive for murder, but she decided not to mention that to Gretchen. Gretchen went up and down in her estimation, and right now she was down.

Thirty-six

When McLeod finally got to the McKays' house that afternoon, Fiona came running down the stairs as Gabriel and Beelzebub came rushing out from the kitchen.

McLeod felt warm and welcomed. What a joy it was to have friends like Fiona and Angus, she thought, with dogs like Gabriel and Beelzebub. She was kneeling to properly greet the dogs, as Fiona said, "I didn't see you before you left this morning. I wanted to tell you that Angus and I have to go out to dinner tonight. I'm sure you won't want to come, or we would have called our hosts and told them we had a houseguest —"

"Of course not," said McLeod. "Where are you going this time?"

"It couldn't be worse, but we have to go at least once a year. It's the Tilleys — can you believe it?"

"Oh, Lord," said McLeod. "Do you really have to go there for dinner?"

"Every now and then."

"Guess what. I found out something today that puts Silly Tilley at the top of the list of suspects."

"What?" said Fiona.

"Tilley is gay — he's come on to students, even," said McLeod.

"Merciful fathers! Where did you find *that* out?"

"Willy Cameron."

"This is quite a piece of news, isn't it?"

"It certainly is. It gives him motive on motive for killing Dan Strong, doesn't it? See, Fiona? Last night I told you Toad Tilley — that's what Willy calls him — had poison ivy on his hands, and you didn't pay any attention."

Fiona blinked. "I had forgotten that. Listen, Nancy, you're right. He should be at the top of the list of suspects."

"You've got it, George, in a nutshell."

"Do the police know this?"

"No. The police questioned Willy Cameron last night and they wanted him to name names — gay people at the seminary who haven't come out. He wouldn't do it. He's a great kid. He just told me about Tilley — I guess to get it off his chest. The police seem to think, with good reason I'd say, that a closeted gay would have a good motive for murder if Dan had threatened to expose him. I think maybe Willy should tell them. I know it's honorable not to squeal, but in a murder investigation, I think everyone ought to tell the police everything they know."

"Well, you can tell that darling Lieutenant Perry about it, can't you?"

"I don't know," said McLeod. "In a way, it's betraying Willy's confidence. But then there's that poison ivy. Maybe I should. I don't know. Tonight when you're there, watch Tilley and see if his poison ivy is any better — or worse. And ask him what he was doing last Thursday."

"I certainly will," said Fiona. They both scratched the dogs while thinking.

"By the way, Dean Tilley is married? I can't believe it. He's such a monster. What's his wife like?"

"Oh, she's one of those sweet little women who wouldn't say 'boo' to a goose. You know, all sweetness and light, all gush and no push. Anyway, there's some cold ham in the fridge, and I put some potatoes in the oven to bake. If you want something hot, eat one of them. If you don't want one, fine. I'll use them tomorrow for potato salad or something. There's lots of fruit."

"I'll be fine," said McLeod. "I'd much

rather eat what I can find here than go to the Tilleys' for dinner."

"Of course, you would. Any sensible person would."

"And, Fiona, I found out today that Ernst von Kemp left everything he had to Abigail. Interesting, isn't it? She is happy as a clam."

"That's wonderful for her," said Fiona.

"And she told me the story of her life. She was raised a Catholic in Boston and worked at Rutgers before she came here."

"That's odd," said Fiona. "I could have sworn she told me she was raised in Canada and worked in New York before she came here. Enough of this. I've got to get ready to go."

As soon as Fiona and Angus left, the phone rang. It was Willy, calling McLeod.

"I just wanted to let you know," said Willy. "Roscoe's back and he says it wasn't bad. They have some other BGLASS members out there now. They said they just wanted to make sure he kept his snakes under lock and key, and they brought him back and checked his room and they seemed satisfied. They asked him about Dan's sermon and the warning against snake handlers, and he told them about threats down South against his fa-

346

ther, a real snake handler, and he convinced them that a brief mention in a sermon like Dan's was nothing to be concerned about, not compared to the things people threatened to do to his father. Roscoe is so unflappable that I think they realized he just wasn't worked up enough about it to do anything, especially commit a murder. I'm much more eruptive, I guess you'd call it. Anyway, I think Roscoe's all right."

"I certainly hope so," she said. "Thanks for calling."

She hung up, and while her hand rested on the phone, considered her next move. She frowned resolutely, looked up Henry Fairfield Worthington's number, and dialed it.

"Henry Fairfield Worthington," she said when he answered. "This is Mary McLeod Brannon Dulaney. I'm all alone — Angus and Fiona have gone off to dinner with the Tilleys — why don't you come over and eat cold ham and hot potatoes?"

"I'd love to, McLeod, but I have a guest." (McLeod tried to remember how many potatoes there were — enough to feed three people? she doubted it.) "Why don't you come over here? You'd probably like to meet him, and I know he'd like to meet you."

Henry sounded quite chipper, McLeod thought. He must not have heard about the audit yet. "I couldn't intrude," she said, but not firmly. She hoped he would urge her. He did, and she accepted gratefully.

"Do I have time to run uptown and get a bottle of wine?" she asked.

"No, you don't," said Henry. "And we've got plenty. Come on over."

So McLeod went upstairs, washed her face, combed her hair, and brushed dog hairs off her skirt. Then she grabbed her coat from a hook in the hall and went off on the short walk to Henry Fairfield Worthington's apartment.

Henry looked his usual cheerful self, she noted, so the blow had probably not fallen. His guest turned out to be Johann von Kemp, or John Kemp, as Henry introduced him. He was a personable young man, McLeod thought.

"How do you do?" he said to McLeod, bowing when he was introduced.

"I'm glad to meet you," said McLeod. "I'm sorry about your father. I liked him very much."

"Thank you. I did not know him well myself, but I also liked him," said Kemp.

"Sit down, sit down, McLeod. What will you have to drink?" said Henry.

"Dry sherry?" asked McLeod. "I never used to drink it, but the McKays are always serving it to me and I lap it up."

"On the rocks or straight up?" asked Henry.

"Just plain," said McLeod. "Is it cold?"

"Oh, yes," said Henry, disappearing briefly into the kitchen.

When Henry brought her sherry, McLeod appraised young Kemp as she sipped it. He was tall and did not look like the stereotypical Teuton — instead of blue eyes and blond hair, he had brown hair and brown eyes. He had proper manners and spoke formal English with an accent and some Teutonic mannerisms. What else? He was smoking a cigarette. "You were here when your father was . . . killed?" she asked him. "That's terrible that it should happen while you were visiting . . ."

"Yes, it is bad, as you say. Now I am an orphan," said Johann. "But at least I know about it. I feel that if I had not been here I might not have been told. It is strange, but nobody here knows about me."

"Yes, it's very odd," said McLeod, somewhat at a loss for what to say. Henry Fairfield Worthington looked at her sympathetically but said nothing.

"Had he been in touch with you?" she asked.

"In touch?" said Kemp.

"Did he write to you? E-mail? Call?"

"He did not write often," said Kemp. "He came to see me sometimes when he was in Europe. Naturally I wanted to know him better, so as soon as I earned enough money, I came to this country. And he is killed while I am here. Is very strange. And nobody knows I exist."

"Abigail Turner knew you exist," said McLeod.

"True. She did. But she is not happy to see me here."

Nobody could think of anything to say to this for a minute. Finally, McLeod managed to say, "But Henry is happy to see you, I bet."

Johann smiled, and looked at Henry. "He has been very kind," he said, stubbing out his cigarette.

"Come, come," said Henry. "I haven't done anything. I'll leave you two to get further acquainted while I go finish up our dinner. It won't be long."

McLeod was delighted to have a chance to find out something about young Johann Kemp. "What kind of work do you do?" she asked him.

"Computer software," he said, lighting another cigarette.

"That's a marketable skill," said McLeod.

"Yes, I hope so," he said. "I am looking for work in this country."

"Really? You'd like to emigrate?"

"Yes. I am half American, you know."

"Your father loved Germany, I understand," said McLeod.

"Yes, he said so, but he had not been back in years." Johann shrugged his shoulders.

"Did your mother ever come to America?"

"No, she never did."

"And she hasn't seen your father in all these years?"

"No," said Johann. He looked somewhat puzzled. "She has been dead."

"Been dead?" asked McLeod.

"She died twenty years ago when I was five years old."

"I didn't know that," said McLeod. "I didn't know that at all." She tried to think what all this meant. Why had Ernst not married Abigail if his mysterious German wife had been dead for years? Did Abigail know that Lise had been dead for twenty years? Apparently not. What a mess. She stared at Johann. Finally, she asked him,

"Who raised you, Johann? Did you live with relatives after your mother died?"

"Yes. I lived with the mother of my mother and the sister of my mother."

"Is this your first trip to the United States?"

"Oh, yes." Johann lit another cigarette from the end of the one he had been smoking.

"How long have you been in this country?"

"I came four weeks ago. I came here first; I wanted to see my father. Then I went back to New York. I took the Greyhound bus to California. I wanted very much to see the Golden Gate Bridge and to see Hollywood. There was not much to see in Hollywood, I have to say. But I have seen it. To see the whole country is —" he paused, groping for a word — "astounding. It is like crossing all of Europe from the Atlantic Ocean to the Alps and on to the Adriatic. Incredible scenery."

"Yes," said McLeod. "Even if you fly cross-country, you get the sense of enormous distance and splendid landscape stretching out before you."

"Yes," agreed Johann.

"And so now, you will look for a job?" she asked him.

"Yes." He seemed to want to finish the narrative of his travels. "When I returned from the West Coast, I came here from New York on Friday and my father was dead."

"That must have been a dreadful shock," said McLeod.

"It was dreadful shock," said Johann.

Henry came in to announce that dinner was ready, but Johann appeared to be a man who liked to finish what he was saying. "It's a dreadful shock, also," he said, "to find out today that my father has left all his money to his secretary."

"She told me," said McLeod.

"I can make my own way," said Johann. "But it is a shock not to have him advise me as I look for work and to know he did not want me to have any of his money."

Henry, who had apparently heard this before, looked sympathetic for a moment, and then repeated his message that dinner was ready. Johann put out his cigarette and moved with McLeod to the round table in the living room, where plates were already served.

"Quail!" cried McLeod, when she saw the tiny birds on each plate. "I love it, and haven't had it for years."

"You can buy fresh quail over at Griggstown now," said Henry. "I couldn't resist it when I was out there today. Johann, I hope you like it."

"Quail?" said Johann, trying the unfamiliar word a few times. "Quail? Quail?" He pronounced it "kvail."

"Just a minute," said Henry. "You two go ahead and sit down and eat. I'll be there in a second." He pulled a book down from the shelf nearby and looked in it.

"Johann, I think you should talk to your father's lawyer. He may have left you some remembrance that Abigail didn't know about."

"I do not know who he is," said Johann.

"I know who he is," said McLeod. "It's Jim Collins. And he's a respected lawyer in Princeton. I'll look up his address after dinner. You must go to see him."

Henry put the book back on the shelf and joined them. "Quail is *wachten* in German, Johann."

Johann turned to him and beamed. "Yes, I see. *Wachten.* Quail. Thank you." He nodded and returned to his dinner with vigor.

"And wild rice!" said McLeod. "Goodness, I'm glad I got included in this feast, Henry. I really am."

"I'm glad you did, too," said Henry.

Johann ate. Henry poured the wine.

They all ate. Salad followed the quail, and for dessert Henry served apple pie.

"No, I didn't make it," he said. "I bought it at Griggstown, too."

"No need to apologize," said McLeod.

"Who's apologizing?" said Henry. "Have some cheese. My father always said, and I mean always, every time my mother made apple pie, 'Apple pie without the cheese is like the kiss without the squeeze.'"

"Squeeze?" asked Johann.

McLeod cut herself a generous slice of Vermont cheddar while Henry explained the meaning of squeeze.

Over coffee, she asked Johann, who was again smoking cigarettes, if he had talked to the police. Many times, he said. "Lieutenant Perry has questioned me," he said. "He came to see me at the Peacock Inn, and then the police came and took me to the Borough Hall. But they were very kind. They wanted me to tell them about my father. They asked me why I wasn't staying with him, and I said because he was dead. He had a small apartment but I had stayed there when I was here before. I regret that I did not get to stay with him again. Maybe I would have been able to know him some better. But it was not to be. . . ." He sighed and shook his head.

No, it was not to be, thought McLeod sadly. What an odd man Ernst von Kemp had been, keeping his wife a secret, and then keeping the *absence* of a wife a secret. McLeod shook her head, too. "But they can't suspect you of the murder, since you didn't get here until Friday," she said finally.

"They suspect me," said Johann. "You see, I came straight here from New York when I return from my travels. It was about two or three o'clock in the morning. I got off the bus at Palmer Square. I walk down to my father's apartment on Bayard Lane and policeman on guard. I ask what is the matter and they say a seminary professor has been murdered. I do not tell them who I am and I go to the Peacock Inn and sit on the gallery, the porch, in front until someone opens the door and I can check in."

"And you can't prove you didn't get here before Ernst was killed? Is that it?"

Johann looked at her with admiration.

"Correct," he said.

Shortly after, when Johann left, McLeod lingered. Henry offered her brandy, which she refused.

"You're okay?" she asked him.

"I'm fine," he said. "And you?"

"I'm fine, too." She hesitated. "Well, I guess I should be going."

"I'll walk with you to the McKays'," he said.

As they walked down Mercer, she could see the McKays' house was still dark. "Fiona and Angus aren't home yet," she said.

"They're at the Tilleys', I think you said."

"That's right."

"But isn't this Tilley walking up the walk to their house?"

McLeod looked up and saw the figure approaching the stoop. "It sure looks like him. I hope he's not bringing bad news — I'm not sure I could take anymore."

They reached the bottom of the porch steps just as Tilley turned away from the front door and saw them.

"Good evening, good evening," he said. "How are you, young lady? And Henry Worthington."

"Aren't Fiona and Angus at your house?" asked McLeod.

"Yes, indeed, they are," said Tilley. "I just stepped out to get a breath of fresh air. And while I was out, I decided to come and see you" — he stopped, breathed in, and said in a hurry — "to see if you could come and have coffee with us. Mrs. Tilley did not know that you were staying in the house of our guests or she would certainly have included you in the invitation. I was just trying to make amends for that oversight."

"Thanks so much," said McLeod. "But I've had coffee. I was lucky enough to be invited to dinner at Henry Fairfield Worthington's. You can get back to your guests now."

"All right," said Tilley and scurried off.

He should hop, like the toad he is, thought McLeod. She turned to Henry and shrugged.

He looked at her. "What do you suppose really made him come here?"

"If you want to know what I think," said McLeod. "I think he thought I'd be alone. I think he slipped out and came over here with some evil deed in mind."

"Really?" asked Henry. "You can't be serious."

"I am serious. Where does he live? Where's Toad Hall?"

"It's just two houses down," said Henry.

"I see," said McLeod, who could tell that Henry wasn't taking her seriously about Tilley. That was all right. She didn't particularly want to go into detail about her suspicions. No, they weren't suspicions anymore. They were stronger than that.

McLeod unlocked the door and greeted the two dogs, who were leaping about in a frenzy of welcome. "They know I belong here," she said. "Isn't that nice?"

"Do you have to walk them?"

"Oh, no, Angus will do that when he comes home. Won't you come in?"

"No thanks. I've got to get home and clean up."

"That's right. I should have helped before I left."

"No, no, I don't like people helping me in my kitchen. I'm glad you came to dinner, McLeod. Johann's a nice boy, isn't he? Although he does smoke a lot."

"Very nice," said McLeod. "But Europeans smoke more than Americans. I don't envy him. How did he find you anyway? You didn't even know he existed until I told you about him on Monday."

"I don't know, but I was delighted to see him. He just came by the apartment this afternoon and I asked him to stay for dinner. Fortunately, I had the quail. I was going to freeze them, but I was happy to cook them. And then you called. The rest is history."

"Thanks," said McLeod.

Thirty-seven

The next morning, Thursday, McLeod astonished Fiona with the news that she had met Johann von Kemp.

"In the flesh?" asked Fiona.

"In the flesh," said McLeod.

"Tell it all. You have the best luck. You meet everybody and everybody tells you everything. What did Johann look like? How's his English?"

McLeod did the best she could with description and told Fiona that Ernst's wife had been dead for twenty years.

"Good heavens! Does Abigail know? I guess not."

"I guess not, too." McLeod suddenly thought of something. "Fiona, did you notice that Dean Tilley left the house last night while you were there?"

"No, I didn't. He excused himself briefly when we were about to go in the living room for coffee, but I didn't realize he left the house."

"He didn't say anything about your houseguest, or going to ask me to have coffee with you?" asked McLeod.

"No, nothing like that."

"That's funny. He was at your door when I came home. Thank heavens Henry Fairfield Worthington was with me. I really think Toad was up to no good."

Fiona did not express the same doubts that Henry had shown. Thank heavens for that. So she wasn't crazy, McLeod thought. "You know," she said, "I'm still worried about Henry Fairfield et cetera. He's entirely too happy and chipper for a man who's accused of stealing a quarter of a million dollars from the endowment. I guess he doesn't know yet that he's been accused, and thinks he's safe."

"It is a very gloomy prospect, isn't it? What are you going to do today?"

"I'm not sure," said McLeod. "Go over to the library and make sure I've squeezed out every drop of information they have about Elijah P. Lovejoy and his times."

First, she settled down with the *New York Times,* to which Angus always seemed to have exclusive first rights until he left for work. When she had finished, she put the paper down. "Fiona, do you know any German?"

"Very little. We lived in the German part of Switzerland for a semester, and I picked up a little."

"Let's go see Johann," said McLeod.

"Let's invite him here for lunch," said Fiona. "That's so much cosier."

"Are you sure? I'll call him."

Johann declined. He had an appointment, he said.

McLeod put her hand over the receiver and consulted Fiona. "What about dinner?" she said into the phone.

Fiona was grinning and silently clapping her hands in applause for McLeod's quick thinking. Johann accepted.

"Dinner's better anyway," she told him. "Dr. McKay will be here for dinner, and he'd like to meet you."

She hung up the phone and said she thought that she and Fiona were a great pair of detectives, especially the way they fed people whom they wanted to question. "The road to a confession is through the stomach," she said.

Fiona agreed, and began to talk about what she'd serve. "German," she muttered. "Noodles? Weiner schnitzel? Sauerbraten? Sauerkraut? Come on. That won't do. Not German. What then? American. I know, pork loin roast with apples and potatoes."

She was rapidly making a list.

"I have to tell you that Johann smokes like a chimney," she said.

"That's all right," Fiona said absently. "Remind me to put out ashtrays. I'm off to the store."

"Shall I come along and help?"

"I don't need help, but you can come along and cheer me ever onward."

After shopping for groceries, they ate a quick lunch and McLeod made a lemon pie as her contribution to dinner. Then in a further effort to be useful, she volunteered to take the dogs out for a walk.

Beelzebub and Gabriel, dancing with joy, departed with her. Coming up Mercer Street, McLeod saw Hester Hardin coming out of the huge gray and green house at the corner of Library Place and Mercer Street that held Henry Fairfield Worthington's apartment. She looked back and saw that Henry had come out after Hester and was walking with her. Did that mean that Hester had finally told Henry that he had been found out? Was he under arrest?

She took the dogs on past the house, turning back once to see if Henry was visible. He wasn't, so she and Beelzebub and Gabriel hurried down the hill toward the canal. Long before she got that far, she had, with some difficulty, turned the dogs around and headed back up the hill. She was glad she had when, as they got near Library Place, she met Henry coming up from the campus. He looked distinctly troubled.

"Henry Fairfield Worthington!" she called.

He stopped when he heard her and waited. "I see you've gone to the dogs," he said. "Or gone with the dogs."

"We went for a short, but brisk, walk," she said. "You look troubled. Are you all right?"

"I'm fine, but I am troubled," he said.

"What's the matter?"

"Oh, nothing worth talking about," he said. "I guess."

"Come on, Henry."

He shot her a sharp glance. "You do like to know everything, don't you? I listened with admiration while you interrogated young Kemp last night."

"I can't help it," said McLeod. "I don't want to pry into your affairs, but I want to help you if you're troubled. You do look worried. You've been wonderful to me; now, can't I help you?"

"Thanks, McLeod. I'll certainly let you

know if I need help. But I don't right now."

"Okay, Henry. I'll be here a few days longer, I guess."

"You'll be leaving? Come on in for a minute. Bring those pests."

"Pests? I thought you loved them!"

"I always just pretend to think they're wonderful when I'm at the McKays' house. They're so foolish about the creatures."

"Oh, Beelzebub. Oh, Gabriel. What a two-faced friend you have in Henry Fairfield Worthington," said McLeod. "He speaks with honeyed tongue, but in his heart —"

"Two-faced, but not malicious," protested Henry.

"What about that cairn terrier you said you used to own?"

"It was my sister's. I kept it for her one time. I guess that's my fantasy I trot out for Angus and Fiona."

The dogs skipped up the carpeted stairs to Henry's apartment with great zeal, unaware of their host's feelings toward them, and walked around appraising the place as though they might make an offer on it.

"I'll make a pot of tea," said Henry. "Won't take a minute. Sit down. I'll be right back." When he was settled with teacup in hand, he looked over at McLeod and said nothing for a minute. "I don't quite know how to begin," he said.

McLeod sighed. "I was afraid you might find it hard to talk about, but I think it's better to face up to it and share it with a friend," she said. And then to help him along, she said, "I saw Hester Hardin coming out of here earlier."

Henry was clearly startled. "What? You know about it? Is it common knowledge that I was thought to be an embezzler?"

"Not at all," said McLeod. "Gretchen Green knows. She's the student auditor who discovered the — er — discrepancies. And she told Hester Hardin, and before that she came over and consulted Angus and Fiona about what course of action to take. But no one else. You see, she likes you and she hated to bring it out. Everybody loves you, Henry."

"I see. So Angus said to her, 'Do what's right and damn the torpedoes.' Is that it?"

"Essentially," said McLeod.

"And nobody thought about asking me about it, did they?"

"Actually, I did. I asked Gretchen if she was going to talk to you before she talked to Hester, and she hadn't decided then how to handle it."

"Well, she talked to Hester first and

Hester came over here like Christ on Judgment Day. 'Henry, I regret that I have received the most distressing news from our accountant, et cetera, et cetera, ad infinitum.' 'Hester,' I said, 'What are you talking about?' 'The theft, not to put too fine a point on it, from the Discretionary Funds. It has been revealed.' 'Oh, Hester,' I said, 'I just kept quiet about it. I don't like the man, but I didn't want to expose him to the cruel light of — well, exposé.' 'What are you talking about, Henry?' she said. 'Why, Ted Tilley's plundering of his Discretionary Fund,' I said. 'What?' she shrieked. 'You're going to blame it on the dean?'

"And on and on it went. We finally got it straightened out after I walked over to the Administration building and showed her the books, and the cancelled checks, which I had thoughtfully saved and carefully put away. They were made out to cash and endorsed by Ted Tilley. Hester's not too bright, actually, but she's teachable. She finally caught on. And then she was furious with me for not doing anything about it at the time. I just let her blow off steam about that. I can't understand why anybody would think I would steal money from the seminary, retire, and then hang around,

367

waiting to be caught. Well. Do you feel better? I do. You were right — it was a relief to share it with you."

"Talk about relief!" said McLeod. "It's the biggest relief in the world. I am so glad. And the villain is poor old Toad Tilley, as the students call him."

"And now they've caught up with him. Well, I'm sorry. I don't like to see anybody in the toils of the law."

"Neither do I," said McLeod. "But if it's Toad Tilley, I find I'm a little more anxious to catch the perpetrator. Even then I'm not sure I trust our criminal justice system."

"It's like Churchill said about democracy: It's the worst possible system, except all the others," said Henry.

"Listen, come to dinner tonight," said McLeod. "Johann is coming. It will be so much nicer if you'd come, too."

"Are you empowered to invite people to your hosts' house for dinner, McLeod?" asked Henry.

"I'm empowered by the laws of Southern hospitality and kinship, I'm sure. But if you don't have faith in them, I'll check with Fiona when I get there and make sure. I'll call you."

"Thanks," said Henry.

"I'll be on my way." The dogs got up as she did, and twitched in anticipation.

"Hey, don't forget your little friends," said Henry. "I don't want them left here."

"I won't forget. And I shall keep all your secrets, including your true feelings about Beelzebub and Gabriel."

"Thank you," said Henry. "Thank you for everything."

Thirty-eight

McLeod brought the dogs in and told Fiona about her visit with Henry. "Fiona, he didn't steal the money from the seminary. It was Tilley."

"Tilley!"

"He says it was. Henry knew about it when he was in the business office, but he just never said anything about it and let Tilley get away with it. He never dreamed he'd be accused of embezzlement himself."

"Oh, what a relief! One does hate to find out that people one really likes are guilty of heinous crimes," said Fiona.

"I agree with that one. Oh, by the way, I invited Henry to dinner. Is that all right? He wouldn't accept until I cleared it with you."

"That's fine," said Fiona. "I've got plenty of food. And it's all ready to go."

Angus, informed of the expected guests (and of the good news about Henry

Fairfield Worthington) when he got home, said that was fine, since he had also invited Rob Hillhouse, whose wife was out of town, to dinner. Fiona gulped and said that was great. "I'll call Lucy to see if she can come," she said, "so we won't have four men and two women."

"Rob Hillhouse is the man who's interested in the Jesus Seminar, isn't he?" asked McLeod.

"And several other things," said Angus. "He's the one who conducted the ceremony for two gay men. And he's a truly fine New Testament scholar."

McLeod volunteered to race off to the grocery store and get another pork loin, just in case. As she left, Angus was happily building fires in the living room and dining room. McLeod hurried back to set the table for seven, and then went upstairs to dress up — at least put on a long skirt instead of pants. Fiona quartered more apples and potatoes and finally arranged the flowers she had bought earlier.

They were, by a miracle, all ready when the doorbell rang. Henry Fairfield Worthington was the first to arrive, and McLeod eyed him knowingly as he stooped to greet Beelzebub and Gabriel. Unfazed, he winked broadly at her and gushed over the dogs.

Rob Hillhouse was next and McLeod was delighted to meet this controversial figure in person. He was a tall, handsome man, clear-eyed and clear-skinned, smiling broadly at the world. "I've heard so much about you," he said, "and I'm pleased to meet you at last. How's the work on Lovejoy going?"

"I've finished here," said McLeod. "Now it's on to Alton, Illinois."

"Oh, yes, that's where the mob lynched him, isn't it? It's right outside St. Louis?"

McLeod said he was right.

"You entertain Rob and Henry," said Fiona to McLeod. "I'll run to the kitchen for a minute."

"And I'll take drink orders," said Angus.

McLeod immediately began to question Rob Hillhouse about the Jesus Seminar, but their discussion was interrupted by the arrival of Lucy Summers. As soon as she had settled down, Johann von Kemp arrived, looking cheerful and carrying a small briefcase. "I hope I am not late," he said.

Reassured, he sat down and was soon the center of kindly interest from people who offered condolences and asked him questions about his plans. Johann answered slowly, in his precise English. He wasn't sure how long he would stay in Princeton, or whether he would move to this country or not, he said. He would stay here until his father's funeral.

"I saw my uncle today. The brother of my father." He took out a cigarette and a lighter and looked around. Angus rushed out and returned with an ancient-looking brass ashtray. Johann looked up at him, smiled gratefully, and lit his cigarette and then went on talking. "He is also staying at the Peacock Inn. I had met him before when I rode the bus to California and I stopped in Missouri to see him. So it was good to see him again today."

"We didn't know he was here," said Angus. "We would have asked him to dinner, too."

"*Ja, ja*," said Johann. "That would be nice."

"I knew he was supposed to come, but I didn't know when," said Henry Fairfield Worthington.

"He told me he left and went to New York and came back yesterday," said Johann.

Conversation faltered, as everyone realized how negligent each one had been in finding Ernst von Kemp's family. Lucy began to talk to Angus, and Rob Hillhouse turned to Henry Fairfield Worthington. McLeod stuck to Johann and asked him when his father's funeral would be.

"I don't know," he said. "The police have not yet released the body. I have something to tell you and Mr. Worthington; you are my friends here. I went to see my father's lawyer today."

Just then Fiona appeared and summoned everyone to dinner. Johann stubbed out his cigarette and stood up. He and McLeod trailed everybody to the dining room. She was dying to know what the lawyer had told Johann, but apparently it was going to have to wait until after dinner.

"I didn't help get things on the table," said McLeod to Fiona. "I'm sorry."

"Don't be sorry. You were helping to entertain so I could relax and finish up in the kitchen."

They sat down and Fiona served the plates from her end of the table. "You've outdone yourself again, Fiona," said Henry Fairfield Worthington, admiring his full plate.

They ate, with enormous deliberation, McLeod thought. She was seated between Henry and Rob, and could only look curiously at Johann sitting across the table with Lucy. After everybody had eaten pork loin and apples and potatoes and salad and lemon pie, they got up to go back to the living room for coffee.

McLeod intercepted Johann. "What did the lawyer say?" she asked him.

"Excuse me, I must have a cigarette," he said.

McLeod dashed into the living room for the brass ashtray and waited while he lit up. After the first long drag, Johann said, "He told me my father had left me everything. Everything. Just as my uncle had said he would. Is that the correct use of the past perfect subjunctive?"

"Yes, wonderful," said McLeod. "But Abigail told me and told you . . . you said —"

"She was wrong," said Johann. "He left it all to me. And left me a mystery bequest also. Wait, I'll show you." He went into the hall, retrieved his briefcase, and came back. First he stubbed out his cigarette and opened the briefcase and pulled out some sheets of paper. "He left me what his lawyer says is his big find in the Middle East. He cannot give me the real thing yet because the will is not — what do you call it?"

"Probated?"

"That's it. But look at this. These are photocopies. The original is a manuscript on papyrus. In Aramaic, I think. But I don't know what it is. The lawyer did not know either. But he said my father was very excited about it."

"Johann, you've come to the right place. Rob Hillhouse is a New Testament scholar and he's here tonight. I'm sure he can read it and tell you about it. Show it to him."

"Perhaps you could ask him to come out here."

"Sure," said McLeod. She went into the living room, where a fresh fire blazed on the hearth, and went up to Rob Hillhouse, who was sipping coffee, and asked him to come with her for a minute.

In the dining room, Johann handed him the photocopies. McLeod explained where they had come from. Hillhouse pulled reading glasses from his inside coat pocket, put them on, and looked at the papers. After a minute or two, he looked up at Johann and McLeod, who were standing, waiting. Then he pulled a chair out from the dining table and sat down and turned back to the papers. Then he got up and said, "This is extremely interesting, but I need more light."

McLeod, who had been holding her

breath in suspense, managed to breathe again and led him to the library where she turned on a bright lamp. Hillhouse sat down and turned his attention back to the documents.

"What's going on?" demanded Fiona, who had just come in. "Why have half my dinner guests abandoned the other half?"

McLeod explained what was going on, and Fiona's mouth opened and her eyes widened. "That's it? The big find? Right there?"

"It's a copy," said McLeod. "The lawyer has the original."

"On papyrus," said Johann.

Fiona went and peered over Rob Hillhouse's shoulder. "It's Greek to me," she said.

"No, it's Aramaic," said Hillhouse, looking up to smile at Fiona, who said agreeably that she didn't mind being Rob's straight man.

Hillhouse turned to Johann. "May I take this with me? I find it extremely interesting. Extremely. But I need to take more time with it."

"Yes. Certainly. You will let me know . . ."

"What do you think it is, Rob?" asked Fiona.

"I think it is very exciting," said Hillhouse. "It may be the most exciting thing I've ever seen. But I don't want to say what I think it is right now. Give me a little more time. I'll just finish my coffee . . ."

"Let me get you some fresh, hot coffee," McLeod said.

It wasn't long before everybody departed. Angus took the dogs out while Fiona and McLeod set to work in the kitchen.

"That was an exciting evening," said McLeod, rinsing off dishes at the sink, while Fiona loaded the dishwasher.

"I know," said Fiona. "Do you think they'll put a historic marker on this house? Something like, 'On this site, the existence of such-and-such extremely rare document was discovered'?"

"Of course they will. And it will continue, 'while world-famous cook and hostess Fiona McKay entertained the crème de la crème of theological society.' "

"I'm sure," said Fiona.

When Angus came home with Beelzebub and Gabriel, Fiona said, "Let's have a nightcap. I'm too excited to go to bed. Henry Fairfield Worthington didn't steal money and Ernst von Kemp didn't disinherit his son and his discovery may be a world beater."

"I think I'll have hot chocolate instead of any more alcohol," said McLeod. "Even though this has been an exciting evening."

The other two concurred, and she made three mugs of cocoa from a packaged mix and took them to the living room, where they sat beside the remains of the fire.

"Have you thought of the significance of Henry's innocence?" she asked. "It just occurred to me. This all gives Tilley yet more motive for the murder of Dan Strong, doesn't it? I mean, if Dan was threatening to expose him, for two things — homosexual harassment and embezzlement, too — he could hardly help murdering him, could he? By the way, did you ask him where he was last Thursday night?"

"He said he and his wife were in New York," said Fiona.

"Well, that lets him out. I suppose," said Angus. "If it's true."

"Knowing him, he could have nipped down here and killed Ernst and gone back to New York," said McLeod. "Anybody who would leave his own dinner party to come looking for me — Wait a minute! Fiona, you remember when Abigail was over here the morning after the murder and she said the police called the dean and he came over and identified the body. So he *was* here."

"He must have gotten the date wrong," said Angus.

"Oh, Angus, you always take up for him!" said Fiona.

"Have you ever heard of Christian charity?" asked Angus.

"Never," said Fiona. "What is it?"

"There's something fishy about this," said McLeod.

"Of course, there is. Dean Tilley is still a suspect. So it's still a mystery," said Fiona.

Alas, thought McLeod as she finally made her way to bed, it was still a mystery.

Thirty-nine

All night McLeod struggled to get to sleep, turning over on her stomach, then her side, then her back, trying to relax and sleep. No luck. Or at least no luck that she knew of — she had read those articles that say if you just lie quietly in bed when you can't sleep, you won't lie awake all night, it just seems that way. You're really sleeping in brief snatches and don't realize it.

"If I'm sleeping in brief snatches and don't know it," she asked herself, "what good does that do? I don't *think* I'm sleeping."

Who murdered Dan Strong and Ernst von Kemp? Could creepy Ted Tilley have lied about being in New York? He must have gotten home early. How early?

And what about Johann? Could he have killed his father? When did he find out Ernst didn't leave him anything? Wait a minute, Ernst left him everything. Why did

Abigail lie to him? And lie to me? She told me that Ernst had left her everything. What is going on around here? Is anybody telling the truth?

What about Sharon? If she killed Dan, where did she do it? And why? And how did she get his body to the tow path?

The field is wide open. The murderer could be Rob Hillhouse, or any other faculty member. Or Victor Lord — his alibi may be spurious. Or Willy or Roscoe or any other student? Maybe Lucy — with the tent stake. It could be anybody. The field wasn't narrowed at all.

Why did people lie so much?

Just as all the articles said she would, McLeod went to sleep.

When she woke up the next morning, she felt groggy and something nagged at her while she showered and dressed. What was it? She had forgotten something. What? The first one downstairs, she made herself some tea and toast and felt somewhat better when Fiona and Angus — with Beelzebub and Gabriel — appeared.

The doorbell rang. Beelzebub and Gabriel sat up, looked at each other, and began to bark furiously. "Who can that be?" said Angus. "At this hour?"

"Go see," said Fiona sensibly.

The dogs followed him to the front door. They heard him say, "Come in, Rob, come in."

He brought a rumpled, sleepy-looking Rob Hillhouse back to the kitchen, where he was greeted cordially by Fiona and McLeod. Angus offered him coffee, and poured it for him.

"Thanks," said Rob, as everybody sat down around the kitchen table. "I'll tell you why I came so early. I forgot to find out how to get in touch with young Kemp — is it Kemp or von Kemp? — and I want to talk to him."

"Is it about the manuscript? Ernst's great find?" asked McLeod. "He's staying at the Peacock Inn. But tell us what you think it is."

"It is indeed about Ernst's find. It's a tremendous discovery. It really is. I labored over it all night. You know Marian is out of town, so I just stayed up all night. And I'm convinced this is a historic treasure."

"What is it?" McLeod asked. The other two stared at Rob, speechless.

"I think it's a new gospel. In fact, I'm sure it is. The gospel of Mary and Martha," said Rob.

"Mary and Martha?" said McLeod.

"You mean the two sisters? The sisters where one stayed in the kitchen cooking for Jesus and one sat at Jesus's feet and listened to him teach? I remember that story from Sunday School."

"And the one that cooked complained to Jesus and asked him to tell her sister to come help her," said Fiona.

"And Jesus said, 'Martha, Martha, do not worry. Mary has chosen what is best,'" said Rob. "That's exactly who I mean," said Hillhouse. "And this seems to be an account of what those two sisters remember about Jesus. At first, I thought it was another version of the Gospel of Mary — Mary Magdalene, that is — you know, one of the Gnostic gospels."

"Gnostic gospels?"

"McLeod, you've heard about the Gnostic gospels," said Angus.

"I have?"

"They were found in Nag Hammadi, Egypt, in 1945," said Hillhouse. "Well, copies of some of them had turned up in the eighteenth century. A German bought a manuscript copy of the Gospel of Mary Magdalene in 1896."

"The Gospel of Mary Magdalene figures in *The DaVinci Code*," said Fiona. "Surely you read that — everybody did."

"Of course," said McLeod. "I just didn't realize it was a Gnostic gospel."

"The Gnostic gospels were manuscripts that the early church fathers did not want to include in the canon," explained Angus. "The Gospel of Thomas is the best-known one, next to that of Mary Magdalene."

"Oh, I've read about that," said McLeod. "The early churchmen were sexist and didn't want to include anything that might give women a larger role or anything that might cast doubt on the divinity of Jesus. Isn't that it?"

"Roughly," said Hillhouse, "very roughly. Some of the Gnostic gospels definitely include feminine elements in the divine and some of them regard the Christ's resurrection as symbolic. One of them includes the story of creation from the viewpoint of the serpent."

"But tell us about this gospel they wrote," said McLeod. "I'm on pins and needles."

"It is, as I said, what Mary and her sister remember about Jesus when he was on earth, and contains things he said. The Jesus Seminar will be really interested in this. Everyone will be. In the Bible, it's in the tenth chapter of Luke, where Jesus visits Mary and Martha and their brother

Lazarus in Bethany, and Jesus tells Martha that Mary is doing the right thing when she sits and listens to him, while Martha cooks. But there's a much fuller account of this in their gospel that makes it more complex."

"I always felt sorry for the one doing all the work in the kitchen," said McLeod.

"Mary is the star of the piece, all right," said Hillhouse. "At one point she pours expensive oil on Jesus' feet and wipes them with her hair. The sisters saw Jesus often, according to the New Testament — he went to their house in Bethany many times and even more often according to this account. They talk about the time Jesus raised Lazarus from the dead — that's also in the Bible, of course. But this account is entirely different — the sisters recall the event as a vision, the way some of the Gnostic gospels view Jesus's appearances after he was crucified. Jesus helped them to realize that Lazarus was alive in another place and another way. And they mention Mary Magdalene as the greatest friend of Jesus. The sisters write down what Jesus said to them and what he said to people at their house who came to hear him."

"How can you tell it's authentic?" asked Angus. "I have to say, I'm a little skeptical."

"Of course you are," said Hillhouse. "I'm skeptical, too, in a way. I haven't seen the original manuscript. It hasn't been tested to establish its age, and it may be a complete hoax. But right now it's fascinating. Fascinating. I want to talk to young Johann about it and talk to the lawyer who's holding it and see if I can look at the original. Where did Ernst get it?"

The others shrugged hopelessly. "He bought it from an antiquities dealer in East Jerusalem, I imagine," said McLeod.

"It would have to be some place dry to preserve it," said Hillhouse.

"So it wasn't found with the Dead Sea Scrolls or the Gnostic gospels," said McLeod.

"The funny thing is, copies were always made of all ancient manuscripts, always, and so somebody should be turning up a copy of this. Some museum or library may have one and not know what it is," said Hillhouse.

"This is incredible," said Angus. "What a thing to happen. Why didn't Ernst tell anybody what he had found?"

"He may have wanted to hug it to himself for a while," said Hillhouse, "or get it appraised by somebody else. I'm sure he had a good idea of what it was."

"And he knew it was exciting," said McLeod. "He told everybody it was the biggest thing he'd ever found. And he put it where it would be safe, so nobody would steal it from his office."

"Oh, so that would be why his lawyer had it," said Hillhouse, getting up. "Well, thanks for the coffee. I think I'll walk on over to the Peacock Inn and see the new owner of this treasure. I want to be allowed to study it and write about it. Thanks again."

Fiona urged him to eat some breakfast, but he refused. He wanted to see young Kemp as soon as possible, and if he ate, he would fall asleep from exhaustion right then and there.

Fiona showed him to the door, asking when Marian would be back and begging him to stay in touch. When she came back to the kitchen, Angus said he had to go. "I bet you ladies have a lot to talk over, don't you? What do you plan to do today?"

Fiona looked at McLeod. "Detection?" she said.

"I'm going to go see Abigail Turner and ask her why she lied to me," said McLeod. "And I want to talk to Nick Perry, if I can get into his presence."

"It is odd that she would tell that

whopper about inheriting the money to you and to Johann. She must have known the truth would come out."

"Maybe I misunderstood what she said, or something."

"Be careful," said Angus. "And let me say that I'd rather both of you cook than have either sit at my feet and listen. But that's just a personal opinion."

"And un-Jesus-like, but we'll keep it in mind, darling," said Fiona, as she got up, tucked her hand in Angus's, and walked with him to the front door.

"Well, what he had to say was more worthy of listening to," said Angus as he left. The Scotties peered longingly after him through the screen door as long as Fiona held the inside door open.

Forty

McLeod went upstairs, got her purse, and went back down and put on her coat. "I'm going over to Lenox House. Right now," she told Fiona. "Maybe I'll get to talk to everybody I want to right now." She told the dogs good-bye and departed.

She first went up the Lenox House stairs in search of Nick Perry, but again received the news that he was with somebody. The officer promised to tell him she was in the building, in von Kemp's old office.

"Thanks," said McLeod, going back down the stairs. In her office, Abigail Turner was at her computer, looking grim.

"Good morning," said McLeod cheerfully.

"Good morning," said Abigail, not looking cheerful.

"I came to offer my condolences," said McLeod.

"Condolences? On what?"

"Well, I guess the best way to put it is the loss of your inheritance. I met Johann von Kemp and he says his father left everything to him. I immediately thought of you and your expectations. I think it's worse to find out something like this if you expected it to be otherwise. I'm very sorry."

"You met Johann?" Abigail said. She was definitely no longer the pleasant person she had been yesterday, happy and free of mourning and exultant about her inheritance. She was in fact red-faced with what apparently was anger. "I didn't know he was in town. I knew he was in this country . . ."

"Oh, I guess I misunderstood him. I thought he said he had talked to you since his father was murdered. He said you told him you inherited everything."

"Oh, he never gets anything right," said Abigail. "He doesn't speak English very well and he gets things mixed up."

McLeod hesitated. "Abigail, dear, I think he knows what he's talking about this time. Ernst's brother is here —"

"Ernst's brother is here?" Abigail interrupted her. "My God, are they all here?"

"What do you mean, 'all'?"

"All the people who are against me. The son, the brother, the wife."

"Abigail, Johann said his mother, the wife, is dead."

"Dead? She's not dead, or Ernst and I would have been married . . ."

"She is dead; she's been dead for many years, so she's not here, but the son and the brother are here. And they're not 'against' you," said McLeod.

"They certainly are," said Abigail.

"Anyway, when I met Johann yesterday I told him to talk to Jim Collins." McLeod decided to lay it on thick. "You said Collins had told you Ernst had left you everything. But I thought Ernst might have left his son some keepsake, at least. Johann talked to Collins, and he told Johann about his legacy. Did Collins make a mistake? Did he really tell you Ernst had left everything to you? Because he told Johann about Ernst's latest find, and that was left to Johann. Collins had it in his safe. Abigail, it's a manuscript, an ancient manuscript, and of course he couldn't turn the original over to Johann right away, but he made a Xerox copy of it and Johann brought that by the McKays' house last night, and Rob Hillhouse — you know, the New Testament scholar — studied it all night and he thinks it's a new gospel! Isn't that fabulous?"

Abigail looked stricken.

"Are you all right?" asked McLeod. "I'm worried —"

"I'm all right," said Abigail. "A new gospel?"

"It's the gospel of Mary and Martha. It's by Lazarus's sisters — what they remembered about Jesus and what he said to them. They write more about women, and give a new interpretation of Jesus raising Lazarus from the dead."

"So that's what it was," said Abigail.

McLeod tried to puzzle out the whole situation. Had Abigail not known that Ernst's wife was dead? Had she lived in denial all these years? Why had she told people she was Ernst's heir?

"Let's have some tea," said Abigail. "I need a cup. That Collins! He's a piece of work, isn't he? Telling us both we were inheriting." She put tea bags in mugs and was standing with her hand on the hot pot while she talked. When it boiled, she poured the boiling water in two mugs and opened a file drawer to get out sugar and creamer for her mug.

"Oh, this is hot," said McLeod, when Abigail had handed her a mug.

"Well, you've been a busy little bee, haven't you?" said Abigail.

"Me?" said McLeod.

"Asking all these questions. Getting things stirred up."

"I didn't stir up anything," said McLeod.

"If it hadn't been for you, Johann would never have gone to see that lawyer. And the lawyer wouldn't have known how to find him and I would have inherited everything. I deserve it, you know. After all I've been through."

McLeod stared at her.

"Drink your tea, McLeod, it's good." Abigail took a healthy swallow from her own mug. "I put up with Ernst all these years, even when he abused me. He didn't marry me. I knew he wasn't still married, you know. I knew she had died. I knew he loved Johann — in his way. As much as he could love anybody. Drink your tea."

McLeod, frozen, held her mug, her arm stiff as she listened to Abigail, who continued. "He couldn't love anybody really, of course. Too twisted. I finally got fed up. DRINK YOUR TEA!"

"Don't drink that tea!"

McLeod looked up as Fiona flew through the door and shouted again, "Don't drink that tea!" Paralyzed, McLeod didn't move, as Fiona knocked the mug from her hand to the floor.

Abigail stood up and started toward them.

"That tea may have cyanide in it!" said Fiona.

Abigail grabbed Fiona by the shoulders and knocked her down. Just like that. Then she put her hands around McLeod's neck and began to choke her. McLeod tried to pull off the hands but they choked harder. Abigail had the strength of frenzy. McLeod thought, she's going to kill me. Oh, I do hope Harry finishes his dissertation. Is that my last thought? McLeod closed her eyes and breathed what she thought might be her last breath, when, like a deus ex machina, Nick Perry appeared at the door.

When Abigail saw Nick, she suddenly dropped her hands from McLeod's neck and looked at him. She was gasping for breath, as much as McLeod was, but she said, with astonishing aplomb, "What's all the excitement? This is my office, you know."

Nick grasped her by the elbows and said he was arresting her for assault.

"Take your hands off me," said Abigail fiercely, as Angus came bounding in.

Angus went to Fiona's side — she had scrambled up from the floor and they clung to each other for a second — and then he looked at McLeod. "Are you all right?" McLeod nodded and he said, "I just began to think, and it all sounded so fishy I thought 'I'd better get over there to make sure the girls are all right.' "

There were now five people in the office, and, to make it a real crowd, in came two uniformed policemen, who looked at Nick for orders. Abigail began to scream. "Cuff her," said Nick.

"And here's some evidence, I'm sure, Lieutenant Perry," said Fiona, picking up the mug from the floor. "Abigail made McLeod a cup of tea and she was about to drink it when I got here. I'm sure it has cyanide in it. Won't there be traces?"

"Good work," said Nick.

"My cup runneth over," Fiona said to Angus and McLeod. "I helped a detective."

"You sure helped me," said McLeod. "If indeed it does have cyanide in it, you saved my life. She was demanding I drink it, and I'm sure I would have. Thank you, Fiona. George."

The two policemen left with Abigail, who was still screaming and struggling. "How did you know?" McLeod asked Nick.

"We're not stupid," said Nick. "And I began to realize everything she told us was a lie. Nothing checked out. And when we went over the office — you know it was ransacked at the time of the murder — we didn't find anybody's prints but hers. They were on everything. We talked to Johann several times and to von Kemp's brother and we got a pretty good picture of what was going on. Both she and von Kemp were shifty characters. They deserved each other, but finally it looks like she had enough, and she apparently fed him some cyanide in a cup of coffee and then went home and waited for us to call."

"And she killed Danny Strong because he was going to expose their affair?" asked McLeod. "Is that it?"

"That's another case," said Nick. "That's the Township's affair. I can't talk about it."

"You mean they're not related?"

"Talk to Lester Brasher. Look, I've got to go. I'll be in touch. I promise."

"Nick! You can't do this!" said McLeod.

"Lieutenant, I want to help," said Fiona.

"Who should we watch out for?" asked Angus.

"Everybody," said Nick, and left.

Forty-one

The McKays and McLeod left Lenox House. "Girls, I've got to get to work," said Angus. "Do be careful. Please. Promise me, Fiona."

"I promise," said Fiona.

"Me, too," said McLeod.

"Okay," said Angus, "but I know what those promises are worth." He crossed Mercer Street to the main seminary campus, while Fiona and McLeod walked back to the McKay house.

Beelzebub and Gabriel seemed immensely relieved to see them and gratefully received a dog biscuit apiece from Fiona. "I think I'd really like a cup of tea," said McLeod. "Plain, with nothing, *absolutely nothing,* in it. How about you?"

"There's coffee left, thank heavens."

McLeod boiled water while Fiona heated a cup of coffee in the microwave. By common consent, they moved to the library. Beelzebub and Gabriel trailed after them, hoping for more dog biscuits.

"Well, this hits the spot," said McLeod after a few sips of her tea. "Do you suppose there was really cyanide in that cup?"

"I'll bet my bottom dollar there was," said Fiona. "And you know I've always thought the tent stake in the head was just like Abigail. Didn't you?"

"And remember what Gretchen said that night she was over here, about how thorough and assiduous Abigail was? And she certainly did a thorough job of adding the tent stake to deflect attention from herself. But I was really slow to catch on to her. I kept thinking she would explain all the discrepancies when I talked to her. What made you think I wasn't safe with her?"

"After you left, I got to thinking — Abigail is okay, I guess, but the truth is not in her. When she told you the story of her life, it wasn't the same thing she had told me earlier. And telling you she had inherited the money — when she hadn't — it was just too much. I decided she was crazy, and you shouldn't be alone with her. I thought, I'm going over there and see about my pal Nancy . . ."

"I'm glad you did. She lied, too, about the time Victor Lord left Kemp's office.

But George, who killed Danny Strong? Didn't you get the idea that the police don't think it was Abigail?"

"I sure did," said Fiona.

"I thought the same person did the murders because cyanide was used in both of them," said McLeod. "How did Abigail know about cyanide?"

"Maybe she read about it in the paper and that gave her the idea," said Fiona.

"No, it couldn't have worked that way because it wasn't in the Trenton *Times* until after von Kemp was murdered. I remember that from the time."

"It's a puzzle, isn't it? You know, I almost feel bad for her. He treated her horribly. And Johann turning up was just too much."

"I think the last straw was that manuscript, the Gospel of Mary and Martha. When she realized he hadn't even told her what it was, never showed it to her, just hidden it away in his lawyer's safe, I think she just flipped."

"Well, but they don't think she killed Dan Strong?"

"Apparently they don't," said McLeod.

"So, who did?" asked Fiona.

"It must have been Tilley, as I've been saying all along."

"You mean he's a murderer as well as a thief?" said Fiona.

"Has he been unmasked as a thief yet? Let's see, when did Henry tell Hester Hardin about Tilley and the Contingency Fund? Was it only yesterday? So much has happened I lose track," said McLeod.

"Who wouldn't lose track? Henry was fine last night, wasn't he? But old Ted Tilley — does he know yet he's been found out?" said Fiona. She yawned. "Nancy, I'm tired."

"We've got a right to be tired," conceded McLeod. "What a morning. But we can't stop now. Let's figure out who killed Dan."

"We can't," sighed Fiona, yawning again.

"We can at least find out what's happening to Tilley. I'm too curious not to try." McLeod stood up. "Come on, Fiona, let's take the dogs out. We can walk them around the seminary and maybe we can find out about Tilley."

"Oh, all right," said Fiona. "No rest for the weary." Beelzebub and Gabriel, never ones to miss a walk, were already getting up and shaking themselves. All four set out.

"Fiona, what time is it? We haven't had lunch," said McLeod, as they walked down

401

the quadrangle behind Alexander Hall.

"It's noon," said Fiona after a glance at her watch.

"I thought so," said McLeod. "People are beginning to go to the cafeteria. Maybe we'll see old Tilley."

"And if he's in chains, we'll know he's been arrested," said Fiona.

"And we'll know he's been arrested for murder, not embezzling," said McLeod. "We can't go inside the cafeteria, though: we have the dogs."

"If he comes out of the Administration Building, we'll see him," said Fiona.

"Okay, we'll just walk idly back and forth between the Administration Building and the cafeteria."

On one lap, they saw Sharon Leland walking from Hodge Hall toward them. She saw them and stopped to speak, greeting the dogs affectionately. "Do be careful," said McLeod. "Your rash —"

"Oh, that's all right," said Sharon.

"What rash?" said Fiona.

"She gets a rash whenever she's around Beelzebub and Gabriel," said McLeod.

"You didn't get it when you spent all that time at our house," said Fiona. "You know, when you were working for Angus. Did you?"

"Oh, yes, you just didn't notice," said Sharon.

"Let's see," said Fiona. "Where is it? On your hand? That looks really bad. Have you seen a doctor?"

"Oh, it will be all right, Mrs. McKay. Don't worry about it. What are you two doing, just walking the dogs?"

"These are our trusty bloodhounds," said McLeod.

"We are ready to apprehend the murderer!" said Fiona.

"The murderer — you're going to apprehend Abigail Turner? I just heard that the police had already, as you say, apprehended her."

"They have, but that was for Professor von Kemp's murder," said McLeod.

"We're after Danny's murderer," said Fiona, looking grim and fearsome.

"You are?" asked Sharon, awed.

"Oh, Sharon, I'm so sorry," said McLeod, who knew that Sharon and Dan had liked Dean Tilley, had planned to have him officiate at their wedding. She impulsively hugged Sharon.

"It's awful, isn't it?" said Fiona.

"Yes," said Sharon. "But I won't go." She pulled herself away from McLeod. "I won't go," she shouted, as she began to run back toward Hodge.

"Sharon!" called McLeod. "What's the matter?"

"What is her problem?" asked Fiona.

McLeod gasped. "I know what her problem is. She thinks we were going to apprehend *her*."

"But we were talking about Tilley," said Fiona.

"Of course, we were, but think back on the conversation. We never mentioned Tilley's name. We just said the perpetrator and rolled our eyes significantly. And I hugged her — that was because I knew she liked Tilley, but she thought I was sorry we were going to apprehend her. She thought we were taunting her . . ."

"And she thinks we are after her. Did she do the murder?"

"Apparently," said McLeod slowly.

"Let's go tell her what we really meant," said Fiona. "Come on, Beelzebub."

"Come on Gabriel," said McLeod, hurrying after. "I know where her room is. I came here that Sunday night when the students came to dinner. Up these stairs." The Scotties' legs were too short to make it up the stairs, so each woman picked up a dog and hurried upward.

They got no answer to their knock.

"Sharon! Sharon!" called Fiona.

"We know you're in there! Please let us in!" said McLeod.

Another student came out of a room and looked at them curiously, then went down the stairs. They tried the door — it was locked. A second student came out of a room, the one next door to Sharon's. "Are you looking for Sharon?" she asked.

"Yes, she was very upset when she left us just a minute ago, and we wanted to see her. Make sure she's all right," said McLeod.

"Is she in there?" asked the student, who was plump and red-haired and capable looking.

"I'm sure she is. We saw her come flying over here, just minutes ago."

"You know, I think I have a key to her room," said the student, somewhat in doubt. "Are you Professor McKay's wife?" she asked Fiona.

"Yes, I am. I'm Fiona McKay."

"Glad to know you. I'm Tracy Cone."

"How do you do. And this is my friend, McLeod Dulaney."

"I've seen you around," said Tracy. "I guess it will be all right. We gave each other keys to our rooms in case we got locked out or something. Let me get hers."

She disappeared into her own room and came back almost immediately.

"I guess this is all right," she said again, and put the key in the lock. They opened the door, and saw Sharon sprawled on her bed. "Wake up, Sharon!" Tracy Cone said.

McLeod walked over to the bed, looked at Sharon's red face, picked up her wrist, and felt no pulse. "She's not asleep," said McLeod.

"She's not asleep?" said Fiona.

"No, she's dead!" said McLeod. "She must have taken cyanide. It acts so quickly. Call 911."

"You mean she really was the murderer?" said Fiona. "How could anything have gone so wrong?"

"I don't know, Fiona, but she is the murderer apparently. She probably didn't want to have to face trial."

"I guess so," said Fiona, "but no jury would have found her guilty."

"She would have found herself guilty," said McLeod.

"What are you talking about?" cried Sharon's neighbor. "Sharon didn't murder anybody."

"I'm afraid she did," said McLeod. "And I'm sorry. I thought it was —" She interrupted herself and changed what she was about to say. "I thought it was somebody else."

"Me, too," said Fiona.

"Call 911," said McLeod wearily. "Not in here, from your room, Tracy. Please do it now." Tracy bustled away.

When they were back home around the library fire, having large, solid drinks with Angus, Fiona and McLeod were still in shock. "Naturally," said Angus. "It's hard to believe. That nice girl."

"That nice girl," agreed McLeod. "I liked her."

The doorbell rang, startling them and stimulating Beelzebub and Gabriel to frenzied barking. Angus answered the door and they heard him saying, "Come in, Lieutenant."

"I came to chew you out," said Nick Perry, ushered into the library by Angus. He settled in a comfortable wing chair and said he'd love a Scotch when Angus offered him a drink.

"I never saw you have a drink before," said McLeod.

"I never was so free — for a minute, anyway," said Nick. "This is really Brasher's case. You ladies cleaned up mine this morning."

"What are you going to chew us out for?" asked McLeod.

"For cheating the prosecutor," said Nick.

"He's got Abigail Turner," said McLeod.

"That's right. Thanks to you, we caught her red-handed — for assault, if not murder."

"But she did murder Ernst, didn't she?"

"She did," said Nick. "She says she did. And she had good reason, apparently, even if she is slightly off her rocker."

"That's what we said this morning," said McLeod. "But she knew all along that Ernst's wife was dead, didn't she? I can't figure that out. She told us about the wife's existence."

"Oh. I understand that," said Fiona. "That was to justify his not marrying her."

"Oh."

"But why tell me she inherited everything?"

"That's just fantasy, wish fulfillment," said Nick. "By that time, she was out of it. You know, I gather from talking to her all day that what made her the angriest was his not telling her about the manuscript. He hid it from her. She didn't know what he'd just found. He was pretty rotten to her, all right."

"Do you think they'll convict her?"

"The prosecutor's not wildly happy with the case. He says she's so nutty a good lawyer and a good psychiatrist can get her off."

"And there were two separate murderers," said McLeod. "I'm still trying to adjust to that one. It just began to dawn on us after we found Sharon — we had no idea."

"We thought it was Tilley," said Fiona.

"Fiona, you've got no respect for the dean," said Angus.

"You always take up for him, and you know he's a thief," said Fiona.

"I guess he is, at that," said Angus. "But a man is innocent until proven guilty. Anyway, he's taking early retirement, I heard today."

"Good," said Fiona. "That means Mc-Leod can stay here as long as she wants to."

"I'm leaving tomorrow, actually," said McLeod. "I've finished my research, and I'm going home tomorrow and leave again Tuesday for Alton, Illinois. Tell Tilley."

"I will," said Angus, "but you can stay here as long as you like."

"Back to Sharon for a moment," said McLeod. "Did she leave a note, Nick? I forgot to look."

"I'm glad you didn't poke around the scene," said Nick. "She wrote it earlier. It was very involved. I think this had been preying on her, and she was already thinking about killing herself. The note explained that she had to kill Dan because he was causing so much grief to so many people. He didn't just threaten people in his sermon, he sent them warning notes. That got Abigail Turner stirred up, and Ernst von Kemp, and I don't know who else. Sharon's note said he was crazy and she tried to break up with him but he wouldn't have it. He turned on her and threatened to expose her as a whore of Babylon. She was afraid of him. She had already told us that her story about last seeing Dan at the cafeteria was not true — several students had told the Township police that they didn't see them in the cafeteria together that night. She and Dan had a picnic down at Turning Basin Park the night he disappeared. She had started carrying a vial of cyanide around with her, planning ahead, as it turns out. In the note she said he became violent at the turning basin, so she just put some of the cyanide in his lemonade. She got the cyanide from the Internet — just like the policeman told the press — and finally was pushed far enough to use it."

"So she didn't have to get the body from the seminary to the canal," said McLeod.

"There she was with a body on her hands," said Nick. "She said they had come in her car and her old garment bag was in the trunk, so she hung around until dark and somehow managed to stuff him into the garment bag. Then she dragged it down to the tow path and threw his clothes in the Dumpster down there."

"And stabbed his arm to make it look like a snakebite," said McLeod.

"That's right. That's because she didn't like that student with the snakes. She said she was sorry she did that."

"Then she came back to the seminary and acted as though nothing had happened?" said Fiona.

"She took a long time to report that Dan was missing," said McLeod.

"That's right," said Nick. "The Township police asked her about that. It took her several days, all right. But then she told the dean — I think other students began to bring pressure on the dean. All this was a strain on Sharon. She couldn't carry it off."

"Looking back, I can see how she vacillated between grief and guilt and anger —" McLeod said.

"And denial and everything else," said Fiona.

"Denial and everything else," said McLeod. "That's like a book title. Or like a murder case."

"Well, a lot's happened, hasn't it?" said Angus. "Two murders, a theft exposed, a new Gospel found. Do you suppose that's all, Lieutenant?"

"All for now," Nick said.

"Do you still think the seminary is a peaceful place?" Fiona asked McLeod.

"As peaceful as it can be," said McLeod.

"With a peace that passeth all understanding," said Angus.

Fiona's Veal Stew

(This can be cooked in a slow oven or, as Fiona did, in a slow cooker.)

6 small onions, peeled and sliced
1½–2 pounds veal cubes
1 can chicken broth
6 medium red potatoes, peeled and sliced
3 large carrots, peeled and sliced
¼ cup raisins
2 tablespoons mustard
¼ cup soy sauce
herbes de Provence
pepper

Preheat oven to 350°.

Place onions in a large casserole. Arrange meat on top of onions.

Sprinkle with mustard and raisins.

Slice potatoes on top of meat. Add black pepper and salt. Slice carrots on top of potatoes.

Pour in chicken broth and soy sauce. Bake, covered, at 350° for at least two hours. Serves 6.

Fiona's Apple Dumplings

Pastry

2/3 cup shortening
2 cups flour
1 teaspoon salt
4 tablespoons ice water

Mix shortening with flour and salt, using two knives or a pastry blender. Add ice water until dough can be pressed together. (You may need a little more than 4 tablespoons.) Divide dough into 6 equal portions and roll out separately.

Apples and Filling

6 apples, peeled and cored
Sugar
Butter
Cinnamon

Place an apple on each piece of pastry. Fill cavities with sugar, butter, and a little cinnamon. Moisten edges of pastry and bring them up over the apple, sealing well.

Place in buttered casserole just large enough to hold them.

Syrup

1 cup sugar
2 cups water
¼ teaspoon cinnamon

Boil all ingredients for 3 minutes. Pour around but not over dumplings. Bake at 425° for 40–45 minutes, until brown and tender.

The employees of Thorndike Press hope you have enjoyed this Large Print book. All our Thorndike and Wheeler Large Print titles are designed for easy reading, and all our books are made to last. Other Thorndike Press Large Print books are available at your library, through selected bookstores, or directly from us.

For information about titles, please call:

(800) 223-1244

or visit our Web site at:

www.gale.com/thorndike
www.gale.com/wheeler

To share your comments, please write:

Publisher
Thorndike Press
295 Kennedy Memorial Drive
Waterville, ME   04901